A SPY IS BORN

A STARSTRUCK THRILLER, BOOK 1

EMILY KIMELMAN

A Spy Is Born
Star Struck Thriller, Book 1

Girls, we run this motha, yeah
Girls, we run this motha, yeah
Girls we run this motha, girls
Who run the world?
Girls
Who run the world?
Girls
Who run the world?
Girls

-Beyonce, Who Run the World (Girls)

PROLOGUE

I AM NAKED, bruised, and clutching a blood-stained Oscar statue.

I didn't mean to kill him. The last thing I want is the director of my film—my first big role—dead.

Now the cops are here, and even though it's obviously self-defense, I'm done for…my life is over. I'll never work in this town again even if I manage to avoid jail time. I'll be infamous instead of famous.

Unless…

CHAPTER ONE

I GRIP MY KEYS, the point of one protruding between my knuckles. The entrance to my apartment is right beyond the dumpsters. *Ten feet away.* Water mists the air, swirling in gray tendrils, turning the dark alley foggy and creepy. Brick walls rise on either side of me, closing me in—the street at my back is quiet, deserted.

Fear tickles over my skin, raising hairs on my arms and the back of my neck. A scuffling comes from near my door, and I freeze, my heart hammering. A shadowy figure steps out from behind the stinking trash dumpster. I stay frozen, breath gone, blood rushing loudly in my ears.

"Hey, cutie," a man's voice says behind me. *There are two of them!*

I whirl around, panic closing my throat, my fists tightening—one clutching my purse strap and the other my keys. *My weapon.* A tall man with greasy hair, wearing a peacoat and a smug expression, blocks my only exit.

My gaze ping-pongs between the two men. *I know what they want.* The shadowed figure by my door steps forward, revealing dark eyes and the low brow of a Neanderthal.

They move in unison, closing in on me. Peacoat's smug smile morphs into a hungry grin as his gaze falls onto my heaving chest.

Even through the trench coat, it's obvious I'm stacked. *That's half the reason I got this job.*

Crap. Stay in the moment.

I plant my feet, the stiletto, thigh-high boots I'm wearing both an asset and a liability. Taking a deep breath, I bring my purse up fast and hard, whipping it at Neanderthal's face. He steps back in mild, almost amused, surprise, and I lash out with my back leg at Peacoat.

My heel catches him in the stomach, and he stumbles away with a muttered curse. I pivot, twisting around, and step forward into a roundhouse kick that catches Neanderthal in the chin. The heel of my boot gouges him, and blood pours down his neck as he gives a cry of pain.

"CUT!!!"

"I'm so sorry," I say, stepping forward toward the actor playing Neanderthal. He is holding his chin, blood spilling between his fingers.

"What the hell, Angela?" Jack Axelrod, my director, asks from his perch above me—he and the camerawoman, Darlene Jackson, are in a cherry picker, getting the scene from the air. A medic rushes up to Neanderthal.

"I'm sorry!" I yell up to my director.

Jack shakes his head and says something to Darlene. She nods.

Please don't fire me.

"Let's take a break," Jack says, waving his hand to be lowered to the ground.

"I'm so sorry," I say again, but no one is listening.

My manager, Mary Genovese, hurries over, heels clicking on the concrete floor, Birkin bag swinging from a well-muscled arm as she pushes past the medics. "Come on, sweetie," she says, taking my elbow. "Let's get you to your trailer."

Her heavy floral perfume stings my eyes as I follow her. We move off the set, weaving through the equipment and stepping over cords. Mary pushes open the door of the studio, and bright LA sunshine blinds me for a moment. Mary keeps moving forward, talking the entire time. "Don't worry about it. They're not going to fire you for *that.*"

"Fire me?"

"They are *not* going to do that." She pulls open my trailer door and pushes me up the few steps into the air-conditioned, plastic-scented space. "Have some water." She points to a row of bottles lined up on the green granite counter.

I obey, opening a bottle and taking a long sip while Mary sits on the couch and starts to type on her phone. My eyes are drawn to my Kindle, which is plugged into the wall. *Can I just curl up in a ball and read now?*

"I've got a surprise for you," Mary says in a sing-songy voice, pulling my attention back to her. My chest tightens. *What now?* "A little present for completing your first week on set."

"It's not over yet," I point out, sitting next to her on the white faux-leather cushions. She smiles at me. Mary's dark lashes are painted with thick layers of mascara, and her brown eyes are sparkling. She is full of energy and enthusiasm.

Mary believes in me and is one of the top agents in Hollywood, so I ignore the spray tan and the heavy perfume and the annoying way she orders me around. She got me this job. She's convinced I can be a star.

There's a knock on the trailer door, and Mary pops up. "Here it is!" She opens the door, and a PA stands there, his long hair pulled into a man bun, his T-shirt and jeans just the right amount of distressed. He's holding a cardboard file box by the punched-out handles. He passes it to Mary. "Thanks, sweetie," she says before closing the door.

"Here you go," she grins, handing me the package. Something inside it moves, and I screech, almost dropping it. "Careful!"

"You should have warned me it was alive," I grumble, placing it firmly on my lap and taking off the lid. Inside is a tiny little fluffball— a puppy. It looks up at me with giant brown eyes surrounded by soft white fur, the little black nose sniffing the air.

The puppy jumps up at me with a squeak. I don't know what to say. *I can barely handle taking care of myself, what am I going to do with a puppy?*

"It's one of those new designer dogs, part poodle, part Dachshund. Pick it up!" I glance at Mary; she's smiling, her gold hoops swinging back and forth as she gestures for me to pick up the dog. "It's going to be great for your image." Her eyes widen. "People love puppies."

I look back to the animal and scoop a hand underneath him…or her. It's warm and soft. *So tiny.* I can feel ribs through the fur, and its heart flutters quickly against my palm. It wriggles, and I move the box to the floor, bringing my other hand up to clutch the small thing to my chest.

"You two look adorable! Hold on." Mary whips out her phone and aims it at me. My face breaks out into a smile, the one I've perfected for social media. *I'm so normal and happy and LOVE sharing with you.*

"Perfect," Mary says, head bending over the phone as she posts it on my accounts. "What are you naming him?"

I look down at the little guy. With the long body of a Dachshund, and the curls of a poodle, he's funny looking. *And super cute.* The puppy yawns, showing off tiny pointed teeth, then spins once before curling up on my lap. *He is falling asleep on me.*

I kinda melt.

"Should it be something funny?" I ask, scratching under his chin. He makes a little sound, a vibration of pleasure.

"Sure. Anything you want."

"How about Lump?"

"Loomp?" Mary looks up from the screen, her lip raised in distaste.

"Yes, but spelled L–U–M–P. It was Picasso's Dachshund."

Mary shakes her head. "I don't think so."

I scratch the puppy's head, and he cuddles closer. "Okay, how about Amos or Archie? Andy Warhol's Dachshunds."

"Those are cute. Either one will do. How do you know that, anyway?"

I shrug. "That's the kind of stuff I remember." *Useless.*

She nods and turns away. "I'm saying Archie. Amos might offend people who remember that old show Amos and Andy—very racist."

"Okay, Archie." The little dog blinks his eyes open. "Do you like that name?"

He whines and wiggles closer. I bring him up to lay a kiss on his head. "That's perfect!" Mary says, holding up her phone again. "So sweet!"

Another knock at the door, and Mary goes to answer it. "Oh, hi, Jack," she says, stepping back. I wince at the sound of the director's voice.

"Mary, can I get a moment alone with my star?" *My star.* I like the sound of *that.*

"Of course." She reaches back into the trailer to grab her bag off the couch and raises her brows at me. *This is your chance to apologize and show him you deserve to be here.*

Jack steps into the trailer once Mary is gone. He's tall and strong, with gray hair and round glasses sitting at the tip of his sculpted nose, exposing his bright blue eyes. He gives me a warm smile. "Sorry I yelled at you."

My shoulders relax, releasing the tension gathered there. "Sorry I screwed up."

He shrugs, sitting down next to me. "This is your first action movie."

I nod. "My first major role," I say with a grateful smile. *You're giving me a chance, and I appreciate it.*

"I think you've got a lot of potential. And I know you've been training hard."

Seven days a week with my trainer and still managed to screw up. Ugh.

"I have, but I can train harder," I say, determined to get this right.

His eyes dip down to my body for a moment. "You look great. But we need you to have…" His eyes make it back up to mine. "More control."

"I know." I nod. "I'll work on it. I swear. I'm so sorry."

His hand lands on my thigh. "I'm sure you will." He gives my leg a squeeze before standing. "Back on in ten," he says as he opens the door. "Oh." Jack turns back to me, his hand on the knob, the door half open. "Come by for dinner tonight. My place in the hills. We can go over all this. I want to make sure you're having a good experience."

"Okay," I say, my instincts sounding an internal alarm. *That's a bad idea.* He smiles and, after one more up-and-down glance at my body, heads out the door.

Mary comes in, grinning. "He invited you to his house," she says. "That's great. Means he's taking an interest in your career."

"Is that what it means?" I ask, placing Archie back in his box. He turns in a circle before nuzzling in among the shredded newspaper.

"Of course. Now come on. You're needed back on set."

I pick myself up and glance in the mirrored wall before stepping out of the trailer. Taking a deep breath, I put on a smile. *I can handle whatever comes my way.*

THE STEPS UP to Jack Axelrod's house are white marble. The whole thing is classic, fashionable, 1920s Hollywood glamour. Lights twinkle in the gardens surrounding the mansion. The brick driveway behind me doesn't have one weed creeping through the crevices.

I grew up with a dirt driveway.

Taking a deep breath, I continue up the fabulous steps. This is the stuff old Hollywood dreams are made of…everything I want. Everything I came to this city to get. Determined to make it all work and make this dinner a success, I knock on the imposing wooden doors, releasing a long, slow breath.

The sun is setting, bright orange and glimmering in the smog over the ocean. The sky is that dark, luscious blue of almost night. A few of the brightest stars twinkle overhead.

Are they smiling down at me?

The door slides open on well-oiled hinges, and a woman wearing a pale blue maid's uniform —including the crisp white apron—stands before me. Gray curls frame her smiling face. She nods to me, as if I'm important.

I'm the daughter of a welder and a laundress. *She doesn't care.* Nothing matters here except what you make of yourself.

This isn't Kansas, Toto.

I heft the bag Archie is sleeping in and smile. "Hi, I'm Angela," I say.

"Of course, we've been expecting you." She steps aside to usher me in. "Please come in. Mr. Axelrod is on the back patio."

To describe the entrance hall as anything but grand would be madness. The ceiling soars above me, arching into a domed skylight—like that ancient church in Rome. Not that I've been there in person, but I've seen it in books.

I smile at my uniformed greeter and follow her, my ridiculously high heels clicking on the tile floor as we move past a staircase that winds up the wall to the second floor. *Grand.* The brass railing sparkles, and thick carpeting in the same blue as the sky runs down the steps. Photographic stills from black and white films line the walls.

We pass under an archway into a huge sitting room with multiple couches and chairs…lots of places for people to sit. My feet stop as my eyes catch the gold statues on the mantel. *Oscar.* Oh, sweet Oscar.

The housekeeper, whose name I don't know because I'm too nervous to ask, stops with me. She waits patiently. This can't be the first time she's stood next to some starstruck newbie. Does she know how dry my throat is? Does she know how much I want one of those? There are four of them. *Four!*

Best Director awards over a three-decade career, and the man still has *it*. I take a stuttering breath, pulling my guts back into myself from where they've spilled all over the fancy carpet. *It looks so soft!*

I glance over at my guide. "They're beautiful," I say. What a load of crap. They are powerful. They are *everything*.

She nods. "Yes."

She must clean them. Gets to touch them. I wonder if he'd let me if I asked. A giggle bubbles up in my chest, and I repress it. *Asking to touch a man's Oscar.* What would my grandmother say? *Slut, whore, filthy woman.* The anger and hate in the old woman's voice seems to grab me around the middle in a vice that squeezes all those guts I just stuffed back into myself, threatening to spill them out again.

I swallow. "What's your name?" I ask as the woman starts to walk again. I follow, my legs leaden but loosening with each step as I get further away from those statues. It's as if they have some kind of aura around them—some kind of witchcraft spun into the gold.

"Nancy," she answers quietly, almost like she doesn't want me to know.

Somehow, it reminds me of something…but what? *A lamb to the slaughter.* An image of the sheep we raised on our small farm flashes across my mind—they are standing in the rain, the lambs close to their mothers, my father striding through the storm to do his duty.

"My real name is Stacy," I admit boldly, strangely, out of the blue.

Nancy turns to look over her shoulder, her brows conferencing in confusion. *Why did I tell her that?* She gives me a half smile. "I'm sure lots of actresses change their name. You're Angela now, dear, as long as you want to be."

I nod, blushing. I'm acting like an idiot. *And that is so not new.*

But I got here, didn't I?

Nancy reaches the sliding glass doors we've been walking toward and pulls one open, revealing the back patio. The view stops me again. All of LA is spread before me. It's glittering. And there—oh, right there! The Hollywood sign is lit up, seeming so tiny in contrast to the sparkling city.

Archie stirs from within the purse Mary gave me to carry him around in and pokes his head out, looking around for a second before licking my hand. All he sees is a blurry screen of black and white, from what I've read about puppy development.

Maybe I really should have named him Toto…

Jack rises from a cushioned chair and steps forward, his movements as elegant as his pressed linen shirt and casual jeans. He's barefoot, and something about that sends a thrill through me. It's strangely intimate. Jack Axelrod, Oscar-winning director, is smiling at me, holding out a hand…not wearing any shoes…all of LA behind him. Almost like he's offering it to me.

But what is the price?

Your soul, my grandmother's pinched voice pierces through me. A smile comes to my lips as I boldly walk through the opening. It's just me and Jack, here to talk about my starring role in his movie.

I throw on my warmest, most intimate smile—the one that says

I'm totally fascinated by the person in front of me. And in this case, it's not acting.

JACK POURS me another glass of wine. My second and last, I note to myself, as a warm flush is already moving up my neck.

So far, it's going well. My limbs are loose, my laugh genuine, and Archie is doing a good job of being a cutie pie.

Jack has bright eyes—they look like sapphires and emeralds had the most beautiful babies. They remind me of the deepest waters of the Caribbean… I went there once. On a photo shoot. Was sick as a dog on the boat.

But I got the shot.

And I saw that pristine turquoise water, I luxuriated in it.

"Are you ready to eat?" Jack asks me.

"Yes, please."

He smiles and stands, offering me a hand. *Gentlemanly.* He's not coming on to me. *Doesn't mean he won't.* But I'm prepared. I'm not going to sleep with him. Not only is he old enough to be my father, he's also my boss. I might be from Podunk, Kansas, but I know that's a bad idea…lessons can be learned the easy way sometimes.

The light breeze is sweet, and it plays with my hair, almost like a lover's touch. *This city loves me.* I trip, falling forward a little. Jack catches me, his arm warm and tight on my waist. *I'm drunker than I thought.*

"Sorry," I say, my speech slurring enough that a flicker of concern tightens my gut. *I only had one glass.* This is three-whiskey drunk Stacy, not one-glass-of-fine-Sancerre tipsy Angela.

Jack's eyes are close, so glittering…like the city.

Will he hurt me? What a strange thought. I shake my head, trying to clear the fuzziness. "Do you need to lie down?" he asks, his voice filled with concern. He's a good actor, too. Started out in front of the screen back in the late 70s. He was a real hottie then. Still is in his early 60s. But I don't want him to touch me. There is an edge to that glittering gaze, the sharp edge of hard stone.

He does not care about me.

You're a slut. My grandmother's seething voice sends a wave of nausea through me.

"I think...I'm not sure what's happening," I admit, bringing a hand to my forehead. It's clammy. *I'm clammy.* Archie pokes his head out of the bag again, licking my forearm.

"Here," Jack says. "There is a couch in the living room; you can lay down and take a rest. We can eat later."

He's moving me into the house. My feet are numb, and I'm tipping side to side, the only thing keeping me moving is Jack's hold around my waist. I wince; God, he's holding me tight. It's like the pain is the only thing holding me *here.* I'm on the verge of drifting away. I'm on the verge of losing something...

He drugged me.

The realization is a shock of cold water—like falling through a frozen pond.

I stop...or I try. My legs are not working right. Archie gives an alarmed yelp as his bag swings wide with my unsteady movement.

"Wait," I say...or at least I try to say. Blackness is edging my vision. The icy pond is sucking me under, the weight of my clothing dragging me down.

Swim! Something inside me screams. It's not my voice. It's not Gramma's. It's not any voice I've ever heard before.

I spin away, the martial arts classes I've been taking pulling muscle memory from deep inside me. Jack's hold breaks, and I flail widely, my arms pinwheeling, Archie's bag drops onto the floor. He squeaks at the impact. I keep moving, my vision a swirling mix of colors.

I slam into something hard, and air *oofs* out of me. A lamp tips, the shattering of broken glass accompanying our dip into near darkness.

My eyes are not working.

I grasp the table that stopped me, holding on to my mind, to what's left of my vision.

"Dammit!" Jack curses. "What are you doing, you drunk bitch? That was a very expensive lamp."

He's grabbing me again; pain, a dangerous, burning pain, lights in my bicep at his touch. "Let go of me," I slur.

"Shut up," he commands.

My hand searches across the surface of the table I'm holding. My fingers find something big—a bowl, maybe. I grip it. Hot breath hits my cheek. "You need to lie down." Jack's voice has gone soft again.

"I'm not drunk; you put something in my drink," I think I say, but it comes out all distorted. Distorted like my vision, like the room. Shit, the whole kaleidoscope is spinning. Am I moving?

He's dragging me.

Then Jack picks me up, and everything tilts.

I search for that small, familiar coal of inner strength and, closing my eyes, breathe on it, getting it to glow a bright orange—the way I did when I built the courage to come out here from Kansas. This is how I hunted down the bruises left by my grandma and covered them with makeup because I figured she was better than foster care. *The devil you know.* This burning coal gave me the power to march into Mary's office and tell her she would regret not taking me on as a client.

The light from this latest blaze brightens, and with it my senses return.

My back is moving, something rough underneath me is rubbing my skin.

I hear Archie barking, but far away. There is hot breath on my face...the huff of desire, of sexual satisfaction. Fabric tears, the sound sharp. Air hits between my legs. My breasts are exposed—cold.

Sharp teeth bite a nipple, and the pain throws gasoline onto the flames of the fire I'm tending.

My eyes pry apart. That's when I feel him at my entrance. *Oh no —hell no.*

Rolling, turning with all my strength, I knock him away.

Sharp fingers in my hair pull me back. Jack's eyes are right above mine. They are no longer those Caribbean depths—now they are the shallow, dangerous shores of the Pacific, roiled and dark, with flecks of white swirling.

His lips crush onto mine, stealing my breath, but not my strength. His tongue invades me as he tries to position himself again.

My hands are empty. I lost whatever I was holding. But I still have my nails.

I bring them up—these long, fake, plastic artifices of femininity. *My weapons.* I rake them down Jack's cheeks, cutting through his rough stubble and digging into that famous face.

Warm blood follows the force of my dragging fingers. The smell—that metallic tang of life force—invades me, stoking my fire. You'd think liquid would quell flame, but that's not what happens here.

I want more. *I want to unleash all his blood.*

Jake Axelrod is going to pay.

He cries out, his mouth leaving mine, and pulls away. I blink, struggling to focus. I'm lying on a rug on the floor of a room, the ceiling high above me. I'm naked.

I can't let him get away, because he will come back.

This isn't going to end well for either of us.

He chose the wrong country bumpkin.

I am more than he knows. I built my own damn pyre of strength. He can take nothing from me.

I roll onto my side. Jack is pressed against the side of a couch. *He's not wearing any pants.* One hand holds an injured cheek. "You stupid bitch," he says. His eyes land on me. "You fucking slut."

I don't try to make my mouth work. I can't waste the fire on words. I need to burn *him* down.

Forcing myself onto my hands and knees, I keep an eye on Jack, refusing to lose consciousness again. Refusing to lose sight of *him.*

Jack is staring at his blood streaked hand. *He can't believe what I did.*

I let my eyes track the rest of the room. We are in the living room I passed through to get to the patio. The one the kindly housekeeper led me through. *Where is she?*

A shiver brings goosebumps over my bare flesh. *She knows. She knew.* This is what he does. I'm not the first.

I won't be the last.

His eyes find mine, and a spark leaps into his gaze. He's got his own fire. And the blood on his hand is like kerosene.

Jack launches at me, bowling us both over, knocking into another table hard enough to tip the lamp on it, rolling the thing onto the floor, breaking the bulb and sinking us into near-darkness.

The only light left comes from the city outside and the fires burning in each of us.

I taste the smoke of our contradicting desires, feel the flame of our wills, the soft linen of his shirt and the rough stubble of his beard as we struggle.

Wriggling, slithering, inelegant-but-effective movements free me from his clenches. Fingers tight on my ankle, he drags me back under him. My fists flail, connecting with his jaw, sticky blood coating my knuckles. He doesn't cry out in pain but makes this weird grunt. Not sexual satisfaction, but close.

I kick out, or try, but he's on top of me again. I struggle, my back burning against the carpet.

I inhale a sharp breath as a shard of something cuts me, warm blood blooming between me and the rug.

I have to get out from under him.

His fingers grab at my wrists, and weight bears down on my stomach, making it hard to breathe. *He's got my left hand.* I kick harder, desperate now. Really waking up, all this movement throwing off the shroud of the drug he put in my drink.

Lucid thought beckons, almost in reach.

I stretch out mentally, grasping for clarity, but fall back onto instinct as the drug crowds my thoughts into the hazy, smoke-filled space of my subconscious, where my fire burns.

Strength infuses my limbs, and I lash out, desperate to be on the offense.

I'm not subtle, or gentle. I'm not some little girl. No way! A primal scream rips from my throat, and he is stilled by it. *By my power.*

Using his momentary surprise, I kick my way out from under him. He falls back into shadows, and I scramble to my feet, still facing him.

He rises slowly as I back up, my butt hitting another couch. My hand grasps it, and I move along its solid back. He's blocking the way forward.

I risk a glance over my shoulder. The fireplace is to my right, the patio doors a straight shot down the wall and behind another couch.

My vision jitters as I bring it back to him. He shatters into a kaleidoscope of Jacks, all moving toward me with the slow, steady pace of a man who thinks he's won.

He has won.

His whole life.

A shudder shakes me, my stomach cramping on emptiness and fear.

My hand leads me along the edge of the couch. Archie's barking starts up again as I reach the end of it.

Where is he?

I'm going to have to run, but I don't know if my legs can hold me.

I turn and launch myself from the steady support of the couch, flying forward, ungainly and sloppy. My bare feet touch the cold marble of the hearth. I'm falling forward. My hands fly out, grasping the edge of the mantel.

It's cold and smooth, slippery against my palms—slick with sweat and fear. I grip the mantel, dragging myself along it.

The gold of the Oscar statues twinkles in the low light. Four stoic forms, all lined up—immune to the horror show playing out in front of them.

Fingers dig into my hair, grasping a chunk of it, and rip back my head. I move with the pain for a moment but then lurch forward, trying to twist away, gripping the mantel even harder. Jack grunts.

I grasp the closest Oscar. It's cold and solid and *heavy*.

Jack's arm comes around my bare waist, the softness of his shirt in contrast with the roughness of his hold. He drags me back, and we fall together onto a couch, me on top. My legs are spread, his arm under my breasts, and hot breath on my neck. A swipe of his tongue against my flushed skin turns me wild with rage, with fear, with every instinct out there. They all flare, the perfect fuel for my flame.

"No!" I yell. And it comes out clear. Unmistakable.

Jack thrusts his hips up, the hard line of him rubbing against my bare ass, wriggling to get in. A mind of its own. A member apart.

I thrash, the statue in my hand landing against Jack's shoulder, loosening his grip on my middle. Surging forward, I fly onto the coffee table, pushing big, heavy books off its polished glass surface onto the floor.

I thought that rug looked so soft when I came through here earlier —didn't know how much it could burn.

Weight lands on my back, pressing me into the table, and—oh my God! No, no, no—he has me down. He's trying to…I twist hard, bringing the statue up and around with all my strength. It connects with his temple, the sound a sickening *thunk*. A disgusting cracking. *I just broke something.*

He falls away, limp. My heaving breath is the only sound in the room.

I scramble away, pulling myself up onto a nearby chair. Gray light filters in through the tall patio doors. Scanning the room, I see one of my shoes in the open doorway of the patio. Where are my clothes? They must be behind the couch.

Jack isn't moving.

Is he dead?

I can't look. *I need to leave.* The thought is sluggish, fighting through the loud rushing of blood in my ears and the hard, terrified gallop of my heart.

My eyes travel wildly over the couch in front of me, cushions askew, then to the mantel, where that one Oscar is missing, then down onto the coffee table. A sweaty imprint from my body mars the glass, big art books are open and crumpled on the carpeting below.

A shudder runs over me and my stomach flips, threatening to empty.

My eyes finally, slowly, fall onto Jack, a slumped, pants-less form on the floor. His legs and ass look so white. His pale blue shirt has gone gray in the darkness. Jack's hair looks darker in this light…my eyes drop to my hand, to the statue still gripped there.

Blood. There is blood on Oscar's head. My fingers grip the statue's ankles so tightly they hurt. Throbs of pain suddenly awaken all over me. There is a bite mark on my breast, a cut on my back, bruises all over me.

Tears blur my vision. I can't see again. A deep heave racks

through me, and I double over, retching at my feet, the bile splattering my ankles, wrecking the carpet…well, the blood probably already did that.

What is happening?

I heave again. But there is nothing left, nothing left to release. I got it all out.

Struggling back onto the chair, I curl around the statue, my gaze drifting back to Jack's slumped form. He's not moving. *I should check on him.* A thought passes by, at first like a drifting cloud, then suddenly insistent. Jack Axelrod is dead.

I killed him.

CHAPTER TWO

Time passes. Not so much that the light changes, but enough that the drugs in my system—whatever didn't end up on the carpeting—fade, leaving me awake, alive, and fully aware of the situation.

I've killed a man.

He's lying right there on the floor—his pale ass glowing in the darkness. This is not some thug in an alley who attacked me. This is a world-renowned actor and director dead in his own home. The signs of self-defense are everywhere though...

Doesn't matter.

I'm over. My dreams are dead. As dead as Jack Axelrod.

Should I have let it happen? He probably wouldn't have killed me... the thought flitters past, firing a shot of pain through me. *No. No. No.* I wrap my arms around my legs and start to shake.

I'll shake until it passes then I'll get up. I'll find my clothing. Soon, I will move.

The sound of footsteps raises my head. I'm going to be found. I shouldn't let anyone see me like this. I try to stand, but my limbs are wooden and heavy. I nearly tip off the chair, getting a leg down just in time to prevent the tumble.

The door to the foyer opens, throwing yellow electric light onto the twilight space I've existed in. The shaft of color does not reach us. Jack, Oscar, and I remain shrouded in shadow.

A woman's silhouette, wearing a knee-length dress and flat shoes, is outlined in the doorway. *It's the housekeeper, Nancy.*

She knew. She *let* this happen to me…and how many others?

Nancy steps into the room, and reaches for the light switch. A chandelier glows a soft, elegant gold, casting warm light over the scene.

Her eyes land on me, and she takes a sharp inhale. Nancy's hand comes to her throat as her eyes widen and cheeks blaze with a furious blush of surprise and shock. *She's not breathing.* Seems I have that effect on people tonight.

I don't move or speak. Just sit here, one foot on the floor, the other up, my knee blocking some of my nudity but not all of it.

I am naked and bruised, clutching a blood-stained Oscar statue.

Nancy takes a tentative step forward, eyes traveling over the room. Her gaze falls on Jack, and all the blood rushes from her face. Where my bruised nakedness brought color to her skin, the site of Jack's lifeless corpse takes it all away.

I'm the one that's alive. *I survived.* A savage pride pulses through me.

I take in a stuttering breath. Then another—grateful for my lungs, my lips, my tongue, everything that keeps me breathing. Grateful for every cell that kept me alive tonight.

Archie comes barreling into the room—so small and fluffy in this death-filled cavernous space. Jack must have tossed him into the foyer before turning his full attention on me. He jumps at the chair, trying to get up to me. His long, white body is tall enough for his paws to reach the seat, but his back legs are too short to propel him up onto it. I reach down and take him into my arms, still gripping the bloody statue.

I should put it down. But my fingers won't release. I refuse to let down all my defenses.

Archie licks my face, and I hold him tight. He settles into my arms, whimpering softly.

Nancy approaches Jack's body and stands over it for a moment before crouching down, her skirt hitting the carpet as she leans forward, reaching for his neck, searching for a pulse.

It only takes a moment to find that there is no life there. She could probably tell just from looking. He's a husk. Just a bag of skin and bones. The light and life are gone.

Nancy turns to me. Her eyes are the soft brown of a cow, red-rimmed with the emotions of a human.

"He's dead," she whispers.

I nod. "I know."

"We have to call someone."

"Who?"

"The police?"

"Okay."

"Are you okay?" she asks, standing and approaching, her eyes running over me. I shake my head. She turns back to the couch and grabs a throw that lies rumpled within the pillows. Nancy holds it out to me. When I don't move, she takes a tentative step closer. She licks her lips, clearly nervous. *Is she afraid of me?*

Nancy holds the blanket open and, leaning down, wraps it around my shoulders without letting her skin touch mine. The blanket is soft, so soft. My eyes blink closed, and when I open them she's stepped back again. "I'll go call the police."

I don't answer. I just sit there under that soft blanket, my dog in my arms, Oscar in my grip, and wait for the next person to find me. There is no point in moving. I survived, but I'm as over as Jack.

THE POLICE ARRIVE SILENTLY, the whisper of engines and the soft fall of feet barely reaching me through the shroud of fear and regret that cloak me along with the soft blanket.

A woman crouches in front of me, bringing her dark eyes in line with mine. "Miss?"

I raise my gaze to her. She has an unlined face, almond-shaped eyes, and skin the same camel and gold as Jack's marble entry way. Her thick, black hair is parted in the middle and pulled back, simple and elegant, almost severe. However, there is a softness to her, sympathy in her gaze, as if she's been where I am. Or seen it enough to know the trap I've fallen into…there is no good way out of this one.

The pit I sit in is deep but also provides a kind of safety. *What can happen to me now?*

"Miss," she says again. I blink and give a small nod that I heard her. "My name is Maria. What's your name?"

"Which one?" My voice comes out gruff, as if there is sandpaper in my throat. As if I've been screaming for days. *But the loudest sound was my heartbeat. Jack doesn't have a heartbeat anymore…*

Maria cocks her head slightly. "Your real name."

"Stacy Melon is what my mother named me. Angela Daniels is my stage name."

She nods and looks down at Archie in my lap then over at the Oscar still gripped in my hand. A flash of light behind Maria draws my attention. There is a photographer standing over Jack, capturing him in death. The flash goes again, burning the image into my mind anew. The pale glow of his backside in the dark is joined by this new, stark image of bloodless skin under bright lights. *I came here to be under the lights.*

Now I'm deep in a pit. I shake my head and swallow. I don't want to be in a pit. I climbed out of one to get here and fell right back in. *You're a slut.* Grandma's voice seethes in my mind.

I'm a killer.

The truth vibrates through me, seeming to change my very cellular structure and reassemble me in some new way.

I return my attention to Maria. Is this the first time she's been called out to Jack's house? Couldn't be the first time she's seen this scene. *It's a cliché.* Not Jack's death, but the hungry starlet getting more than she bargained for…

There is a twitch of humor in my gut. This time the director got more than he bargained for. He thought I'd lie there and take it.

"He drugged me," I say.

A man behind Maria answers me. "You sure you didn't just have too much to drink?"

Maria shifts, looking over her shoulder at the guy who spoke, a deep scowl darkening her face. The man is wearing a long overcoat—another cliché in a room filled with death. He's even got a fedora in his meaty fists. Where's his cigarette? Oh right—wrong era.

I meet his gaze. Smug assurance infuses him. He is a white man in a world controlled by men just like him. He is the law, the judge, and the jury. He is the ruler of this society, and I am a naked, beaten woman—hardly more than a girl. He knows me. *He knows everything.*

"I can handle my liquor," I say, swallowing away the gravel in my throat to speak clearly—to speak like a queen, a priestess—the only feminine energy in the world that can control men like him. "I drank one glass of wine. And I blacked out. Woke up with him on top of me. I fought him off. I didn't mean to kill him."

He sneers, this man who thinks he knows so much. "Pretty brutal."

"Yes," I agree, my voice strong now, accented with something almost English, certainly not a whisper of Southern or Western, which would hint at my true nature. "It is a brutal thing, trying to rape me like that." I hold his gaze, prepared to force *him* to look away.

I just killed one of you; I'm not going to back down from another.

Time ticks by. Maria looks between the two of us, and out of the corner of my eye I can see her lips twitching into a smile. Archie stirs in my lap, spinning once before resettling himself.

"Detective." A uniformed officer comes into the room, addressing my staring contest partner. His jaw clenches. I raise my brows and let the barest hint of a smile tug at my lips, which are still swollen from the rough kisses Jack forced upon them.

"You've got a call." The uniformed officer holds out a phone. The detective takes it and brings it to his ear, keeping his eyes locked onto mine.

We stand on our citadels, neither willing to climb down and fight in the mud.

"This is Jacobs." It's when he gets a response that the detective's eyes blink and flick away, and he turns to step outside.

Maria is shaking her head, a smile on her lips. "You've got balls," she says.

"I'm an actor," I answer, letting honey coat my voice, making it thick and sweet and pretty. "I've got to have balls. And a lot more."

"You ask me, this is obvious self-defense." She says it low, like the truth might get us into trouble.

"Thank you," I say, allowing some of Stacy to slip into my voice, letting Maria know we are on the same side. I see her: we battle on the same field.

"Our photographer needs to take some pictures of you," Maria says, her voice professional, the moment of intimacy gone.

I nod, and Maria waves the photographer over. The camera flashes; I don't meet the lens with my gaze. It cannot have me now. Take my body, take my wounds…but I will stay here at the top of my citadel. I may be covered in mud, but I am a priestess and a queen. *A conqueror.*

Pride flickers in my chest. I killed him. He tried to take me, and instead I took him.

I won.

CHAPTER THREE

THEY DON'T GIVE me my clothing back. Instead, Maria brings me a pair of what look like doctor's scrubs. They won't let me take a shower, either—just escort me down the hall into the kitchen.

Nancy makes coffee before retiring to her room, and Maria pours me a cup, adding cream and sugar.

The kitchen is large but clearly built for staff—this is not the casual dining space of a warm and loving home. The only table is small and pushed into a corner, out of the way, with only two chairs.

It's Nancy's hideaway. There are gossip magazines on a shelf under where her apron hangs. A flash of Nancy sitting where I sit now, leafing through those rags as she hides from the horror of her boss's proclivities, comes to me. How many cups of tea has she drunk while a woman fought in the other room? Or just laid there... asleep...while he...

My jaw clenches as anger cuts through me.

The door swings open, and that smug detective, Jacobs, comes in with another man. Tall and broad, with dark brown skin, closely shorn hair, and a walk that oozes confidence and power, his eyes land on me. *This man is a knight, perhaps even a king.*

I lift my chin and release the cup warming my hands, placing them on the table.

"Hello," the knight says, offering me a smile of greeting. "May I sit?" He gestures to the chair across from me.

I nod, and he pulls it away from the table to allow room for his long legs. "My name is Temperance Johnson."

"Temperance," I roll the word around in my mouth.

He gives me a half smile. "My mother was religious."

"Do you live up to your name?"

He gives me a shrug. "I do my best."

"All any of us can do," I say, just to keep the cliché theme of the evening rolling.

"You did pretty well out there." He nods his head toward the living room…toward the dead body.

Detective Jacobs waves for Maria, who's leaning on the counter near me, to follow him. She glances back at me, giving me a look. *I'll be right outside.*

I nod back. *I've got this, but thanks.*

Temperance shifts in his chair to watch them go then returns his attention to me. He is relaxed and in no rush to get to his point. I sip my coffee, letting the sweet, milky brew soothe me.

"You've had some martial arts training for your most recent role, is that right?"

"Yes."

Temperance sits back in his chair, his broad shoulders eclipsing it. He's assessing me—I've seen it a thousand times. The way a man sits there and looks at me. *Am I right for the role?* But that doesn't really make sense here. He must be wondering if I'm guilty or dangerous.

Temperance shifts slightly, his shirt moving with him. It's crisp and white—someone ironed it this morning. Was it him or a girlfriend…or a boyfriend?

"You're special," Temperance says, and my eyebrows raise.

"Special?" I ask, the word curling around my tongue.

"I'd like to work with you," he says, leaning forward.

"Are you a director?" I ask, confused.

"No. I work for the government." He says it quietly, almost like it's a secret.

"The government," I mimic back. I'm a parrot on its perch, articulate yet senseless. Temperance nods, a small, quiet admission.

An air of secrecy floats around us. My gaze drops to where Archie lays curled up on my lap. There's blood under the nail of my pointer finger. *They took the Oscar and put it in an evidence bag.*

"What do you want me to do for you?" I ask, staring at my nails, those long talons of mine, painted a sweet violet to match my character. They are all rimmed with blood.

"You have access," Temperance tells me, "and you can act." He pauses so long that I look up. He holds my gaze. There are specks of green and gold in the brown depths of his eyes. "And you can kill." A shudder passes over me, but I don't break eye contact.

"I'm not a killer," I say, the defense sounding weak and strange. Why? I hadn't made it believable yet. But I would. I'm an actor.

Temperance sits back, licking his full lips, and gives me that slow, secretive nod. "You killed in self-defense here."

"Yes, of course it was self-defense. You think I planned this?"

He shakes his head. "No." His voice is so deep, so brassy. *He should be an actor.* "But I think you could do it again under different circumstances."

A harsh laugh escapes me. "Do it again? You want me to kill someone for you? I'm not an assassin. I just play one in the movies." I quirk my lip into an ironic smile and raise my brows—trying to make this into a joke instead of a sick proposition.

"You're an actor. You're beautiful, and you have unique skills and access. I need people like you. Your country needs you."

The laugh that comes out this time is almost hysterical. "Oh really, Uncle Sam?" I say. Archie pops his head up and looks across the table at Temperance. The small dog cocks his head, and the big man smiles at him.

"Cute puppy."

I shake my head. "I want a lawyer." For some reason that comes out shaky, like I'm some scared woman who needs protection. And I guess I do—from this man across from me and the system that empowers men like Jack Axelrod.

Temperance shifts again. He has the smooth, assured grace of a predator: fearless, capable, and deadly. "I work with a number of people in your field," he tells me, his voice a deep resonance that touches something in my chest and vibrates there. "Your celebrity status and skills have great potential to enhance the safety of this country. We've worked with Hollywood for a long time."

"Are you serious?" I ask, suddenly realizing this conversation isn't some joke or dream.

"Hollywood assets have a great history." One side of his mouth twitches up. "We couldn't have won World War II without them. The assets who've worked with us are heroes."

I'm speechless, shocked by his admission and invitation.

"We make all this go away"—he tilts his head slightly toward the mess in the living room—"and you continue your life." He shrugs slightly. "Just helping me out every now and then."

I stare at him for a beat. "How do you make this go away? How do you disappear a famous man's death?" Temperance gives me a smile, a clandestine knowledge lurking behind it.

"You don't need to worry about that. The less you know about it the better, really. You came here. You had drinks. Ate a nice dinner. Talked about the movie. And went home. And tomorrow on set you'll find out that he died. A tragic loss." Temperance leans back in his chair, assessing me again. *Am I right for the role?* "I'm sure you can act that part, can't you?"

My head is nodding almost without my permission. The consequences of this evening had barely begun to penetrate, and now the idea that there could be none…

I can almost taste it on my tongue—the freedom this man is offering—but it has a metallic tang to it. The metal oil lingers in the air, as if with this freedom comes a set of chains.

"What do I have to do for you?" I ask. He gives another one of those slight shrugs. "I'm not an assassin," I tell him.

His eyes flash green. "Not yet, anyway."

A chill runs over me, raising goosebumps. I hug Archie closer, feeling the small warmth of him, the steadiness of his little heart behind his chest wall. "I'm not an assassin," I say again, my voice strong.

Temperance shakes his head and sits forward as if I have misunderstood. "It would be unusual—very rare—for me to ask something like that of you. It's more about going to parties and telling me what you see."

"You want me to be a spy?"

"A spy," he says, rolling the word around in his mouth. *He likes the taste.* A smile blooms across his face—one that looks incredibly genuine. But I live in Hollywood. I work with the best. And I know that anything can be faked. "An asset," he says. "Though"—another shrug—"we can call you a spy if you like the sound of that better."

"I don't like the sound of any of it," I say, sitting back into the chair, feeling the hard lines of it pressing against the raw burns from the rug. "How do I explain this?" I wave a hand up and down my body to the blooming bruises and the cuts and scrapes.

"We can make up a fender bender." He nods, almost to himself. "That offers you an iron-clad alibi, too." My eyes widen, and he goes on. "No one will suspect what happened. Why would you kill Jack Axelrod? The man offered you a bright future." He says it like he's now the man offering me the bright future. I'm cold all of a sudden—so cold.

I killed him.

I killed the director of my freaking starring role. I mean, I had to. No, I didn't—it was an accident. I try to think back to the moment when I grabbed that statue. I wasn't thinking of killing him; I just wanted to get him off me. I just wanted Jack to stop.

Some strange humor comes over me and a laugh tickles my gut, working its way up my throat until a strange and distorted sound escapes me…a sob? A guffaw?

Temperance cocks a brow.

My gaze drops to his chest—rising and falling the way chests do when a person is alive. I close my eyes as that strange laughter rises in me again. *What is so funny about life and death?*

The hysteria passes, and my eyes, damp with tears, open. Temperance is still there. I'm still in this kitchen meant for staff. *A kitchen should be for family.* There should be comfort here, but it's all bright lights and hard stone, with a stove big enough to feed a soup kitchen but largely used for just one man.

The man I killed.

"Angela?" Temperance's voice thrums low. "Can I drive you home?"

My leased Lexus, dark blue with tan leather seats, is parked out front. The payments, which six months ago felt like a burden, are now such a small portion of my pay that it's a miracle.

Mary Genovese is going to be upset if the truth of this evening comes out—dramatically so. Her tear-filled green eyes, thick mascara running down her cheeks, flash before my mind's eye.

The thudding of my heartbeat is suddenly loud. *Am I going to accept Temperance's offer?*

"What?" I'm not even sure what to ask. This feels like the wrong time to make a decision which will affect the rest of my life.

"I can answer any questions you have on the drive," Temperance says, standing. I stare up at him. He's tall and strong, his muscles moving smoothly under his suit jacket. Is *he* a spy? Of course he is—what a dumb thought.

"But, which agency do you even work for?" I ask, grasping the question out of the air, just one of many that float by me.

A faint, knowing smile graces his lips. "We don't have a name, Angela. Officially, I don't exist. And your role with us won't either."

I nod, as if I can handle that. Which I *so* can't. I am the person who tells the waitress when she forgets to charge me for a glass of wine. I'm not a thief…or a killer. Certainly not a spy.

Temperance stands next to the table, waiting, as if my decision has been made. *But I never said yes.* That thought firms my will. "Just wait a second now," I say, pulling out an old character, a sassy hairdresser I played in high school. "You can't just say I'm going to work for you. I have to agree." I meet his eyes. They grow shadowed and deeply, terrifyingly knowing.

"Say yes," he commands in a voice that brokers no argument. Not from me. But I'm not me right now. I'm a character who is brash and brave and takes no crap from anyone.

I stand, holding Archie tight to my borrowed scrubs. Reaching my full height, which without my heels is just barely to Temperance's chest—which is still doing that rising and falling thing—I stare up into his dark, knowing eyes.

"I just killed someone by accident. In self-defense. The fact is I've got nothing to be ashamed of. I don't have any reason to lie. I should tell the world what happened here. You have to know I'm not his first victim."

Temperance does not respond—not a twitch of a facial muscle. Not a hint of anything. He is a statue, as solid as the Oscar I used to bludgeon Jack to death.

"You can't make me." It comes out petulant, but I'm not backing down. I'm not walking off with this man—walking away from the truth and into the dark without a fight, without a decision on my part. I won't be walked into my future with a hand at my lower back.

"I can." Temperance says it low, so low. "I can do anything I want."

I clench my jaw to keep it from trembling, seeking to cloak my shaking consciousness with sass.. "I'll call the press."

He smiles, a glorious flash of white in a face so hard its relation to stone could be verified in a lab. "You're stubborn. That's good. And..." He takes a moment to think, and I watch his eyes, hoping to catch some hint at his next words. "And brave. You're going to do well."

"I am doing well," I remind him. My gut shakes at the lie. Standing in a dead man's kitchen with his blood rimming my nails, wearing a pair of borrowed scrubs, could hardly be considered doing well.

Temperance nods slowly. "What do you want?"

The question throws me off; I wasn't thinking about what I wanted, just about protecting myself. About not getting sucked into a vortex. "I—" Swallowing, I keep talking just to avoid creating a silence that exposes my confusion. "I want to understand more clearly what you're offering. I don't want to follow you into the darkness."

He cocks his head. "That's dramatic."

I cock a hip and raise one brow. "I'm an actor."

He lets out a sharp laugh. Real or fake? I can't tell. "Let me drive you home."

"Is that me agreeing to work with you?"

"This is done," he tells me. "You're going to work for me. For your country. Because we need you. Consider yourself drafted. But I don't want our relationship to be adversarial. You'll see that I can be very helpful to you. This loss…it will be temporary. I'll get you plenty of work." A grin slips across his face at the scent of his own power. "I'm going to make you a star."

I jut my chin up, holding Archie tighter. "I am a star."

He grins. "Thatta girl."

I shake my head. "You condescending prick. I want a lawyer. Where is my phone?" I'll call Mary. She must have someone for things just like this. I am not the first actor to end up in legal trouble. One of Mary's other clients recently got on the expressway going the wrong direction, and *she's* not in jail. I turn around, scanning the kitchen, trying to remember where I last saw my bag. The patio.

"You can't call anyone." Temperance's voice remains even.

"Am I your prisoner? If so, I get a phone call."

"That's not how this works." I look back over at him. He's standing very still, that chest just going and going. Nothing to stop it. "Your country needs you."

"For what, exactly? I don't understand what you're offering. It's like you want me to take a role without reading the script. How do I know there isn't full frontal on page sixty-two?"

He lets out a short laugh. "I can't promise what the future holds. What did Jack promise you?"

"I knew who he was. I had read the script and I knew the role. I have no idea who you are; you won't even tell me who you work for. And I have no idea what you expect me to do."

"Jack lied about who he was. I won't lie to you." The oath sounds real, but I know how to make anything sound real. *His words mean nothing.*

"I have no reason to believe you."

"You have no choice." The first stirrings of anger edge his voice.

A smile crosses my face that is not my own—my sassy character has taken over. I don't even need to think about her now. She is me—I am gone.

"There is always a choice." My accent has even gone a little Southern. I back away from him, heading around the table, toward the swinging door that leads into the dining room. From there I can get back to the patio, grab my bag, and call Mary.

Temperance does not try to stop me. Cold tile chills my bare feet, but I move calmly, slowly, like what Beyoncé proclaimed is real...I move as if girls run the world.

Pushing through the swinging door, I run right into a uniformed officer. He's shorter than Temperance but still a lot bigger than me. "Excuse me," I say, going to move around him, but he steps with me, blocking my path.

"Sorry, I can't let you leave."

I raise my chin, that old fallback. *I'm not afraid of you. Let me pass.* "I want my phone call."

He shakes his head. "You'll have to talk to the detective about that," he says. "We are still working in here."

"Fine," I nod. "I'll wait." Turning around, I return to the kitchen. Temperance is where I left him.

"You don't want to go downtown." He shakes his head. " Mug shots are the press's dream come true."

"Martin Luther King, Jr.'s mug shot was a badge of honor. I'll take the punishment society deals me."

"I can tell you what punishment society will deal you. You'll be a tabloid sensation for months to come, crowding the Kardashians and their ilk off the covers of all those magazines. An object of sympathy perhaps, but too identified with the gaudy events of this evening to ever resume a respectable acting career."

A shiver runs over me at his words. Suddenly the cool tile is a frozen block, the thin scrubs porous. I stand on an iceberg deep in the arctic. I am alone and in danger. Temperance is a passing boat, a boat that's on fire. Leap into the raging flames or stay on the ice?

Temperance takes a step toward me, his eyes warm in that stony face. *I am your friend,* they say.

"I promise you, I swear"—he looks up at the ceiling, toward the heavens—"I will take care of you." His eyes meet mine. There is that sincerity again, so hard to fake unless you know how.

"I want to talk to Mary, my agent," I insist.

"I can't let you do that. You can't tell anyone about me or about what happened here tonight."

"Secrets are the weights which sink us."

He steps closer. There are only a few feet between us now. Archie lets out a soft snore, exhausted from the evening's excitement. The sound reminds my own body of its need for sleep, and its as if a lead blanket is thrown over my shoulders. I grit my teeth to keep from slumping under the weight.

"You're sitting at the bottom of the ocean, and you're worrying about sinking?" Temperance asks.

"You can always sink lower."

"Not if you grab the life raft I'm throwing you."

"It might be an anchor."

"It's not."

"I can't trust you." I stick my chin out again, but my exhaustion doesn't let it go very high. The weight of the water above me is so heavy.

Temperance's lips remain firm. "I admire your fortitude in this moment. But I want you to understand that I will take care of you. I will take care of everything. You will get roles, and you will be safe."

"My grandmother warned me about men who promised me the world."

"Is that what Jack did?"

I shake my head. "He offered me a drink." I take a deep breath. "You're asking me to follow you blindly."

"I'm not asking." His voice is low—gentle—but his meaning is clear. *You have no choice.* "I'll take you home now; you can sleep. We can talk in the morning. If you don't want to work with me—don't want to serve your country—then we can discuss that once the sun is up."

I glance toward the windows. They reflect the kitchen back to me —a clean, orderly space. "What time is it?"

"Three o'clock."

"I'm supposed to be on set at 7:30 a.m."

"You don't want to be late." Temperance doesn't move to touch me, but I can almost sense his hand on my elbow. He's smart not to take it. I'd jerk away. His stillness is a much more powerful motivator.

And he's right; I don't want to be late. But I also don't want Jack to be dead. I don't want his blood on my hands and the mess that's sure to follow.

"You won't take no for an answer?" My gaze is still stuck on the kitchen window reflecting back the glistening counters.

"You are better off that I don't. You deserve better than what Jack did to you, better than what this evening would turn into without my interference."

"Do I?" My eyes are drawn to his. "How would you know?"

Those dark, jewel eyes hold me. "I know a lot about you. That's part of *my* job."

"But you won't tell me what your job actually is?"

"I'm an actor like you. Except I perform for the safety of our nation." The way he says it…well…it sounds noble. Like what he does matters. "Join me." He offers his hand, palm up, exposing pale skin with dark creases. I stare down at it.

I'm standing at the edge of an abyss, the wind rushing in my ears. The arctic ice is no longer underfoot, the burning ship vanished. It is just me on the precipice and this offer of salvation…this open palm.

I shift Archie into one arm, and he wakes, snuffling closer, as I reach out and accept Temperance's hand: warm and solid, rough with hard work.

Temperance leads me out past the uniformed officer, and where there should be throngs of cops, there is just Maria and the photographer, chatting in the entranceway. The front door is open, the driveway shrouded in darkness, the lights of the city glittering beyond it. *We are up so high above it all.*

I glance toward the living room, catching a glimpse of a sheet sticking out from the other side of the couch. They have not moved the body.

I don't see Nancy anywhere. How will they keep her quiet? All these people will have a secret. It won't just be me. The burden of

Jack's death lifts a little, as if someone has stepped under it, shouldering a small amount. While this secret leaves me exposed, it also shields me. *That's what shared secrets do.*

Temperance, still holding my hand, leads me through the open door and down those old Hollywood steps to where a black SUV waits. Not an amped-up reporter or photographer in sight. A man behind the wheel gets out to open the back door for us.

He does not speak and neither does Temperance, who motions for me to get in first. I stare into the backseat, black leather lit by the dome light. I glance behind me to the mansion. My heart gives a powerful thump. *I survived.*

Climbing into the SUV, I settle into the seat. Temperance gets in next to me. My eyes burn with unshed tears, but I force them away. The perfect topiaries blur as we pull down the drive.

This isn't what I planned. This isn't what I want. But it is what's happening.

A small spark of pride ignites. I'm joining something larger. Like when acting in a play—the way you lean on the actors around you and submerge your ego into something larger than yourself.

Now I'll be doing that again. Joining with others to keep our nation safe. The nation that gave my grandmother a home. That gave her freedom when Nazis wanted to exterminate our people—Roma, a nomadic people with no claim on any nation.

A laugh bubbles but does not burst. I'll be serving a nation rather than just roaming through it. My gut tightens with worry and a fear passed down through my DNA. *Putting down roots leads to death.*

CHAPTER FOUR

SUNLIGHT STREAMING through my windows wakes me before my alarm has a chance to sound. I blink against it. *I didn't close my blinds last night.* That's strange.

Rolling over, I feel pain in all sorts of places, and the events of last night crash back into my consciousness like a bad dream.

Nausea swirls, and I lean over the edge of my bed, gripping the mattress. *Please don't puke.* Taking deep breaths, the spinning slows, and reality settles into place around me.

I am a killer.

And an *asset* of the US government.

This is not a role I'm playing.

This is my life.

But I have to pretend to be the woman I was yesterday.

Pushing myself into a seated position, I slide out from under the covers and set my feet onto the carpeted floor. The soft plush sends a new shiver of disgust through me. *Will carpet ever feel good to me again?*

Light-headed, spots dancing in front of me, I try to summon the strength to stand.

When did I last eat? My salmon salad at lunch yesterday comes to mind, and bile rises again. My eyes catch on my Kindle, sitting on my bedside table next to my phone. The Kindle, my clothing, computer, cell, and the rotary phone are the only things of mine in the apartment; everything else came with the rental. I bought the phone, a classic from the 60s, when I first came to the city as a model. It's white, with a long, curled cord and heavy base. The kind of thing James Bond would use to take out an attacker.

How about I just crawl back under the covers and read for the rest of the day?

Instead, I push off the bed and make it to the bathroom, gripping the door frame and taking a few deep breaths to regain myself. Glancing back at the bed, I consider climbing between the sheets again. It's as if my Kindle is actually calling my name.

Archie lets out a small yip, drawing my attention to his crate. "Just a minute," I say, stepping into the bathroom.

There are two sinks set into white marble—the majesty of the space meant for two. Most mornings that second sink gives me a moment of sadness. *When will I have a partner? Will I ever find love?* This morning, gratitude fills me that I only have to worry about myself... and Archie.

My gaze finds the mirror and my reflection. *Crap on toast.* I took a shower before collapsing into bed last night, too tired and wiped out to dry my hair. I just left it. And now there is a price to pay for that laziness. My long pitch black hair—inherited from my grandmother's Roma roots—is a tangled mess. The contrast of my dark hair and violet eyes often gets me compared to Elizabeth Taylor.

A flash of Jack's still body—the pale curve of his hip in the darkened room—crosses my vision, blocking out my rat's nest of a hair do and forcing me to grab the marble counter and breathe. I need to lock that thought down and wipe that image away.

It was just a dream, I lie to myself. *No, not a lie. It. Was. Just. A. Dream. Forget it.*

Taking a deep breath, I look back at myself and firm my jaw. I have an hour and a half before I need to leave. There is no time for this weakness. *This wallowing.*

I flick on the radio, tuned to the news, and grab my brush off the marble counter, beginning to work through the knots, the pull bringing tears to my eyes. Yes, that's why I'm crying. It's the pull of knots against my scalp. I'm not crying because of a stupid dream. I wouldn't do that. I'm stronger than *that*.

The news anchor drones on about the upcoming election, and I concentrate on his words, using them to blot out the memories trying to surface. "Reginald Grand and Natalie Stone will debate tonight in the first contest between the two presidential candidates. A billionaire business tycoon and television personality, Mr. Grand brings no political experience to the presidency but his strong, nationalist rhetoric and hard-right politics have fired up the base…"

Hair brushed and pulled into a tight ponytail, I pull off my pajamas and inspect the bruises I found last night. They've blossomed. Handprints on my hips, fingertips on my bicep. Turning my back to the mirror, I see the rug burn on my back, the long shallow cut that runs across one shoulder blade—darker and scabbier this morning.

Last night in the shower it stung—burned right through my exhaustion and dragged me back onto the floor…dragged me across it.

No.

Just. A. Dream.

I shake my head and try a smile, something sweet and gentle. A little tired. *Up late last night, got banged up in a fender bender. No big deal. I'm fine.*

The news anchor's voice cuts through my act. "Jack Axelrod, Oscar winning director and actor, died unexpectedly last night at his home…" A buzzing fills my ears as the fake story plays out just the way it's supposed to. No mention of me, of our violent struggle. A heart attack. Natural causes. Tragic but not scandalous. *Because last night was just a dream.*

Pulling on a pair of jeans and a long-sleeved, high-necked black shirt, I grab boots from my closet—ones that I'm steady in. Last night turned me off high heels for a while.

When I open Archie's crate, he leaps out, standing up to place his small paws on my shin, just above the boots. "Good morning, cutie," I say.

He jumps a couple of times, and I pick him up, putting him into his black leather bag with the mesh sides.

Outside the apartment complex, I set him down in the "pet relief area" and pull my sunglasses on. It's a gorgeous LA day: high sixties, the sun blasting through the haze of the city and making everything sparkle.

"Good morning," a deep voice says behind me, sending a chill up my spine, sending me back to that iceberg I stood on last night.

I turn and smile at Temperance.

He wears a baseball cap, pulled low over his eyes. He's got on mirrored sunglasses—like a cop. But he moves with an air to him, something that is different than regular police. This is not a man who follows the rules of society or enforces them. This is a warrior, who wakes up each morning and battles forces unseen by most. A sorcerer or a wizard—that's how he moves, like he's got some special knowledge the rest of us don't, like he can bend time and reality to his liking.

Will I learn enough secrets to give me that power? A thrill brushes over me as he approaches, two cups of coffee in his hands.

He holds one out, and I take it, smiling behind my own shades—dark brown so that no one can see my eyes. I'm a celebrity, after all.

Temperance is wearing a short-sleeved white T-shirt, and his arms, dusted in dark hair, are glistening in the sun. The aroma of coconut wafts off him...he's wearing sunscreen. *We all need protection from Mother Nature.*

I scan down, my eye catching on the waistband of his dark jeans, then continuing to his fashionable sneakers. He does not appear to have a gun on him.

But that does not mean he is helpless. The guy looks like he could kill with his bare hands. *Of course he can.* He's a freaking secret agent.

"So." Temperance sips his coffee. "How are you feeling?"

I bring my gaze back up to his face. Hidden behind my sunglasses, I stare at myself in the reflection of his aviators. "Fine," I say. *It was just a dream.*

"Good," he nods. "Ready to head into work?"

I nod, my eyes flicking down to my watch. It's a platinum Rolex, each hour marked with a diamond—a gift from Mary when I got this role. The joy it brought me that day whispers at the back of my mind.

A starring role, in a famous, respected director's film. The arrival of my stardom. The moment I'd been working toward and dreaming of...

"I'm leaving in a few. Just letting Archie do his business."

"Good, the police report about the fender bender is in place; your car, with appropriate dents, is in the garage." I hadn't even thought of that. I'd left my car at Jack's house, not even considering how I'd get to the studio this morning.

"Thank you." It comes out quiet and sincere. I'm not faking.

In the bright sun of the morning, facing this day as the me from yesterday, with all of last night as a dream, is better than facing it as a killer.

"I guess I'll have a lot of free time," I say.

"Nah." Temperance shakes his head. *Will I be working for him right away?* "The production will continue with a new director. You're going to be fine, Angela."

I search my reflection in his sunglasses, wishing I could see his eyes. His voice is assured, though. He is not worried about me. But maybe that's because he does not care about me. Maybe it's because I am just a weapon to him—a piece of equipment to be used and discarded like any other. *An asset.*

"That's good news, I guess," I say about the new director.

He nods. "I told you I'd take care of you." Temperance tips his head. "Call me if you need me."

My brows raise. "I don't have your number."

"It's in your phone."

Of course it is. "Will you call me?" *I sound like a lovesick teenager. What the hell?*

He smiles, slow and seductive—I'm a mouse, and he is a teasing cat. "When I need you. But you can call me anytime. I want to help you. The American government is now invested in your success. You need anything, just let me know. Even if you don't think I can help."

Archie pulls on his leash, and I follow him, Temperance trailing behind me. "Really? So, I just keep living my life."

"That's right."

"Where is the catch?"

Temperance laughs and shakes his head. "You want to help your country, and we want to help you. It's all working out just the way it should."

"Okay." I say it slowly, doubt clear.

"Don't worry," he says. "Just concentrate on today, on each step. They will have a new director by the end of the week, and filming will continue. Work with your trainer and memorize your lines."

He's my acting coach now?

"Okay," I say again, glancing down at my watch.

"You need to go," Temperance says, reaching into his pockets and pulling out my car fob.

I stare at it for a moment, and he shakes the chain, stirring me to take it. "Thanks," I say again.

He sips his coffee and nods. "See you soon, and remember, call me if you need me."

I nod, and he turns, walking away from me, back across the pet relief area, into the shadow of the apartment complex and disappearing around the corner.

My phone beeps—my alarm telling me I need to leave.

Scooping up Archie, I head to the garage. My car is in my spot, the dim, florescent lights overhead exposing scratches and an ugly dent in the back bumper.

I open the passenger door and place Archie's bag on the seat. He pops his head out, but doesn't try to escape—he likes it in there. Feels safe, probably.

I go around and get behind the wheel of my fancy sports car. Pushing the button to start the engine, I take a deep breath. *Here we go.*

It was all a dream.

As I pull out of the garage into the bright LA day, that line becomes easier to believe. My entire life feels like a dream—and has for some time. Starring role in a movie, fancy car, plush apartment. Now add in dead director, secret agent…what's real about any of this?

My grandmother's voice resounds in my head. "They will come for you. They always come for us."

I shift gears, speeding up on a straight of way. *They* are *not* coming for me. I am *them* now.

CHAPTER FIVE

THE CLICK of the cameras is like the chatter of bugs in brush. I give them my shoulder, letting my long hair brush down my exposed back and smile, more with my eyes than my mouth. Like the femme fatale I play in the film.

The full-length, black shimmering gown slips across my skin, making me feel that much more seductive. That much more *wanted*.

My publicist, Jeremy Talons, nods and smiles from the side, his phone gripped in his hand. I shift, giving the crowd of photographers another angle, keeping my chin down, body angled to show off the dip of my lower back and the swell of my ass. The last nine months of filming and training have brought me up to peak physical shape.

"Over here! Angela!" They yell for me, and I slowly, carefully, evenly, draw my eyes across the forest of lenses, connecting with each one, watching them click, feeling the power they offer and letting it in.

"Okay," Jeremy says, stepping forward. He takes my arm, and I duck my head as I move down the line with him. "We have Jamie Novis from Celebrity Fit TV," he says quietly as we step up to a woman dressed in a full-length emerald green gown, standing next to a camera man. She gives me a giant smile that creases her heavy makeup, and I return it.

"Angela Daniels," she enthuses. "I love your dress. But more than that, I love your arms." I laugh good-naturedly…what a silly thing to say. *Aren't we having so much fun right now?* "So, I've heard the workouts for this shoot were grueling."

I nod, my hair sliding over my shoulder, "Yes, it was super intense. I worked with Synthia Taylor every day to stay in top shape, and I had to give up all my favorites."

"Like what?"

"I'm from Kansas, and we love our barbecue—I haven't had a bite since January."

She laughs and nods. "So what have you been eating?"

I tell her about tofu, green leafy veggies, and broths…bone broths. We laugh at more ridiculousness.

Jeremy takes my arm, and we move down the line.

Harold Jaspers from HLTV is the first reporter to bring up Jack's death—a tragic massive heart attack. The reporter's eyes get all serious right before the question, so I have a moment to prepare, to put on the expression I've practiced for this moment. "What was it like, losing your director so early in the shoot?"

"Well, Harold—" I put my hand on his arm, and his eyes light. *He's getting something good here.* "I really admired Jack. Everyone did." Harold nods, his brow drawn down, drooping under the weight of the sadness, the grief of such a loss. "He taught me so much in the short time we worked together. It was just so sad, to pass now, when he still had so much to offer."

"I've seen the movie," Harold says, and I nod. *Yes, Harold, you're important enough for an early screening.* "And you're amazing. What a powerful female character you play."

"Thank you." I bring a soft blush to my cheeks by thinking about a dumb comment I made at a party years ago that still stings. "I'm so happy to have had the opportunity to play this role." Badass chick in tight leather, kicking ass…*cliché.* But how can we show women's strength without also revealing how tight her ass is?

The strength of the single mothers of the world, the struggling waitresses and endangered teenage girls, are hidden in dreary dramas that no one goes to see. *We don't see them as strong.* Maybe one day I'll win an Oscar for my portrayal of an unattractive woman surviving, and Harold will ask me about my strength in that film… but more likely he'll ask me about my intentional weight gain and makeup job.

I pull my attention back to him. He's asking about the replacement director, and I am smiling, talking about how talented he is and what a wonderful film we made. "I'm really lucky," I say, the words coming out on a gush of emotion that I practiced for two weeks with Mary. Harold loves it; he laps it up like Archie going after the frozen peanut butter in his chew toy.

My publicist's hand at my elbow ends the conversation and moves me down the line until we are in the theater, where Mary is waiting for me. "You did great, honey."

"You saw me?"

"Jeremy texted. Let's talk after-parties," she says as we step into the theater. "I have several options for you…" I zone out as she goes on about where I need to be seen and with whom.

My eyes catch on a broad back. Is that Temperance? The man turns, and it's not him. My heart is pumping though, sending adrenaline through my system.

I have not heard from Temperance since he gave me a cup of coffee that first morning. Several nights, late, when I was being haunted by that dream that never happened, I've thought about calling him…just to see if he's even real. But time has passed, and the nightmare has faded. As long as I get in my training, my yoga, and my work, I'm fine.

I'm great, actually.

A hand stretches across my bare lower back, and I jump, startled. Mary grabs my arm as I bump into her. "Sorry, love, didn't mean to scare you." It's my costar, Julian Styles. "We're sitting together." He puts his hand onto my lower back again and points to the row of seats.

"Enjoy the show, honey. I'm going to make some calls, and I'll see you after," Mary says, raising on her toes to kiss my cheek.

She rushes off before I can even reply. Julian ushers me into the aisle, and I sit in my assigned seat, arranging my long skirt around me.

The fabric bunches up and flows over Julian's tuxedo-clad leg. I try to pull it off, and he just shakes his head. "No worries. I don't mind."

I smile at him, and he grins back. His star power is dangerous… enticing. Mary suggested I date him. But, I am not dating at the moment. Julian flashes his dimples at me, and I wonder if I should reconsider my position.

The theater darkens, and the screen lights. A tribute to Jack begins to play. My skin grows clammy, and my fingers fidget in the folds of my skirt. Julian leans over, bringing his lips close to my ear. "You okay?" he asks.

"Yes, of course."

Julian reaches down and winds his fingers through mine, stilling them. I let him, let him believe it's just normal grief, not guilt or repressed memory that makes me shake. *I have to believe it too.*

As Jack's accomplishments flash across the screen—clips and snippets from his long filmography—I take in measured breaths, pushing one thought through my mind.

It was just a dream—a nightmare. It never happened.

By the time the movie starts, I've convinced myself again that none of it was real. Now I'm ready to enjoy the movie I spent most of the last year making. *My first major role. The film that will make me a star.*

THE AFTER PARTY IS LOUD, and the drink in my hand is cold. I sip the strong vodka and smile at Julian, who's leaning over me so we can hear each other above the noise. His hair falls across his forehead, and his dark blue eyes sparkle.

Mary, a ways behind him, is involved in another conversation but gives me a small knowing smile. *She approves.*

My heart beats faster as I think about her sending me off to Jack's that night. Did she know what was going to happen? Could she have guessed? Julian leans closer, his lips brushing my cheek. "Want to get out of here?"

"Let's stay a little longer." I turn my own mouth to his ear. "I've only had one drink."

"Yes, I know." His hand cuffs my elbow loosely. "I don't want you to drink anymore."

He leans back to catch my eye. *He wants me sober.* A thrill runs over my body, and a shy smile pulls at my lips. It's coy, and I note it—this is a good smile, authentic and subtle. Perfect for a close-up. I take a mental snapshot of this moment to use for later.

Maybe Julian Stiles—heartthrob, drop-dead gorgeous, pretty damn good actor—is also a pretty darn good man.

"Okay," I say. He grins, those dimples of his setting loose a flock of butterflies in my stomach.

Julian's hand moves down my elbow, and he intertwines his fingers with mine. He pulls me forward, and I put the still mostly-full martini glass down on a passing waiter's tray. "I have my car," Julian says as we move through the crowd.

Mary watches us go, giving me that smile again. It almost makes me stop. The fact that she wants me dating Julian is annoying. *I may need to fire her.* Should I ask her if she knew about Jack?

Knew what? *That was just a nightmare.*

I squeeze Julian's hand. Because he's here, now, and this is not dream. This is reality. I just left the screening of my first big movie.

As we step outside, the world explodes with flashes of cameras. I almost stumble, but Julian is holding me tight. He smiles for the cameras. People are yelling questions, but Julian doesn't answer. *He's used to this.*

We move through the crowd, and Julian speaks with the valet, handing him the ticket.

Julian leans in. "You'll get used to it, love," he says.

That smile comes back, the genuine one. I look up at him in the strobing lights of the paparazzi's flashes. They are capturing this moment—seeing the reality that I like him. It's authentic. *It can help sell tickets.*

His car pulls up, a black Bentley with tan leather interior, classy and super expensive. Julian opens the front passenger door for me. I get in, arranging my skirt so he can close the door.

Julian climbs in behind the wheel and pulls into traffic, using his turn signal. *A good driver.*

"Want to come back to my house?" he asks.

"Where do you live?"

"I've rented a place out in Malibu." That's a long drive, plenty of time for me to fully sober up. "Don't worry." He looks over at me, his famous sparkling blue eyes sincere. "I don't expect anything from you —just looking for a quiet place to talk. So we can get to know each other better. Somehow, that seems easier now that we're not both absorbed with making the movie." A short laugh escapes, and he cocks his head before turning his eyes to the road. "What?" he asks.

"Sorry, it's just—you're acting like such a gentleman."

He shifts as we get onto the highway, turning to me and flashing a smile. "Don't all men treat you like a lady?"

I just shake my head, looking down at my hands nestled in the black folds of my skirt. "Not exactly."

He moves into the left lane, accelerating. "I actually have some insight into what it's like to be a woman in this business. My sister, you know, she's an actor, too. We're very close."

"Right, I've heard that." His sister is not nearly as big a star as Julian but has had some interesting roles in indie films. She's tall and thin and shares his dimples, but with green eyes instead of blue.

"She's told me stories." His hands tighten on the wheel. "Even told me some stuff about Jack." My lips go numb, and I don't respond. "Not to speak poorly of the dead or anything, but I heard the guy was a real jerk." Julian shifts again, the engine purring with delight as we speed up.

"Yeah," I say. "A lot of people in this business are jerks." I glance up and see the turnoff for Malibu.

"We could go to your place instead," Julian suggests. "I'm happy to hang out and leave."

"I think that's a better idea," I say, giving Julian the address.

"Thanks for the invite," he smiles, changing lanes and speeding toward my apartment.

I open the door with my key fob, and we step into the darkened living room. The landline phone rings as I flick on the light.

"Just a moment," I say, passing into my bedroom. *Almost no one has this number.* Just my grandmother and Mary. The white rotary phone blares again—I love the weight of it, the look of it, its incredibly loud ring. The whole thing harkens back to an era when phone calls were important.

"Hello," I answer, curling the cord around my finger, my eyes landing on Archie's crate where he is still fast asleep. *Quite the watchdog I've got.*

"Angela." His voice is a deep rumble, a tiger's purr. *It's Temperance.*

"Oh, hey," I say. *So he is real.*

"How are you?" he asks.

"I have a guest."

Temperance chuckles softly—the butterflies in my stomach dip and whirl at the sound. "I know. That's why I'm calling. You need to get rid of him."

"Excuse me?" *What is he, my father?*

"Get rid of him. We need to talk." The line goes dead. I return to the living room. Julian is looking around my apartment, at the white couch with its artfully thrown pillows, the flat-screen TV and the array of vases on the mantel. None of it mine, all of it rented.

"I'm sorry," I say. "But you have to...have to go. That was my grandmother..." *Ugh, when did I become such terrible liar.*

Julian's brows arch. "Everything okay?"

"Yes, I'm sorry... I just need you to leave."

Julian takes a step toward me. His tie is loosened, hanging casually around his neck, and the top button of his white shirt is undone, exposing the dip at the bottom of his throat. *Seriously sexy.* Julian smiles softly, offering just a hint of dimple. "Can I see you again sometime?"

"I don't think you have a choice." I raise one eyebrow. "Aren't we going to be doing a massive press tour together in the coming weeks?"

"I mean just the two of us. Can I take you to dinner?"

That smile is sneaking back onto my face—the real one. *He seems so sincere.* He is *so* cute. "Sure," I say, trying to hide the smile. "I'd like that."

He nods, smiling, and starts to move toward the door. I follow in his wake. Standing on my threshold, he leans back in, catching my eye. "I hope everything is okay."

I nod, guilt at the lie sending the butterflies into a circling pattern.

"Thanks." He hesitates for a moment and then steps into the hall. I close the door behind him, leaning my forehead against it. How can I enter a relationship with someone when I've already had to lie to him before we've even gotten started?

I take a few breaths, my eyes closed, breathing in the scent of wood and the last wisps of Julian's cologne. *Should I change out of this dress?* It makes me vulnerable while also providing protection—hard to run in, but gives me an air of untouchability. The low neckline does expose enough to make any man hungry for me, which gives me a certain kind of power.

I'VE GOT on jeans and a T-shirt when the knock comes. My hair is still up in a complicated twist, a few loose strands tickling my neck and cheeks for effect, and my makeup is still thick, showing off all my best assets and hiding any flaws. But the gown now hangs on my closet door, the full skirts spilling out onto my bedroom floor, far too ample to be contained.

I answer, affecting an air of nonchalance. I'm not afraid to have a master spy in my apartment. This is totally normal for me—a figure from a nightmare strolling into my living room and turning to close my door. Temperance puts a finger to his lips, telling me to stay quiet. I give a small nod, adrenaline seeping into my system, raising my heart rate and sending fluttering waves of nausea through me.

He moves smoothly across the carpet, his footsteps silent. I follow him into my kitchen. Temperance glances around quickly before going to my table, pulling out a chair, and climbing onto it. Reaching up, he takes the cover off the recessed light and holds it out to me. I step forward, taking it. Temperance reaches up past the bulb and pulls out a small something with wires sticking out of it. He slips it into his pocket and then holds out his hand for the cover again. I hand it to him, and he puts it back, his eyes never meeting mine.

I stare at his forearms as he screws the shade back into place—his shirt sleeves are rolled up, exposing dark skin over taut muscle. There is something very sexy about this guy. Is it the power he exudes? All the secrets he keeps, seeping out of him in a pheromone perfume of danger and protection?

He keeps secrets safe.

I turn away as he climbs down from the chair, to keep myself from checking out his ass. Temperance puts the chair back under the table with a scrape of legs against tile and then starts to move toward my bedroom.

He knows his way around my apartment. Did he put whatever that was in that light socket or did someone else? The invasion of it strikes me as I follow him. Someone is listening in on me. Or are they filming? A surge of nausea pulses at the thought.

Temperance enters my bedroom, and I'm glad I took the time to make my bed and tidy up before heading for the premiere. He goes to my bedside lamp and flips it over, the shade tinkling against the bulb. Archie lifts his head and watches him for a moment, then nuzzles back into the blankets. Temperance pulls out another device and slips it into his pocket.

Replacing the lamp, his gaze finally reaches mine. The golden brown is soft, almost amused. He gestures with his chin for us to move back into the living room. I go first this time, feeling him at my back, the experience sending trills of sensation up and down my spine. I'm afraid and turned on, and confused…and somehow feeling all kinds of safe. *Wtf?*

Temperance points to my sneakers by the door, and I grab them, moving to the couch to put them on. He waits for me, standing, his arms crossed over his broad chest. Moments later, we are down in the garage getting into my car. He pulls out a screwdriver and leans toward my stereo. I wince as he pries the front off. *It's a lease.*

Reaching behind the plastic casing, he pulls out one more device, slipping it away into his pocket with the other two.

He then climbs out of the car. I follow, locking the doors in our wake, with a flash of lights and a beep of assurance.

I hold my tongue as we take the elevator back up to my apartment. Temperance waves a fob over my door, and it opens. Did he take mine? No, it's in my hand, along with my car fob. Temperance holds the door for me, his eyes meeting mine again.

Anyone can get into your apartment, his gaze warns.

I suck my bottom lip between my teeth as I pass him. He nods toward the couch, and I sit down. Temperance holds up a hand—*stay here*—then leaves, closing the door behind him.

I stay on the couch, staring at the closed door, my hands fisted by my side, chewing on my lip. Is he coming back? Am I supposed to sit here all night? Is he watching me? My eyes scan the living room. There could be devices anywhere. Were they just listening? Or also watching? And who the heck is they? Are there more?

I'm starting to go stark raving mad when I hear the lock turn. Standing up, I hold my breath, bracing myself for whatever might come through the door. My training kicks in, and my heartbeat actually slows down. I can fight. *I can kill.*

Temperance steps into the apartment and smiles when he sees me, giving a small nod of approval. I've dropped into a fighting stance without even realizing it. He closes the door. "Next time," he says, "don't stand in the middle of the room. You're better off tactically where I can't see you."

"Are you a danger to me?" I ask. "What are those things you took out of here?"

"TMZ." He answers my second question first, referencing one of the largest celebrity gossip sites. He strolls toward me. The collar of his white shirt is open and he looks like a businessman after hours. If businessmen spent a lot of their time at the gym and walked like they knew all the secrets of the world…which most of them think they do.

I jut my chin up, as good a defense as any punch in my world, and narrow my eyes. "TMZ? The tabloid news site?" I ask.

"Yes, they want dirt on you. That's a good thing. Means you've made it." He pauses on the far side of the coffee table for a moment and then looks toward my kitchen. "I'd like a glass of water."

I'm thrown off, but my hostess instincts kick in. "Right, of course," I say, moving toward the kitchen. "Sparkling or still?"

He smiles at me. "You worked as a waitress, right?"

"Yeah, one of the worst of all time, I'd say. And I think my former boss would agree."

"Still water is fine," he says, his voice is smooth and rough—how does he do that? The man should be on the screen, not behind the curtain.

I grab a glass out of the cabinet and fill it from a bottle in the fridge, turning to hand it to him. He takes a sip, looking around the kitchen. "Nice place," he says.

"It's a rental. That apparently you have a key to."

"Locks are no protection," he brings his gaze back to mine, sending another thrill through me. I cross my arms over my chest. "But don't worry," he smiles. "I'm watching out for you."

That does not make me feel better for some reason. Like having the devil watch your back for just a small price…your soul.

"So…" I lean against the counter, hiding my concerns. "You came by to get those…what were they?"

"Listening devices. No video. They stopped that after the last lawsuit burned GTB to the ground."

I nodded, remembering the case—Holly Manster won a big enough settlement to shut that gossip site down after they published video footage from inside her house exposing her extramarital affair.

"They don't ever publish the recordings from the bugs—just use them to figure out where you are going to be, who you are dating." He raises a brow. "That kind of thing. They call them background bugs." His eyes are holding on to me, and I have to look away.

Staring down at my sneakers I nod. "Thank you," I say.

"You're welcome. They installed them while you were at the premiere. I didn't want them hearing you and Julian."

"Is that the only reason you stopped by?" For some reason my voice comes out sounding like a jilted girlfriend. What the what? I force myself to look up at him, one professional to another.

Temperance watches me, not answering the question. His eyes remind me of tiger stones, black and gold swirling together. But also there are flecks of green in there. "No," he finally answers. "I'm here to discuss your first assignment."

I swallow, keeping my eyes on his. *I won't look away. Won't be afraid.* And yet my body is reacting, adrenaline going again, my heart rate increasing. I keep my face smooth, expressionless…this happens to me every day.

"Okay," I answer.

A smile tugs at his lips, and he takes a sip of water…to cover it?

"You're going to be traveling on this press junket, for the film." I nod. "You'll be in Shanghai for two days." I nod again. "You'll be invited to a party at the American consulate."

This is news to me, but I nod anyway.

"A Russian oligarch will also be there. Vladimir Petrov. He has a crush on you." I raise one brow. "Don't worry," Temperance smiles. "I'm not asking you to do anything untoward." Oh, because spying is so very *toward*. "You just need to slip something into his drink."

Both brows shoot up this time. "Drug him?"

Temperance nods slowly, gauging my reaction. "You can imagine that I would have a problem with that, can't you?"

"You've had a bad experience with being drugged. I get it."

"You get it?" Sarcasm drips off each word. *Really, big, strong guy? You get what it's like to be drugged and helpless?*

"Vladimir is a bad man."

I let out a jaded laugh. "A bad man. What am I? A toddler?"

"You're an asset." The way he says it makes my stomach drop. I'm not a person. I'm a thing…a thing that has an assigned value. Like a stock or a bond. I swallow and narrow my eyes again. *I am a queen.* Temperance smiles back… he is a wizard. "I understand your hesitation, but you need to trust me."

"Trust you?"

"Yes." He drops the word like it's a bond, a chain with a lock on it. Something sturdy. Something that will hold.

I want to argue. Somehow, I want to grasp some control over this thing. But all I can do is take hold of the chain and hope it doesn't break.

CHAPTER SIX

Shanghai glitters brighter than LA.

It's the seventh stop on our Asia tour, and by the time our flight is circling the city, I'm exhausted and nervous as a turkey on Thanksgiving.

Over the last few weeks I've fought for sleep, tossing and turning, Jack's corpse haunting me and Temperance's eyes watching me. I've missed Archie, who's staying with Mary while I travel.

Julian sits next to me, reading a newspaper, not staring out the window like a country bumpkin. But he's missing the spires and peaks of the skyscrapers thrusting up toward us, the lights of the city shining into the blackness of night. It's beautiful.

It's where I'm expected to prove my value as an asset.

What would happen if I just didn't do it? That question has flittered through my mind a million times. And there is no answer.

Besides, I made an agreement. I agreed to the transformation of that night in LA from bleak reality to a bad dream for this...for control over me...for the chain with its sturdy lock that I carry with me now.

Someone will meet me in Shanghai to give me the pills—I'm assuming they are pills—to drop into Vladimir's drink.

I Googled him. The guy is richer than Midas and more corrupt than Judas. In his early fifties with small, pale blue eyes and a low furrowed brow, Vlad looks like a retired bodybuilder: tall with bulging muscles, broad shoulders, and narrow waist. His hands are like meat cleavers—blunt and big. There are lots of pictures of him at galas, and he looks terrible in a suit—all bunched up and forced into it.

What was I going to do to him?

"You okay?" Julian asks, leaning over me. I turn to him. The skin around his blue eyes is wrinkled with concern.

"Yeah." I nod.

He glances down at my hands, and I follow his gaze; they are gripping each other as if one is trying to pull the other up from a cliff. I consciously unclasp them and give him a smile. "I'm just tired."

Julian nods, his hair flopping forward. He's growing it out for his next role—it looks roguish and handsome. I've avoided any more dates with him—I can't start a relationship while living a double life. Things are complicated enough.

Julian hasn't pushed, though he continues to show me attention and find ways to touch me that I can't seem to hate. "I get that," Julian says with a sigh. "These things are murder."

I swallow and force a smile. *Holy crap, what if I'm slipping Vlad poison?* Not just something to knock him out but something to actually kill him.

Julian's gaze narrows. "You're pale. Are you sure you're okay?"

I nod, my throat too tight to respond. He reaches over and takes my hand in his, warming it. "You're doing great. The press is loving you. The paparazzi are obsessed. Angela—" He leans even closer. "You've made it. You're a real star."

His words unlock my throat and lift me up. It's what I've been fighting for. *It's my dream.* So many people dream of this level of success, and I've achieved it.

But at what cost?

THE HOTEL IS OPULENT, beyond any of the other amazing places we've stayed on this junket. In the morning we have press meetings for four hours. By lunch time I'm exhausted, and my throat is sore. One of the PAs brings me a warm tea with honey. "Thanks, Sandra," I say. She smiles. In her early forties, with blonde, gray-streaked hair, she has worked as a PA for almost twenty years.

"Never wanted to be an actor," she told me while we were in Hong Kong. "I like keeping things organized. Gives me a thrill." Her words punctuated by a throaty laugh that was absorbed into the luxury of the car we were riding in.

"These things can be killer on your throat," Sandra says. I nod and sip the sweet elixir she brought me. "I'll take you to your lunch appointment—you've got the China *Vogue* interview." My shoulders slump at the reminder that my day is *so* not over yet. But I pull them back quickly. This is what I want. The more press the better.

The reporter for Shanghai *Vogue* is a young Chinese man wearing 1950s prison-issue style glasses, a narrow black tie over a white button down shirt, and shiny black pants. "Angela Daniels," he says, his cheeks rushing with color as he extends his hand. "I'm Sing Chin."

"Sorry I'm late," I say, knowing he's been waiting for at least thirty minutes. "Traffic on the way over was terrible."

"Don't worry about it." He has a slight accent but sounds like he has spent some time in America.

We take our seats at a table draped in white linen, and a waiter hurries over to fill my water glass. We are in the lobby restaurant of a hotel, about as fancy as the one I'm staying at. I glance out the plate glass windows to the busy street. *I want to get out there and explore.* The waiter leaves me with the menu, and I glance at it. Sing is setting up a recorder, and I suppress a sigh.

"So, Angela," Sing starts, like every other freaking reporter on the darn trail. "Thanks for taking the time to meet with me."

"Thank you for being interested in me," I say with a self-depre-cating laugh.

"Well," he smiles. "You are blowing up right now."

I glance down at myself and grin at him. "Hey, I know I have not been in training as often, but I think I'm doing okay." He looks confused, and I lean across the table toward him. "Are you saying I should order a salad?"

He goes pale. "Oh no—"

"I'm just messing with you, Sing. I hear what you're saying. It's just hard to believe sometimes. Dreams this big don't usually come true."

He visibly relaxes, but the color in his cheeks may be permanent. "You're surprised by your fame?"

"I think anyone who reaches this level is surprised by it, to a degree. Of course, we all wanted it. But really, Sing, how often do we get what we want in life?"

"What has surprised you about it most?"

"I'm not sure," I say, pursing my lips, pretending to think…even though I've answered this question several times over the last few weeks. "I'm not surprised by the lack of privacy. Because, of course, I knew that was a part of the price. But I'm surprised by exactly what it feels like."

"What do you mean?"

"Well…" I lean toward him again, putting down the menu. "I would love to explore this city. Get some street food, you know. Wander inconspicuously. But I'm in a bubble." I motion to the windows behind us—a perfect metaphor of the fish bowl I'm living in.

He nods. "Yes, I can see how that would be frustrating. There are no paparazzi right now, though," he points out.

"Yes…but you're here." I give him a wink.

He leans toward me, and I get a whiff of cologne—Calvin Klein, I think. Something floral and spicy, very gender neutral. "Would you like me to take you out to some street vendors now?"

My eyes widen. "I would freaking love that."

Sing smiles and nods, grabbing his recorder and starting to wrap it up.

We leave the air-conditioned, rarified interior of the hotel. On the street, it's sweltering, dense with traffic and people. The odor of diesel and exhaust thicken the air. Sing turns left, and I follow. This is the first time since landing in China that I've walked on a city street. Usually I go from venue to venue in the back of a car.

"There is a great market not far from here," Sing says, glancing over at me.

"I'm good to walk," I say, even as sweat begins to break out on my back. I don't care if it seeps through my white blouse.

He grins. "So this is your first time in China?"

"Yes," I laugh. "First time for a lot of places. I didn't grow up traveling but always wanted to."

"Tell me about your hometown." He pulls out his phone and holds it between us as we weave through pedestrian traffic. I glance at it for a moment and then begin to launch into my spiel. Small-town America, family farm and working, loving parents who died in a car accident when I was ten. My maternal grandmother raising me. The high school plays. A modeling contract at sixteen. Acting gigs. And now a starring role in a famous director's final film.

We arrive at the market, and Sing stashes his phone to point out my options. The fragrance of roasting meat and foreign spices is intoxicating. "This stall makes the most amazing noodles," Sing tells me, pointing to where a white-haired woman hunkers behind several silver pots. "The chicken stew there"—he points at a younger man with more steaming pots in front of him—"is very spicy. Really special spicy, though. It starts with a buttery texture and then the spice hits you. The only way to ease the burn is to eat more."

"That's a pretty brilliant recipe," I say.

Sing laughs. "Yes, very good. You want to try?"

"After that description, how could I resist?"

We approach the stall and Sing orders two bowls. The young man opens one of his pots, revealing a creamy-looking stew filled with colorful vegetables and hot peppers. He ladles it into two bowls and puts them on a tray. Sing pays and carries them over to one of the small tables set up on the sidewalk. We sit on the low stools, my knees coming up to my waist, and Sing puts a bowl in front of me along with a spoon and a pair of chopsticks.

The aromatic steam from the soup mixes with the rest of the hot air around me, creating a heady perfume. "Thank you," I say to Sing. "It's so great to get out of the bubble."

"Very glad to help."

I taste the soup—he's right, it's buttery, and there is more to it as well, an entire world of spices. The flavor is deep, layered. I close my eyes, just tasting. Then the heat starts. It begins in my belly and climbs slowly up my throat, finally reaching my tongue and igniting it. It's so hot my mouth goes almost numb. "Wow," I say, opening my eyes.

"Take another spoonful," Sing advises. I do, and start the whole process over again.

By the time my bowl is empty, I'm sweating profusely, the heat of the day and the cooking around me, combined with the spice of the soup, leaving me a puddle of sensations. I gulp the last of my water, and Sing waves to another stall. A kid, about eight or nine, hurries over with a big bottle of beer and two plastic cups. There is condensation dripping off the beer bottle even faster than sweat is trickling over my brow. "A cold beer is the best thing for this kind of heat," Sing explains, pouring us each a small, frothy serving.

It looks so good…"I can't," I say. "I have so much more to do today. If I drink that, I'll just need a nap."

"A little won't hurt," Sing advises. "And it will help with the burning."

My mouth is on fire. And the air is so hot. And that beer is frosting the freaking plastic glass. No one could refuse it.

I pick it up, and Sing raises his cup. "To escaping the bubble," he says.

I click my glass against his.

It's good. *So good.* I smack my lips, and Sing laughs. "You really enjoy food and drink."

"I try to enjoy everything," I say. "We only live once."

Sing gets serious, leaning toward me over the tiny plastic table and empty bowls. "What did you think when you heard about Jack Axelrod's passing?"

I'm surprised by the question and take another sip of beer to gather my thoughts. I've answered this one a million times, but Sing lowered my defenses with his spicy stew and cold beer. "I felt sad for his family," I answer.

Sing nods. "You must have been worried about the future of the film."

"No movie is as important as a man's life."

"Meaning you knew it would go on."

"Oh, no." I shake my head. "But it wasn't my first concern. I felt bad that such a brilliant artist was dead."

The way I said " dead" sounded funny in my ears. Should I have used the euphemistic "passed"?

Sing just nods though. I glance down at the table and discover his phone is out, recording us again. That's fine; I knew this was an interview. I take a breath, and another sip of beer, and smile at him. "This was my first major role, and it's any actor's dream to work with a director like Jack. I was heartbroken on a lot of levels."

"What about the rumors that have come out since his passing? That he took advantage of some of his stars."

I shake my head. "I don't know anything about that."

Sing leans even closer, lowering his voice. "You had dinner with him that night. It must have been shocking to hear of his passing."

"Yes, very." I nod my head and hold his gaze. *I have nothing to hide. Everything is in the public record. These are not the droids you're searching for...*

"And you were in a car accident that evening. Were you on your way home from his house when it happened?"

"Yes, close to my home, in Eagle Rock. Jack lived in the hills."

"I'm not familiar with Los Angeles."

"Well, if you ever come, you must allow me to introduce you to our street foods. The tacos are to die for." *I should not have said die. Crap on toast.*

"I would like that very much."

My phone chirps, and I glance down at it. It's Sandra. I put up a finger to Sing, saying I'll be just a minute, then answer it. "We're here to pick you up, where are you?" she asks, a note of panic in her voice.

"I'm not totally sure," I say with a laugh, looking around, not finding any street signs. "Where are we?" I ask Sing.

He holds his hand out for the phone, and I pass it over. He speaks with the driver, giving him directions, then hands the phone back. "They will be here in a few minutes."

As I slip the phone back into my purse, an old, hunched woman, weighted down by bags of merchandise, approaches our table. She holds out an arm draped with jewelry. I shake my head without glancing at it. But Sing pulls a strand off the woman's arm. "For you," he says, passing the woman some cash.

"Oh, I couldn't," I say.

He meets my eyes, and there is something there. Something new and different. "A gift from Temperance," he says.

My heart races, and I take a quick inhale as the woman moves onto the next table. My eyes fall onto the necklace Sing is holding out to me. It glitters in the light—it actually looks like real gold. I take it from him with a trembling hand. The chain holds a round locket with a dragon image inscribed onto it.

"Ah, and here is your car," Sing says, standing.

I swallow, take a breath, and put my face back on as I slip the chain over my neck. It falls against my chest, the weight of it so light compared to the reality of it.

Inside is something dangerous. A pill, a powder? I don't know. But something I must slip into a man's drink. As I stand, I notice my hands are still shaking. I grip my purse with both of them and smile at Sandra, who is standing next to the car.

"Enjoy the party this evening," Sing says, walking toward the car to see me off.

I smile at him. "Thank you, will you be attending?"

"No, but if you need anything while in the city, don't hesitate to call." Sing pulls out a card from his pocket and passes it to me.

We are standing at the car now, the door open before me. I glance down at the card. It has his name on it, "Vogue Reporter At Large" printed under it, followed by a number. "Thank you."

"Enjoy the rest of your stay in Shanghai," Sing says as I climb into the back of the car. I give him a nod before Sandra closes the door, leaving me once again ensconced in chilled, filtered air and the feel and smell of black leather.

She gets into the front seat with the driver, and we merge into traffic.

"You have a few hours to rest now and get dressed," she tells me. "Then the party at the consulate."

"Okay, thank you." I lean my head back against the seat and close my eyes, willing my mind to settle. But the weight of the necklace around my neck is heavy, my task feeling suddenly very real. My hands itch to open the locket and see what's inside.

I still don't know how I'm supposed to get whatever it is into Vladimir's drink. I'm not a freaking magician...or a waiter. But I guess now I am officially a spy.

CLOSING the hotel suite door I stand for a moment in the hush of luxury. Floor to ceiling windows expose a cloudy day, the high-rises around me reflecting the silver gray of the sky.

My hand comes up to the locket and my head bends down so that I am curling around it—mimicking the pose of the dragon figure depicted on the quarter-sized locket cover. The horned beast, with its long body, delicate wings, and split tongue, has a jade eye set into the gold.

I run my finger over the clasp, heart pounding. *What is inside?* Part of me wants to rip it open, face whatever my future holds. But another part is terrified and urges me to flush the necklace down the toilet. *It's too heavy. It would just sit at the bottom of the bowl.* Fine, then throw it out one of those giant windows. *They don't open.*

There is no escaping this.

Just open it!

My nail dips under the clasp and I pause, holding my breath, blood rushing in my ears. I apply light, sustained pressure, my teeth digging into my bottom lip, and the locket opens with a soft click.

Pulling the two halves apart, I find a ring nestled into a velvet cushion—a gold band with a white stone half the size of my pinky nail. I tip the locket, dropping the ring into my palm and stare at it before returning my attention to the empty case.

There are no instructions.

Casting my gaze around the sitting room, I taste blood in my mouth, and realize I've bitten my lip hard enough to cut it.

Nervous energy forces me to move. Gripping the ring in my palm,

I hurry into the bedroom, drop my purse on the bed and sit next to it, staring down at my fisted hand.

Slowly, I open my fingers and it's still there. I pull the chain over my head and inspect the locket casing again, hoping for a clue. Finding none, I return my attention to the ring. *I should put it on.*

The metal slips over my knuckle, settling onto the base of my middle finger. The stone shimmers like freshly fallen snow. It's a simple and elegant adornment.

Feeling the underside of the ring, I discover a small notch. I press it and the stone pops out, skipping across the white carpeting and disappearing into the thick weave. My heart skips along with it. *Crud, where did it go?*

I drop onto my hands and knees, running my fingers over the floor. Crud, crud, crud. *What kind of a spy loses the damn poison pill?*

Its hard surface brushes my palm, and I let out a long breath as I scoop it up and sit back against the bed. The ring band has small gold tongs, now empty, meant to hold the smooth stone in place. I put the oblong, shimmering gem back in the center of the ring and push at the ridge on the underside again. The tongs grasp the pill, and all is as it was.

So, I just have to get my middle finger over his drink and release the pill. *That's all.* A laugh bubbles up in me, and I bite my lip hard enough to shoot a zing of pain through me.

I check my watch—I have about two hours until I need to be ready. The weight of my day and the last few weeks lands on my shoulders. I'm exhausted and I need to shower after my spicy, sweaty meal.

Putting the ring on the dresser top next to the now-empty locket, I strip and head to the bathroom. I spend a good amount of time in the shower, just letting the water pound over me, getting lost in its hum, letting all my thoughts wander at will. My trainer, Synthia Taylor, is always pushing me to meditate—now that I am actually involved in an operation, I understand why.

Just the fear of the unknown will suck you away, much less the actual heat of battle.

Wrapped up in a big towel, I dry my long black hair, being sure to get every last strand straight before climbing into the king-sized bed. I set the alarm, giving myself thirty minutes to nap, and promptly pass out.

When the beeping wakes me, I have to peel my eyes open. *Not nearly enough rest.* Rolling toward the heinous sound, I smack at the bedside clock until it shuts up, then keep rolling right onto my feet.

The sun, hovering now between the skyscrapers, streams into the bedroom. I blink against its brightness and feel a hot tear hiding among my lashes. *Am I going to kill a man tonight?*

Resolve hardens in my gut as the tear escapes. I reach for my purse, finding Sing's card. He picks up on the first ring. "I wanted to ask you about the locket you bought for me today," I say.

"Just a trinket," he says. There is traffic noise behind him.

"Yes, I do like it, though. Can you tell me what it's made of?" I twine the bathrobe's tie around my wrist, staring down at it, hoping Sing gets my drift.

"Made of?" he asks. A horn honks behind him.

"Yes, the material."

"I'm sure it's just painted metal. Not real gold or anything."

Was that code? Sounded pretty reasonable. *Crap.* I take a breath and try again. "What is it tempered with, do you think?" Tempered sounds like Temperance right? *I want Temperance to call me.* Is that message getting through?

"Sorry, but I don't know, Angela."

"Do you know anyone who might? Maybe they could call me."

"It's just a trinket from a vendor on the street, nothing of value."

"But...I want to know what it is..."

"I can try to find out, I suppose," he relents.

"That would be great," I say, enthusiasm lifting me to my feet. "I don't want it turning my skin green...or giving me a rash." I let out a small, genuine sounding laugh. "Or killing me. You never know with things you pick up off the street."

"Of course, but I'm sure it won't hurt you."

"You're sure."

"Positive."

"What if I was allergic to it? I mean, what if I gave it as a gift to a friend?" I'm pacing now, my brow furrowed.

"I doubt it—" A truck rumbles by, swallowing anything else he says.

"Right, okay, but, maybe you could try to find out. Just to be sure."

"I'll do my best."

I don't want to hang up, but this is going on too long, I'm coming off like a nut bar. We say our goodbyes, and I take a deep breath. It's time to get dressed.

I have work to do.

CHAPTER SEVEN

THE PARTY at the American consulate is black tie—very fancy and sophisticated, as one might imagine a diplomatic reception to be. Our entire entourage is invited, and Julian escorts me up the long, elegant stairs into the grand entryway. The last rays of the sunset cast a pink glow over the handsome, early 20th century building and the other guests making their way into the event.

Julian is in a tux again, looking dashing. My black dress, edged in gray satin, has a tight bodice that pushes me up and clings to my waist and hips, cupping my ass before fanning out into a classic mermaid silhouette.

The designer, a young man based in LA, fitted me personally before the trip. "This silhouette was invented for bodies like yours," he said, marveling at me in the mirror. Clearly gay, his appreciative gaze was all about form and artistry.

But as we walk up these stairs, pass through the high doorway into the large and crowded entryway, the gazes that roam over me—staring at my breasts, my flat stomach and tight, high ass—feel almost like hands touching me, hungry for the feminine form, not as art but as sex.

I finger the ring, careful not to press the clasp but desperate to make sure it is still there. If I lose it, I fail. Temperance didn't call. I still have no idea what the stone is made of, but I guess it will dissolve quickly. That I won't be caught because of a malfunction.

The danger here is me—my own failing.

Julian leans over and speaks into my ear. "You're absolutely stunning. No one can take their eyes off you."

I smile and raise my eyes to him. "You're pretty stunning yourself."

"Can we have that dinner soon? Just the two of us."

I'd been putting him off—scared of myself, of Temperance…of this whole thing. How could I agree to dinner with a man? More than dinner really. Julian's made it clear he isn't looking for *just* an affair. The man is serious about me. *Patient.* And isn't that just the sexiest thing ever?

A flash makes me blink—a photographer, also in a tux, though his isn't nearly as fine as Julian's, bows to us slightly. *Must be working for our diplomatic hosts.*

A waiter holding a tray of champagne glasses offers them. Julian releases my arm to take two, passing one to me. I shiver as I stare at the bubbles. Will the pill on my ring dissolve in a cascade of bubbles?

The room fills, and we mingle with other cast members. The ambassador, who made the trip down from Beijing for this occasion, is introduced to us, a white-haired, handsome man in his late fifties. He smiles at me warmly before introducing his wife, who has one of those rich, white-lady haircuts, all pale blonde seashell.

We talk about Shanghai, what we think of it so far, how much we've traveled, how honored they are to have us, and how honored we are to be there.

"Excuse me." I lean in toward the ambassador's wife, whose name I forgot the moment I heard it. "Where is the ladies room?"

She smiles knowingly. *Nature happens to all of us.* "Down there to the right." I follow her lifted chin to where a guard in Marine dress uniform stands at the front of a hall. I nod and head toward him.

The size of a boulder, the guard's shoulders are almost as wide as the entryway. As I approach he gives me a small bow, his hands behind his back, and steps to the side. "To your right," he says quietly as I pass.

"Thank you." He nods again.

I find the bathroom and push in. I'm alone, and the lightness of that is surprising to me. The weight of so many stares is something I've always craved. The attention usually gives me energy, but tonight I want to be hidden. *I'm used to my secrets being in my past, not my future.*

After using the facilities, I apply more lipstick and am turning to leave when there is a soft knock at the door. "Just a moment," I say, heading to open it.

I step back, surprised to see a dark suit rather than a slim gown. At first I think it's the bouncer, but as my gaze makes it up to the man's face, I realize it's Vladimir Petrov. My heart skips a beat, and the breath I'm exhaling gets caught in my throat.

"Good evening," he says, with a slight incline of his head. His accent is thick but not unpleasant. Something about it makes me want to try to mimic it. *I could play a great Russian spy with that accent.* "I did not mean to startle you."

My hand is still on the door knob, and I nod, not sure what I'm agreeing to but feeling that this is a man who does not do well with dissent. In person, his power is palpable. It's not just his size, or that inherently threatening-to-the-American-ear accent. It's an aura that emanates from him—similar to the one that pulls eyes to my form, but also very different. Both are powerful: one projects sex, the other violence..

"I've been wanting to meet you for some time," Vladimir goes on.

I give a tinkling laugh. "Did you always picture it happening in the ladies room?"

Color creeps up his neck, climbing that thick edifice toward his cheeks. *He's blushing.* "I do apologize. I just wanted to have a moment alone with you." He steps back, as if releasing me from the room. I curl my lips into a subtle smile and beam at him with amused eyes as I step into the hall, letting the door close behind me.

Glancing toward the main room, I'm relieved to find the guard still there. "I am a big fan of your work," Vladimir says.

I return my attention to him, having to tip my head back to meet his gaze. Even in my heels, he's still almost a head taller than me. "Thank you."

"Even when you modeled, I followed your career." He leans toward me, eager, like a schoolboy, not a ruthless oligarch.

"That's very flattering." Checking his hands, I find them empty. "Would you like a drink?" I ask.

"Yes," he almost stammers. "Let me get you one; it would be an honor."

I laugh, tipping my head back again to look up into his face. "I'm just a girl from Kansas. Not the queen."

His face turns serious. There is a glint in his eyes, something that sends a shiver of cold over me. "You are more than that to me." *Oh that's kinda creepy.*

I keep my smile in place, though, making sure none of the alarms ringing inside my head can be seen in my eyes. "Shall we?" I gesture back toward the main room, to the shifting bodies and the imagined safety of the herd. I hope to use the crowd to distract him and slip an unknown substance into his drink. *What are his plans for me?*

"May I?" Vladimir asks, holding out his arm.

I loop mine through his, feeling the pure, terrifying strength of him. *He could break me.* I think back to my trainer, Synthia's, words… "your strength comes not from muscle but from your mind. Use your opponents' size and weight against them."

The pill on my ring does not seem very sporting.

But this isn't a game.

We move down the hall and past the Marine guard. Is that something in his eyes? A warning to me? *That man is dangerous.* I suppress the smile trying to turn up my lips. *I'm not the one who needs a warning.*

Julian spots us and raises a brow, giving me a questioning half smile. I answer with a one shoulder shrug. *A fan,* it says. Julian smiles wider and turns his attention back to the ambassador's wife. She's a fan of his and is soaking up the attention. Julian is making an ally for life.

The crowd parts for us as Vladimir steers me through it. We pass a mirrored wall, and I catch a glimpse of us—it's practically beauty and the beast. His chest is so broad, his brow so low, his hands so large…I look tiny and fragile next to him.

I resist the urge to pull the cloak of royalty around myself, to puff myself up, to spread my feathers and show how strong I really am. In this moment it is best to play the part of the scullery maid who has arrived at the ball in a borrowed gown.

The bar has a line, but it wilts away as Vladimir steps up to the polished wood. "What would you like?" he asks me.

"Something fizzy," I say. "Shall we both have champagne? So we can have a true toast."

His eyes light up, and he leans over, creating a more intimate space between us. "In my country, we toast with vodka."

I giggle, dipping my chin then bringing just my eyes up to meet him, my lashes creating a film of lace between us. "I can't drink vodka and be sure not to make a fool of myself." He laughs, those big shoulders shaking. "Please," I say, "let's have champagne."

"Whatever you like, anything." He turns to the bartender and orders two flutes of champagne. They appear quickly.

We clink the edges of our glasses together. "To new friendships," I say.

"Yes," he says, a throatiness in his voice that makes it clear friendship is not his intention.

We sip from the glasses, and I stare at the bubbles in his. How am I going to get my ring over it? *Wait...he's still drinking. Oh...he's finishing. Crap on toast. That so didn't work.*

He puts the glass on the bar, and it is immediately filled again. He orders one for me as well, but I've barely wet my lips. "You're a faster drinker than me," I say, bringing a blush to my cheeks, as if I'm embarrassed at my failing.

His jaw loosens and quickly tightens. *He does not want to upset me.* "I'm sorry," he says.

"You don't need to apologize." I reach out, placing my hand on his forearm, the ring very white against his black jacket.

He looks down at the hand, and it takes every class I ever took, every moment I practiced in front of the mirror...every acting skill I've garnered from anywhere, not to pull the hand back. Not to give away the danger that slim-fingered, simply adorned hand poses to him.

He covers my hand with his, completely hiding it. "You're perfect," he says, his voice low, accent thick. I swallow the hum of real emotion that wants to rise at his words. *You don't know me. We are strangers. Perfection does not exist.*

"That's sweet," I say. "You're very kind."

His eyes implore me to believe him—he may be powerful enough to make any words he says into truth. *Am I powerful enough to take him down?*

Temperance thinks I am. Sing gave me the weapon; all I have to do is slip it into this man's drink. *No, not sporting.*

"Have you ever been to Moscow?" he asks me, changing the subject.

"No," I shake my head. "But I'd love to some time. It seems like a fascinating place. Is that where you live?"

"One of the places. But I will be spending more time in America soon."

"Really, why's that?" I ask, sipping my drink.

"Business. With the election. Things will change. Reginald Grand is a good man. He sees the possibilities that bringing our two nations closer together can provide."

"I'm not really into politics," I say.

His eyes glitter. "A pretty thing like you doesn't need to be."

I force my face to stay open and happy. *I'm not into politics because they are out of my control and paying attention doesn't do me any good.* It's not like I don't vote. I just don't spend my life worrying about what those a-holes in Washington are doing. Of course, with how things have suddenly changed in my life, I probably should start to pay attention...

"I understand that you like to read," Vladimir says, changing the subject again.

"Love it," I answer, smiling.

"You like spy novels, yes?" Truth is, I'm more a paranormal kind of gal, but I nod and smile—I've been telling reporters I love spy fiction. After all, the film I'm promoting is a spy novel adaptation. "Have you read *The Twentieth of January*?" He asks.

"No, is it good?"

"Yes, you should try it."

"What's it about?"

Before he can answer, a bell rings, and there is a call for us to go into dinner. "We are at the same table," Vladimir tells me. "I arranged it."

I give him a smile. "Then we will have a chance to get to know each other better."

He puffs up a little as his eyes raise over my head. I turn to see Julian approaching, his easy smile, and even easier grace, clearing him a path just as Vladimir's raw, dangerous power does. "Angela," Julian says, his eyes flitting over my face for a moment, searching it, before jumping to Vladimir.

"May I introduce—" I laugh, smiling at Vladimir. "You never told me your name."

He extends his hand, leaving the refilled champagne flute unattended on the bar top. "Vladimir Petrov," he says. Julian covers up a wince as their hands grip.

"Quite a strong grip you have there, mate," Julian says, shaking out his fingers with a little more drama than necessary.

I put my own glass on the far side of Vladimir's and tilt the ring over his as I bring my hand back to myself. A small pressure on the tiny latch releases the stone. It drops with a plunk so loud to my ears I'm surprised that the two men are still staring at each other as I pick up the glass and bring it around to Vladimir. The stone is gone by the time I hold it out to him—dispersed amidst the bubbles. "Here," I say, offering it to him.

He glances down at me and softens his expression. "Let's go in."

I turn to Julian, "Vladimir is at our table," I say.

"Oh, jolly."

"Want a drink before we head to dinner?" I ask. Julian shakes his head. Picking up my own glass, I hold it up to Vladimir for another toast. He gives me a broad smile, but there is something possessive about it. *He wants me and is willing to do what it takes to get me.*

Right back at you, baby.

Our glasses clink, but this time he takes a small sip instead of downing it. *Crap.*

Julian offers me his arm, and I take it. Vladimir reddens but is not deterred, walking right next to me, refusing to cede any space to the crowd around us.

It's not until we reach the entrance to the banquet hall that he has to drop back. I glance over my shoulder to check on him. His glass is still in his hand, and his eyes are trained on me. When our gazes meet, I see frustration that melts into hope at my attention.

A man touches his shoulder, and he turns to him. The crowd shifts, and Julian and I are in a large banquet room, Vladimir still in the stream of people behind us.

Round tables covered in fine linen, fancy china, and boastful floral arrangements surround a dance floor. At the front of the room is a stage with a large screen and a band playing soft music.

Julian leads me along the side of the room to one of the front tables. "That guy is kind of scary."

"Yes," I agree.

"He's at our table?"

"Apparently he's admired me for some time."

"Your first powerful stalker." He nods to himself, as if this is some classic stop on the road we are both traveling. "I had a Dutch princess who kept showing up at every festival. This was years ago." He shakes his head at the memory, a private smile playing across his lips as he pulls out a chair for me. I sit, and his breath brushes my shoulder as he helps push the chair in. "She gave up eventually."

He looks past me to the entrance. "This one might be a harder case. I'll stay close."

Vladimir appears in the doorway, the man who stopped him, short and stocky with silver hair cropped close to his block-shaped skull, still by his side. He exudes *private security*—his eyes roam the room, his head bent slightly as if listening to an ear piece.

Vlad is shaking his head, eyes down as they move across the room in our direction. Julian takes a seat next to me. The room fills with the sound of clinking glasses and murmurs of conversations.

The silver-haired security man moves away from Vladimir, going to stand by one of the large windows, hands behind his back, and his employer continues toward us, putting a smile on. He stops at a different table, placing his large hand on a man's shoulder and making him blanch.

Vlad jostles the seated man a few times, lets out a bellow of laughter, and then starts our way again. The glass is gone. *Shit, did he drink it or dump it?* He said he didn't like champagne that much.

I glance down at my ring. Without the stone, it's odd looking, and I slip it off, pushing it into my clutch. Our table is filling up, and Julian is chatting with the other occupants...but I only have eyes for Vladimir. He takes the free seat to my left and, giving Julian one quick glance of distaste, brings his focus to me.

"Sorry about that," he says.

"No need to apologize," I say, waving a hand. "We have all evening."

The ambassador, upstaging the consul general as our host for the evening, takes the stage and a spotlight focuses on him. "Welcome, dear guests," he says. I can't concentrate on his words; I'm too busy staring at the back of Vladimir's head, wondering...*did he drink it?*

I clap when everyone else does and then a band takes the stage and waiters arrive with salads. I pick at my food. Vladimir inhales his then returns his attention to me. "Would you like to dance?" he asks.

"Dance?" The floor is empty, the band is playing soft, slow music meant for eating.

"Yes," Vladimir says. Are his cheeks pinker? Is it an effect from the substance I put in his drink? Or am I the cause?

"I'm not sure..."

"Come," he stands, pushing his chair back. *Did he stumble slightly?* Vladimir holds his hand out. I hope to see it shaking, but the big paw is steady.

I look up at him. Julian leans over and whispers into my ear. "You don't have to."

Vladimir's expression darkens, but when I nod, light jumps back to his eyes. I take his hand, rough with callouses, and so big that again, I get that sense of smallness, so rare for me. I'm tall and thick for a woman in my profession—hard muscle and lush, full curves. I move through the world with a sense of strength and size, especially traveling in Asia the past few weeks. This man makes me feel tiny and fragile.

I lift my head and smile at him, pretending that I like the sensation of smallness. We make our way to the stage, where he speaks quietly with a sound guy. Then Vlad pulls me onto the dance floor, his stride steady.

His right hand spans my lower back, and I rest my left on his shoulder, our free hands twine, his thick fingers almost painful between mine.

Vladimir steps backward, and I follow, surprised by his sudden grace on the dance floor. In my first film role, I played a secondary character in a film about professional ballroom dancers. It went straight to streaming, but I'll never forget how to fox trot. "You're a good dancer," I say as he whisks me across the floor.

"I was inspired by your film, Ballroom Badness," he smiles down at me.

I tilt my head back and laugh. "You saw that?"

"I've seen everything you've done." Something shifts in his accent...slurred?

"Really? That's so sweet," I say, knowing that the word sweet is the wrong one. Calling this man sweet is like calling a docile pit bull sweet —just before it turns on you..

"Yes," he coughs, his eyes unfocusing and his feet stumbling for a moment.

"Are you okay?" I ask.

He nods, but his feet are slowing down. We grind to a halt, his fingers tightening on mine, the palm on my back slips down to my ass...loose...like he's lost control of it.

"Vladimir?" I say.

His eyes are unfocused; he can't hold me in his gaze any longer. He trips backward, pulling me against his chest, and we both go down, me on top of him. The band falters, and a collective gasp rises up from the crowd when we hit the hard wood floor, his one hand still gripping mine, the other shaking.

His whole body is seizing—stiff and quaking under me as his eyes roll into the back of his head.

CHAPTER EIGHT

A PERFUME OF FINE SILK, musky cologne, vodka, and sweat rises up around me. My pupils dilate, a biological response to my own fear I can't control.

Vladimir's body is vibrating under me, and I push to get away, but he's still gripping my hand. He pulls it close, gritting his teeth, eyes rolled into the back of his head.

My free hand is on his shoulder. I push hard, getting my chest off of his, creating enough space between us that I can see his face. So that I can watch the horror show I've created.

Power flows over me. *I did this.*

A flood of guilt follows. *I did this.*

Hands come around my waist and pull, loosening me from Vladimir's grip. My feet wheel through the air, trying to help propel me away...away from what I've done. From that burst of power, of the pure adrenaline it gave me. *Dear God, I liked it.*

"Angela." Julian's voice is in my ear, his chest pressed to my back. "Are you okay?"

I'm shaking, tremors moving through me as I stare at Vladimir, in his tuxedo, that giant body flailing on the shiny dance floor.

Men rush forward, security surrounding him. The silver-haired security agent crouches by Vladimir's side, hand on the big guy's chest, mouth drawn into a tight line.

I'm staring, can't take my eyes off the scene. Then Vladimir goes still. *So damn still.* It's a relief in one moment—the seizure has stopped —and terrifying in the next. He's not moving…at all.

Silver starts doing compressions on his chest. I count with him… one, two, three.

Julian pulls me backward so that the crowd grows thicker, so that I can no longer see Vladimir through the crush of onlookers. Medics yell, pushing through the throng. The onlookers dash out of the way. This is not the gentle parting for a powerful man but the panicked sidestep of emergency… *they don't want to be the ones who kill him.*

"Angela." Julian turns me to face him. "Hey." He cups my cheek, those big blue eyes of his holding mine, trying to see inside. I blink, not sure what he saw. *Did I leave the shutters open?*

"Julian," I croak, my throat thick with tears.

He wraps me in his arms, my face pressed to his chest. "You're okay," he tells me, one hand on my back, the other coming up to pet my hair. I don't respond. What can I say?

This is horrific. *I did this.*

THE MEDICS, cheeks red with exertion and excitement, take Vladimir out on a gurney, an oxygen mask over his mouth and nose. The silver-haired security agent goes with him. I stand with Julian, my side pressed to his, as they jog out of the room. "Is he—?" I ask.

"I don't know," Julian answers, squeezing me. "Are you okay?"

"I don't know."

The ambassador appears on the stage, drawing the attention of the milling crowd, his voice over the microphone quieting the hush of conversation. "Please everyone, return to your tables. Mr. Petrov is in good medical hands. I'm so sorry about this…." I zone out, my eyes scanning the room.

Is this what was supposed to happen? Is he dead? Did I kill a man…again? But this time on purpose, knowingly?

Not knowingly. I didn't *know* what was in the pill. This is on Temperance. On Sing. I'm just the weapon; they are the ones that fired it. A wave of sickness washes over me, and I lean against Julian harder. *I don't want to be a weapon.*

"Let's get out of here," Julian whispers into my hair.

Steering me with a hand at my waist, we start toward the exit. Security stands on either side of the door—not the decorative Marines this time, but plain-clothed professionals. They watch our approach from under lowered brows. One steps forward, putting a hand out to stop us. "I'm sorry," he says. "But no one can leave."

"Excuse me?" Julian says, his voice loud.

"Everyone must speak with the police before they go." Nausea turns my stomach. "The police?" Julian says, his voice softening in confusion. "Why?"

"Please sir, return to your table."

Julian leans toward the security officer. "She's had a rough night. Can't the police meet us at our hotel? This is very traumatizing."

A laugh tries to escape over the nausea, but I stifle it.

"I'm sorry, sir. We have our orders."

Julian stiffens but does not respond. "Come on," he says to me quietly. "Let's speak to the ambassador."

I let him lead me across the room toward the ambassador's table, but he is still on stage. "The police will be here soon," the ambassador says. "They ask that you all wait until their arrival to leave."

The room quiets, the air thickening with tension. Murmurs start up, people leaning toward each other. The candlelight glitters on the women's jewels, which sparkle almost as bright as the glee in their eyes. This is an adventure. A story to tell.

When the ambassador leaves the stage, Julian moves quickly, leaving me standing by an empty seat. I grip the back of the chair to steady myself and take stock of my appearance. My head feels drained of blood; I'm sure I look it. *Good.* Eyes soft, scared. Yes, that's in line with what happened. My throat is still tight, my stomach upset. *Yes.* This all works. *I am an innocent woman whose dance partner just had a seizure and possibly died underneath her.*

Julian reaches the ambassador and dips his head slightly to speak to the older man. The ambassador nods, listening, understanding.

But will he let us go? Julian's hands are moving now. The ambassador is nodding, but his mouth is firm. *It's not going to work.*

Julian, his cheeks flushed, turns back to look at me. I let all the symptoms of my shock show, let my eyes meet his, let them be glassy and slightly confused.

Lips firming, Julian turns back to the ambassador for one more try. The older man shakes his white head, and Julian gives a sharp and frustrated nod before turning back to me.

"Sorry," he says when he reaches where I stand. "He won't let us leave, but promises that the police will speak to you first."

"This is terrible," I say, my hand rising to my neck.

Julian gives that firm nod again before pulling out a chair. *Ah, it's mine.* This is where we were sitting. There is my purse. I gently lower myself into the seat and reach out to take the glass of water. My eyes fall on Vladimir's empty seat as I sip it.

What happened to the champagne glass?

Will there be any trace in it?

The band begins to play again. Nobody dances. Julian keeps a protective arm over the back of my seat. What would he say if he knew? He probably wouldn't believe me.

I can hardly believe it myself.

The salad plates are cleared as the other diners, who had been milling near the stage, return to our table. A middle-aged woman with fine lines around her eyes and pink rouge on her cheeks leans across the table, ducking her head between the giant flower arrangement to find me and offer a sympathetic smile. "I'm so sorry. That must have been terrifying."

I nod.

"I'm sure he'll be okay," she says.

I lean forward. "You think so?" I ask.

She nods forcefully. "Seizures are rarely actually dangerous or deadly. He probably has epilepsy or something like that. This could be totally normal for him."

"Then why would they call the police, dear?" asks the man sitting next to her, his voice accented and condescending.

"Dotting t's and crossing i's," she responds archly, not looking at him. Waiters start bringing us the soup course.

The husband does not respond verbally, and I can't see his face through the flowers, only his hands. He picks up his spoon and starts to eat the soup. The clinking of silver on china rises up, and the room begins to relax. The waiters move through the space, filling wine glasses, and the guests drink with a new sense of urgency.

Julian points to his own glass, and it fills with dark Burgundy wine. Then he points to mine. I shake my head. "I'm not feeling well," I say.

"Please bring her a brandy," Julian says to the waiter, who nods before moving off.

"I don't think I can drink right now," I say to Julian, low so that only he can hear.

"It's good for shock," he replies, leaning toward me. "At least that's what my grandmother always said." He gives me an intimate smile, and I return it with a small curl of my own lips. But I can't get the emotion, the humor he is trying to breathe into the air, up to my eyes. "Don't worry," he says. "I'll stay with you."

"Thank you," I say.

"I'm sure it's totally customary to do an investigation in a situation like this. But she"—he tips his head toward the woman across the way —"is probably right that he has a known condition."

I just nod.

There is a disturbance in the flow of conversation, and our gazes track with the rest of the crowds to the ballroom entrance, where a group of uniformed Chinese police are filing in. The ambassador is by the door, speaking with a man in plain clothes while the officers begin to move through the space.

The ambassador points in my direction, and Julian stands up. I take a deep breath. *Here we go.*

THEY TAKE us to the consul general's private study on the second floor.

It's decorated in dark wood with leather-bound books, just what you would expect. That sense of cliché washes over me again.

The detective is a middle-aged man with deep pouches under his eyes which make him look exhausted. However, his eyes are sharp and bright.

"Ms. Angela Daniels," the detective says, his accent slight.

"That's my stage name," I answer as I take the seat he indicates. It's a comfortable arm chair meant for enjoying some of the books around me, not to be questioned by police.

The detective takes a seat across from me, and Julian stands next to my chair like some kind of sentry. "Please, sir," the detective says. "Sit." He waves his hand at a chair nearby but outside our intimate circle. Julian lets out a small sound of protest but does as asked.

"My name is Choi Sang," the detective says. "The ambassador says that you were dancing with Vladimir Petrov when he fell ill."

I nod. "Yes, he seemed fine until he wasn't..." My voice trails off, as if I'm lost in the memory, and I look down at my hands, a tear forming in the corner of my eye.

"How long had you known Mr. Petrov?" Choi asks me.

"I only met him tonight." I bring my eyes up to meet his; they are dark, the pupil and iris almost the same color. "He told me he was a fan."

"Yes," Julian piped up. "Said he'd arranged to be at our table. It happens in our business sometimes."

Choi nods. "I'm sure, but Mr. Petrov was not your average ardent fan."

"What do you mean?" Julian asks.

Choi does not respond, instead he keeps his eyes on me. "So, you just met him tonight, and what was your impression of him?"

I give a slight shrug, my bare shoulders catching the man's attention more than the rise and fall of my cleavage. *Interesting.* "He seemed fine. I'm not sure what you mean."

"Mr. Petrov was a very powerful man."

"Was?" I say, my throat going dry. I don't need to fake the choked tone of my voice. "Is he..." I swallow, cutting off my sentence.

Choi's mouth pulls down into a frown. He didn't mean to give away any information about Vladimir's condition.

"Jesus, man," Julian says, running a hand through his hair. I turn to see him perched on the edge of his chair, dark hair tousled in a sexy bouffant of stress and seriousness. "Can't you give us a straight answer?"

"I'm here to ask the questions." Choi says, his voice edging on annoyed.

"We are not criminals," Julian says. "This has been a very hard evening for Angela."

I hold up a hand, and he presses his lips together. "I'm okay, but I would like to go back to my hotel. This is upsetting, obviously. Do you have any other questions?" I lower my hand to my lap, placing it on my purse, careful to keep my grip loose.

There is a part of me that wants to open it and pass this detective the ring, to spill my guts. It's strange. Similar to the sensation I get when standing on the top of a building—the completely repressible but still there urge to hurl myself over the edge. Just to feel what it would be like to fall.

"How much longer are you in Shanghai?" Choi asks.

"Just tomorrow." I look to Julian to make sure I'm right about that. He nods in agreement.

"That's the end of our press junket," he says.

"I may have a few more questions for you." Choi reaches into his coat and pulls out a card. "In the meantime, if you think of anything, please call."

"Think of anything?" Julian says, his voice incredulous. "She's not a doctor. What is she going to think of?"

"Maybe she saw someone put something in his drink," Choi says, his voice low, his eyes staying focused on me.

I let my jaw drop in shock.

"You think someone poisoned him?" Julian asks, his voice a high whisper.

Choi stands, dismissing us.

I take a moment to pull myself together—or at least appear to do so. I'm ready to flee, Cinderella style—just pick up my skirts and run, leaving not even a glass slipper behind. But I take a moment to slip his card into my purse, to bring tears into my gaze. "I'm very sorry this happened to him," I say. "I hope he recovers." I meet Choi's eyes and watch sympathy slowly enter his expression.

A beautiful woman on the verge of tears is hard to resist, even for the most hardened of men. As I rise, I tip forward, pressing my breasts against the dress so that they are lifted and on display for him. When I peek from under my lashes I see him watching them. *He is just a man.*

I give a small nod goodbye and then turn to Julian, who is waiting for me. He takes my elbow, his long fingers warm on my bare skin. "I'll get you back to the hotel," he says.

"Thank you." I duck my head, all scared, sad woman in need of defense. *A wolf in sheep's clothing.*

THE NIGHT IS WARM, but I am chilled. Julian slips off his jacket and wraps it around my shoulders as the black car pulls to the curb. I climb into the back. "Straight to the hotel," Julian tells the driver.

"Yes, sir."

I lean my head against the seat and close my eyes.

Julian is tense next to me. I turn to him, opening my eyes. "You okay?" I ask.

He lets out a sharp laugh. "Me? I'm fine."

"You seem tense."

"I am. That was intense."

"Yes, it was." I rest my head back again but keep my gaze on Julian. The lights of the city flash across his flawless features as we move through the metropolis.

"You were very brave," he tells me.

I flutter my lashes and glance away, feigning shyness. "Thank you, but I didn't do anything."

"You didn't scream with hysterics." *Crap, maybe I should have.* "I'm sorry that happened to you."

"I'm more worried about him," I say, looking up at Julian, pouring sympathy into my gaze. "Do you think he's dead?"

Julian breaks eye contact to look out the window before answering. "I don't know. What causes a seizure like that? Epilepsy? I don't know what else." He turns back to me. "I'm not a doctor...haven't even played one on TV." He gives me a weary smile, and I return it.

"You'd make a very handsome doctor."

His smile grows, and he drops his eyes to the seat between us, playing coy. But we both know that we are some of the best-looking people on the planet. That's how we ended up in the back of this luxury car. For whatever talent we have, there is a genetic component to the placement of our features, the coloring of our skin and eyes, the quality of our hair, that has brought us as far as any ability to pretend.

"I think mothers would be much happier to meet me if I was a doctor. No one wants their daughter dating an actor."

I wrinkle my nose. "They can't be trusted, you know. Fakers, every last one of them."

He lets out a rich laugh that zings right through me. I'm suddenly starving for touch, affection, and oblivion. I don't want to fake anything else tonight.

My gaze drops to Julian's hands...long-fingered, elegant. I don't think I'd have to fake anything with him.

When I bring my eyes back to meet his, Julian cocks his head. I let the heat in my center roll up into my gaze, burning away all the questions and strangeness of this evening.

"Angela." His voice is low, not a question so much as a statement. *He's been waiting for this.*

I give him a coy smile, not fake. Nothing else will be fake tonight.

HE WALKS me to my door, and I unlock and push it open, strolling in. Julian follows, not needing a verbal invitation. Tossing my purse onto the entry table, and slipping out of his jacket, I turn to him. He stalks toward me, the playful gentlemen replaced by a hungry predator.

The intent in his gaze sends a shiver over me, and I bare my throat, tilting my chin up. *Take me.* Take me away.

My back hits the wall, and I put my hands against it, letting him push up to me. No words are exchanged. We don't need them anymore. We've spent the last six weeks dancing around this—*the inevitable.*

His hand touches my waist, gentle and almost tentative except for the desire in his eyes, which have gone deep ocean blue in the dim room.

Julian lowers his head and brushes his lips to mine. I close my eyes, the glittering sparkles of darkness waiting for me, promising oblivion. My hands stay against the wall, feeling its cool smoothness as he kisses me. His tongue caresses my lips, and I open for him.

We've kissed before—under the lights, with the director coordinating each stroke of Julian's hand, every one of my whimpers. Julian has touched my breasts before, caressed along the sides…wrapped his hand into my hair.

But never alone.

Never for real.

Never *not* pretend.

I take a breath, and he smiles against my lips. "Do you know how long I've wanted to do this?" he asks.

My hands come up to wrap around his neck, pressing myself against him in answer. He pulls me closer. Our bodies align, the silk of my dress rasping against the fine cotton of his shirt as he pushes me up against the wall again—steadying me, the better to kiss me, to invade me.

I let out a moan. It doesn't sound like the whimpers of pleasure my character made. It is the satisfaction of a predator's hunger easing, not the relief of a victim's fear receding.

His hand finds my zipper and traces it down my back, loosening the dress's hold on my body, spilling me out against him.

My fingers find the button at his throat.

The dress slips between us, falling to my waist; his thumbs push it over my hips, following to cup my ass, pulling me up. Free now of the dress, my legs come around his waist, and I'm pressed even harder against the wall. *Oh yes.*

His hands are not disappointing me.

Soon there will be no me. Only sensation.

I give myself over to the experience, to the realness. I force my mind to stay here, in my body, where all the pleasure is sizzling, where all the excitement is brewing, where all the anticipation is boiling.

His shirt comes off, and then we are bare skin to bare skin…again. But this time for real.

Julian pulls me forward, and our lips break as he begins to carry me through the suite. His is the same as mine; he knows the layout and strides to the bedroom.

I dip my mouth to his neck, running my tongue along his jaw. *God, he's gorgeous.*

My hands rub over his shoulders, exploring the hard, defined muscle. It sends chills of anticipation racing over me, through me.

Why did I wait so long to do this? *Don't think about the reasons.*

He lays me down on the bed, crawling over me, his eyes intent, genuine…a sweetness behind the hunger. He does not want to hurt me. *Just devour me.*

Exposing my throat again, I wrap my legs around his waist, pulling him forward, forcing him close. Begging with my body for him to take away the thinking, the worrying, the faking—to leave me nothing but physical sensation and satisfied need.

His hands run over my naked flesh, finding the cup of my strapless bra and pulling me free. His mouth finds me, and I gasp in pleasure even as my fingers desperately reach for his waistband.

I need all of him.

He growls, a sound so sexy that it vibrates right through me, and I moan again.

The button gives, and I use my feet to peel the pants down to his knees. He kicks a few times, and they are gone. He rises up for a moment to pull his shirt off his arms. I chew on my fingernail as I watch him.

Julian grins at seeing me staring at his chest. "You're gorgeous," I say.

"You're the gorgeous one." He leans back down. "And not just here," he says, placing a quick peck on my lips. "But here too." He places a slow, steady kiss on my forehead.

Crap, he really likes me.

My heart pounds harder.

Or he's a great actor.

Could we ever truly trust each other?

He brings his lips back to mine, and I close my eyes, slipping deeper into him, into his smell, focusing on everywhere we touch. Focusing all of me on *us*, so as to escape *me*...the woman who dropped a poison pill into a stranger's drink and then danced with him as he died.

CHAPTER NINE

JULIAN FALLS ASLEEP AFTERWARDS, his arm over my waist, chest pressed to my back—intimate and stifling.

I wriggle free and go to the bathroom, ignoring the mirror and turning on the shower instead. As the water rumbles in the stall, I put my hand under it, waiting for the warmth to come.

My body is slack and satisfied. There is the perfect ache between my thighs. I step under the water, and it sluices over me as memories of Julian's touch reawakens the hunger he just satisfied.

Last night's two very different experiences appear to be linked: Vladimir's fall and my hunger for Julian.

Power—there is something about power here.

I soap my hands and run them up and down my breasts, bringing myself back to a place of starvation. *If I keep this up, I'll have to wake Julian.* He won't mind. He'll love it.

I'm smiling under the spray.

Shouldn't I feel guilty? Or afraid?

But I don't.

When I get out I wrap myself in a towel and return to the bedroom. Julian is still asleep, his arms spread wide, his legs apart, a satisfied smile on his face.

Dropping the towel, I climb back onto the bed and pull down the sheets, exposing his naked body. Goosebumps rise as the cool air graces his skin.

Power courses through me. *He is at my mercy.*

Admiring the muscles cording his thighs and waist, I take a tentative lick. He mutters and jumps a little but does not wake. I move closer to him, positioning my knees under me, and lick closer to his belly button. He thrusts his crotch up, and I glance at his face to find his eyes still closed, though his breathing is growing rapid.

I move slowly south, Julian rising to meet me.

By the time I wrap my mouth around him, he jerks into awareness. "Oh God," he says, his hands coming up to my hair. "Jesus, what..."

I look up to find his eyes boring into mine. I smile around him and take control.

I am powerful. I am running this world.

His head flops back onto the pillow—he knows it. And he likes it.

I HAVE a missed call from an unknown number. Swiping over to the voicemail screen, I see there's a 10-second long message. We have press meetings this morning for two hours before our flight.

Julian comes up behind me and nuzzles my neck. I lean into him, closing my eyes, and let the phone fall back into my purse.

"You're amazing," he says into my hair.

I turn in his arms. "You're incredible," I say back.

His lips brush mine, and I bend to give him better access, my purse and phone forgotten...everything but the feel of him gone.

To be lost in this physical space is such sweet relief. Such a decadent escape. My fingers dive into his hair, feeling the thick waves of it. He groans and moves forward, pushing me against the wall. The solidness at my back, and the man at my front, gives me a sense of place, of purpose, and I wrap a leg around his waist as he deepens the kiss, his hands on my cheeks, holding me, angling me.

A knock at the door releases a low growl from his chest. I can't and don't want to stop the giggle that burbles up from my chest. "Angela?" It's Sandra.

Julian breaks the kiss and leans his forehead against mine. "I'm getting addicted," he whispers. A thrill runs through me. His glistening lips are right there, right in front of me. *Mine.*

I can do what I want with him. With anyone. I'm a freaking super spy *and* a famous actress.

The world is mine.

Pure erotic pleasure hums through me.

Sandra knocks again, this time more persistent. Julian leans away, releasing me from the wall. But really I'm the one who released him…

I straighten my shirt before answering the door. The PA, her ear piece in place, wearing comfortable clothing and simple pony tail, is waiting. She holds out a coffee cup for me. "Good morning," she says brightly.

"Morning," I grin, not even trying to hide the good humor I'm in. "Want to come in?"

She glances at her smart watch. How many steps a day does she take? I bet it's over ten thousand. A flash of her circling her small hotel room to complete her daily goal enters my mind. I swallow, something twisting in me. "They need you downstairs in twenty. Did you have breakfast?"

I glance back into the suite. Julian has gone into the bedroom, probably getting dressed. The door opens, and he steps out. God, he looks good. In his tuxedo from last night, his finger-fucked hair twisted over those sparkling blue eyes, his bow tie hanging loose, jacket in hand. Those glorious hard planes of his chest, the rounded perfection of his shoulders, are visible through the fine material of his white shirt.

Seeing me watching him, Julian grins, those damn dimples practically making me tremble. Sandra makes a small sound of surprise but does not comment. "I've got to run to my room, love," he says. "See you later."

He leans over and gives me a chaste kiss on the cheek, lingering just long enough for the stubble around those silky lips to rub me just right.

"Morning, Sandra," he says, his voice husky.

She checks her watch again. "You've got thirty-five," she says, all business.

He grins at her. "Thanks." He steps out of the suite, throwing me one last heated glance. Jesus, he is something else.

"So, breakfast?" she says, once he's out the door.

I have to clear my throat. "Yeah, sure."

"Great." She pulls out her phone and speaks quietly to someone. Moments later, a waiter arrives with enough food to feed half the cast. I sip at the coffee and have a hard-boiled egg, my appetite not focused on food this morning.

We head down to the interview rooms, with their gold paisley carpet and comfortable looking chairs, posters from the movie arrayed around them. The makeup artist works quickly, the hairdresser pulling my hair into a casual ponytail that takes thirty minutes to perfect. My makeup—which makes me look like I wake up this way—takes another forty.

By the time I'm under the lights and miked up, my high from last night is starting to wear off, and the drudgery of the press tour is crowding back in. "Last day," I remind myself under my breath.

By this time tomorrow, I'll be back in my apartment. I can't wait to see Archie.

Sandra enters, holding the door open. My heart leaps into my throat when Temperance follows her in. His eyes meet mine, and I swallow, forcing a calm, pleasant expression onto my face. I stand to greet him. "Greg Martin, for *Entertainment China*—an English-language publication for the big ex-pat community," the PA says.

"Thank you," I say, holding out my hand. "Nice to meet you, Mr. Martin."

"Call me Greg," Temperance says, his accent British today.

"Greg, then." I turn toward my chair, taking the moment with my back turned to suck in a deep breath and relax.

Sandra's walkie-talkie crackles, and she excuses herself, so that it's just Temperance and me. He takes the reporter's chair, one long leg crossed over the other as he pulls out a small notebook and a pair of glasses. Perching the spectacles on his nose, he smiles at me.

I'm staring, waiting, *desperate* to know how he will proceed. "How are you feeling?" he asks.

"Good, you?" My voice is tentative; I'm not sure where he is going with this. I have so many questions but am afraid to ask any of them.

"Great, you did a wonderful job."

"Did I?"

"Perfection." He's practically purring.

"Is he..." I chew on my lip for a moment...do I want to know? I drop my voice to a whisper. "Dead?"

"Don't worry about Vlad; that's not your job."

I stiffen. "I'm going to find out. It's natural that I want to know."

He smiles. "So true. You're good at this. You'll need to find out through regular channels though. How would I know?" He waves his pen up and down his body, referencing his facade of a reporter.

"Okay," I say, brows bunching. "So what are you doing here?"

"Just wanted to congratulate you."

"Really?" I sit back in my seat. "I don't believe you."

He grins again. "You are really good at this."

"What do you want?" My eyes track to the door. How much time do we have?

"I wanted to give you something to take home with you."

"What?" He holds the pen out to me. It's black as ebony, with a gold tip and bottom. He shakes it a little, encouraging me to take it.

Raising my eyes, I meet his gaze. "Why?" I ask.

A smile curls his lips as he shakes his head. "Just take it. Get it home. I'll pick it up from you in a day or two. Don't lose it."

"What is it?" I ask again, and he just shakes his head.

My insistence suddenly seems ridiculous. I'm willing to kill a man, poison his drink with some unknown substance, but not carry a pen over international borders?

I reach my hand out and take the pen from him. It's heavy, as I'd expect an expensive pen to be, slick against my fingers. A chill runs over me as excitement tingles across my skin. *This is dangerous.* And it feels so good—that erotic pleasure is pulsing through me again.

Temperance is smiling when I look up at him. "You've done a great service for your country," he says.

"It—" I cut myself off and shake my head.

"What?" He leans forward, his brows bunching. He's concerned... afraid I can't handle this? He has no idea how much I'm liking it. Should I tell him? *No, keep it a secret.* Temperance is not a friend. He's using me—for a greater good perhaps, but that does not make him trustworthy.

I shake my head. "Nothing." I give him one of my smiles—the one that hints at a sadness behind my eyes. "I'm happy to help my country." I take a breath. "Proud." *This is hard for me, but I'm doing it because I'm a patriot.*

Temperance's eyes bore through me, seeking the reality beyond my words. *Can he see the truth?* He sits back as the door opens. "Thank you so much, Angela, I think I have everything I need," he says.

"Wonderful." I give him a big smile—the one I give to every reporter at the end of an interview. It's broad, and yet, with the way I squint my eyes, feels intimate. It says, *I smile for a living but you've really been a pleasure to spend time with.* "Thank you for your interest in me and our film."

"You're going places, I'm sure," Temperance says as he stands, holding out his hand to shake.

I stand as well and shake his hand. "Good luck," he says then turns to leave.

Sandra watches him go. "Damn," she says under her breath, her voice practically a wolf whistle. I laugh. "Well," she says, turning to me with a smile, "that man is something else, huh? Idris Elba vibes, right?"

I just smile.

"Never seen him before, must be new," she muses to herself, as she checks her watch again. There is a small knock on the door, and the next reporter and his crew step into the room.

I slip the black pen into my purse before taking my seat and putting on a smile as the cameraman sets up.

JULIAN and I ride together to the airport. A group of photographers are waiting at the terminal. "Can I hold your hand?" Julian asks.

He's asking if I'll be his girlfriend in the public eye. The black pen in my purse feels heavy. A whisper of guilt and doubt flitters through me. Is it wrong to be falling into this with Julian when I've got such a big secret?

He's got secrets. Everyone has secrets.

There is a shy smile pulling at my lips, and I let it draw my mouth up. "You sure you want to?" I ask.

He nods. "Yes, for months I've wanted to." Julian scoots closer to me, putting his arm around my waist and pulling me tight to him. "I —" He licks his lips, those blue eyes holding mine, making my body feel weak and pliable, making my mind feel strong and powerful. "I want to be with you, Angela."

I kiss him rather than answer. I want him too. But more than I want him, I'm enjoying the hell out of him right now. I don't know when I'll have had enough, but this...*this could last.*

I blink against the flashes of the cameras as we climb out of the black town car. Julian pulls me forward. In my other hand I grip my purse, the pen Temperance gave me zipped inside an interior pocket. Julian keeps his head down as the photographers yell questions at us.

We move into the airport, where security holds back the throng. My heart is beating wildly. Julian's hand is tight on mine. He moves his arm around my waist as we wait in line, Sandra in front of us. She handles everything, and soon we are being escorted to the front of the security line.

My purse and carry-on bag go onto the conveyor belt, and I breathe through the slight panic from relinquishing the pen to the X-ray machine.

I pass through the metal detector, my socked feet cool against the linoleum floor. My purse appears, but the conveyor belt stops before it reaches me. A bored-looking guard, face etched in deep grooves from decades of frowning, pulls it off and looks up—starting a little when he sees me. "This is your bag?" he asks in accented English.

I nod, my mouth suddenly a desert.

"Come with me?" He moves down the opposite side of the belt, and I grab my shoes before following him to a metal table. Julian picks up my carry-on and his bag, then steps up next to me as the guard places my purse onto the examination table.

He slips on a pair of thin plastic gloves, and I finally find enough spit to swallow. Unzipping my purse, he looks inside before cautiously reaching in to pull out my wallet, phone, a package of mints, and the key fobs for my apartment and car.

My passport and ticket go next to them on the metal table. My Kindle is the last thing from the main compartment to be pulled. An intense need for a comfortable chair and a cup of tea wells up in me. I grip my shoes to keep from grabbing at the device.

When I hear the interior zipper opening, my heart beats heavily in my chest, blood rushes in my ears, and visions of myself in a Chinese prison camp race through my mind. The security agent pulls out the pen and puts it next to the other items. Reaching back into the small pocket, he rummages around. My eyes are fastened onto the pen.

Look away!

I drag my gaze back to the security agent and put a mild smile on my face; I am patient, innocent, and well-behaved. "Ah," he says, pulling out a pointed nail file. He holds it up for my inspection. "This," he says, "is not allowed."

"I'm sorry," I say, impressed with how normal my voice sounds considering that my heart just slipped back into my chest. "I didn't realize it was in there."

He nods, placing it to the side. One more swipe around in the bag, and he nods to himself. *It's secure.*

The agent begins to put the items back in my bag. He picks up the pen and spends a moment looking at it. "Nice," he says before dropping it back into the interior zippered pocket.

"Thank you," I say, clearing my throat.

Julian's palm at my lower back, sneakers back on, I try to keep a natural grip on my purse as we move toward the first class lounge but can't help a tight squeeze, just to make sure the pen is still there. *It is.*

Once in the lounge, Julian orders us both drinks, and we settle into comfortable arm chairs. He pulls out his phone and begins to scroll.

"I'm going to run to the bathroom," I say. *A final check before I pull out my Kindle and slip into the world of fiction.*

Julian nods and gives me a smile before returning his attention to the phone's screen.

In the restroom, I step into the stall and close the door, leaning against it and taking deep breaths, forcing myself to unwind. Opening up my purse, I take out the pen and stare at it for a moment. *Should I unscrew it, try to figure out what it is?*

No. Better not to know.

I hear the door open and a pair of heels click on the tile floor. Putting the pen back into the zippered pocket and securing it, I flush the toilet and then step out of the stall. A Caucasian woman in tight black pants, with luscious dark curls streaked with red highlights cut into a stylish bob, is washing her hands. She smiles at me in the mirror, her lips painted an even brighter red than her hair.

I step up next to her, putting my purse strap across my chest to wash my hands. Her muscles tense, and alarm bells jangle in my mind. Instinct pushes me back from the sink as she twists, her hand chopping through the air, aimed for my throat.

My back slams into a stall door, and I stumble as it gives way. The woman kicks out backward, her pointed heel striking for my gut. I dive into the stall, cornering myself but avoiding the blow.

Her leg comes down, and she stands on it, spinning and aiming a roundhouse kick to my face. My hands thrust up, blocking it and throwing her off balance for a moment.

Red lips drawn tight, my attacker grunts as she catches onto the counter and steadies herself. I take in a breath for the first time since she took a swing at me. *What in the Cornhole is going on?*

Pushing off the row of sinks, she leaps at me again, her fist barely missing my face as I duck. Coming up fast, I bring an uppercut with me, but she's spun away.

She's fast.

I raise my fists in a defensive pose and, with my back leg pressed against the toilet, bring my front foot up, striking out. Red steps back again, leaving me enough room to get out of the stall.

I land on my front foot and bring my rear one up, striking at her again. She catches the foot, her eyes lighting up with power.

With a quick twist, she turns my leg. *I'm forced to follow or break my ankle.* My chest hits the ground, and Red holds my foot at her waist. She twists it again, and again I follow, my face up now, looking into her eyes, black jewels lit with victory.

I bring my free foot up and over her wrists, cracking it down hard. She grimaces but her hands remain locked around my left ankle. Raising on my elbows, I grit my teeth and kick at her hands with my right foot. She twists, and I cry out with pain as my ankle strains. Turning to the side, to ease the pain, I place my palms on the bathroom floor and kick for her stomach with my right foot. She stumbles back, and her hold loosens. I strike out again. This time her grip breaks, and I pull free.

I try to scramble away but she leaps on top of me, a fist hitting my chin so hard that stars dance in front of my eyes. The side of my head hits the floor, and she rolls me over, grabbing for my purse. *She wants the pen.*

Let her have it, a weak part of me suggests.

If you let them take one thing, they will take everything, my grandmother's voice reminds me.

I grip the bag and try to roll away with it, but Red has got her legs on either side of me. She yanks it back.

The scent of her is all around me—floral perfume, fresh sweat, and the soap from the dispenser by the sink. She takes a hand off the purse, bringing it up, telegraphing another punch. I bring my arms up to cover my face, and she strikes my chest instead.

I can't breathe.

Red again yanks at my bag, and I almost lose hold of it.

My lungs are not working.

Spots dance in front of my eyes.

Red rips the bag from my quickly numbing fingers.

She stands up, staring down at me for a moment. I'm lying on the bathroom floor, wheezing…a small sip of air gets through, clearing my vision enough for me to see her rear back. I try to roll away, but she kicks me in the side, pain lighting through my ribs.

Another sip of air makes it through as she turns and starts for the exit.

No!

Barely any oxygen in my body, spots of darkness swirling, I lunge for her, grabbing an ankle right above that sharp, dangerous heel.

Red falls forward, her hands coming out and hitting the wall. I pull off her shoe, that sharp weapon now mine. She looks over her shoulder at me and sneers. Air whooshes back as I bring the heel around and drive it into her calf.

She gives a sharp cry and kicks out with her other foot, the stiletto catching me in the shoulder and shooting pain down my arm. My fingers lose their hold on the shoe, and I fall back.

Red pulls the stiletto from her calf and brandishes it like a knife, my purse in her other fist. I scramble to my feet and drop back into my fighting pose. "Give it back," I pant.

She doesn't waste her breath on words, instead kicking out with her bare foot. It's my turn to grab it and twist. She grunts and turns the way I'm twisting, keeping hold of the purse. The shoe, with its sharp, blood-stained heel, skitters across the floor, stopping when it hits the door.

Dropping my hold on the ankle, I jump onto Red's back. She's warm between my thighs, her waist narrow and hard. *The woman is made of muscle.* I grab a fistful of curls and, yanking hard, force her into a backbend before slamming her face into the tile floor.

Blood explodes from her nose, flowering across the white tile, and she goes still. Where electric energy raged seconds ago now is dead space… like when the lights go out on a stage: brightness to blackness in a split second.

I grab my bag from her loose fingers and stand up, my feet on either side of her waist, my breath coming in heaving pants. *She's not moving at all.*

I use my sneaker to roll her over. A shiver of disgust races over me, and my stomach flips. Her eyes are open, staring up at me, unseeing.

I killed her.

CHAPTER TEN

My eyes jump from Red's destroyed face, hopping around the room like terrified bunnies. They land on a maintenance room door and freeze.

Put her in the closet and get out. Now.

What about the blood?

One step at a time.

I cross to the closet door and rip it open. *Brooms, mops, extra paper towels and toilet paper. A sign that reads "Closed for cleaning" in several languages.*

I pull that out first and step to the entrance door. *It's locked.* Red must have done that when she came in. My hands shake as I open it. A breath of fresh air flows in. Smelling of carpeting and normal life, it brings tears to my eyes.

I slip the sign onto the outside handle and lock the door again, sealing myself in with the blood and the death. I return my attention to the body on the floor.

This makes three people who died at my hand. Three!

There is no time to think about that now.

Lips pressed tight, eyes avoiding Red's mangled face, I grasp her under the arms and drag her to the closet, laying her torso against the shelving and then pushing her legs in. *Do not cry. Do not cry.*

One last thing to do. I grab a mop, wet it in the sink and then proceed to remove every trace of blood from the sparkling white floor.

Lurching into the hallway outside the bathroom, I stumble against the far wall. The sign on the door sways as the door swings shut.

My purse gripped tight in my fist, I push off the wall and start back toward the lounge. There is blood on my shoulder. My hair is loose from the bun it had been in. *I look a wreck. I can't go out there like this.*

The family bathroom is to my right. I step into it and lock the door, closing my eyes against the florescent lights. *I'm shaking.*

I don't have time for this.

Forcing calm, I step up to the mirror. There is a bruise blooming on my chin and a blood-stained tear in my shirt on my right shoulder. I delicately pull the fabric apart; there is a stab wound from her stiletto oozing blood.

Grabbing paper towels, I wad them up and press them to my shoulder, hissing at the pain the pressure brings. Pain is screaming to life all over my body as the adrenaline drains away. I pull the paper towels away, and they are bright red, the wound still bleeding.

Crud, crud, crud. How am I going to explain this to Julian? Would they even let me on the plane looking like this?

Sing. I open my purse with my free hand, keeping the other pressed to the wound. Pulling out my phone and wallet, I find his card and dial the number. It rings twice before he picks up.

"It's Angela," I say, my voice coming out breathless.

"Angela, I didn't expect to hear from you."

"I'm having some trouble at the airport..." Was it safe to say anything over this line? Why the hell didn't Temperance give me more information—a better way to reach out for help? *Because I'm not going to get any.* I shake my head, pushing away the paranoid thought.

"At the airport," Sing says. "Your flight is in about an hour, right?"

"Yes, but..."

"It's okay," he says, low. "This is a secure line."

My shoulders relax. "I just got attacked in the bathroom of the first-class lounge. On the far side of freaking security!" I bite my lip as emotion wells again.

"Oh," Sing says.

A long silence follows. Long enough for me to find my gaze in the mirror, look at the wad of red paper towels at my shoulder, and see the mark on my chin darkening into a hell of a bruise. "Sing," I finally say, prompting him. "I need some help here. I look like I've been in a bloody fight. And..." I drop my voice to a low whisper. "There is a body in the maintenance closet."

"I can send someone." He sounds way too calm. Like this happens all the time. *It probably does.* There is a shadowy world filled with spies —good guys and bad gals—waging a war under the surface of our calm society. "Tell me precisely where you are."

I tell him, and he hangs up.

I sit down on the closed toilet and put my head between my knees, just breathing.

What did I sign up for?

My phone buzzes. It's Julian. He must be worried about me. I send him to voicemail and then type a text. *There is a woman getting sick in the bathroom; I'm helping her.*

Doesn't that just make me sound sweet?

Okay, he writes back. *Let me know if you need anything.*

Returning to the mirror, I pull out my makeup bag and start to work on the bruise on my face. A knock at the door jerks my head up. "Cleaning service," a perfect American accent says.

My heart thundering hard enough that I can feel fresh blood pooling to the surface of my wound, I stand and creep to the door. I throw away the bloodied paper towels and take a deep breath, putting my purse back over my chest.

Unlocking the door, I tense, ready for another attack. The woman is petite, barely five feet tall, and waif thin, with long black hair and a serious expression.

She pushes into the bathroom then closes and locks the door, her gaze raking me up and down. She turns to the sink and puts a case on the counter next to it. "Take off your shirt," she says.

I don't move as she opens the bag and begins to pull out instruments in sterile packaging. *She comes prepared.*

Throwing a look over her shoulder, she says it again. "Take off your shirt."

This time I start to move, gingerly unbuttoning the blouse and hissing as I pull it off my shoulder, keeping my purse strap over my body. The woman points for me to sit down on the toilet.

I sit, exhaustion beginning to take over my limbs. She stands in front of me, wearing latex gloves, and starts to clean the wound. "I'm going to stitch you up," she says.

"I need stitches?" I ask stupidly. *Obviously I need stitches.*

"Yes."

"My…boyfriend will notice," I say.

Her eyes meet mine. "You shouldn't have a boyfriend." She says it simply, matter of factly.

My mouth opens a little in surprise. "Excuse me?" I say, pulling on my cloak of queendom.

"You wouldn't have to explain this to him if you didn't have him in your life."

I don't argue with her, just narrow my eyes. *I can have my boyfriend and eat my cake too, lady.*

She pulls out a hypodermic syringe and, without even a *this will only pinch for a second* warning, stabs me in the shoulder. I wince, but it's over quickly, and a wonderful numbness spreads from the injection point. She begins to stitch me up.

My phone buzzes again. *Everything okay?* Julian writes. *They're boarding our flight.*

Yes, out in a few, I write back.

The woman ties off the stitches and cleans around the wound before putting a bandage on it. "There," she says, turning back to her bag. "Anything else?"

"My ankle hurts," I say. She steps back and I raise it up. She holds my sneaker in her hand and examines the ankle. It's only slightly swollen. Feeling it with deft fingers she nods to herself.

"Just a mild sprain. You'll be fine."

She turns back to her bag and pulls out a black cashmere sweater. It will look great with my jeans. I can tell Julian that the woman in the bathroom got sick on me.

I pull the sweater over my head, feeling the stitches pull. *How the hell am I going to explain the puncture wound in my shoulder?*

"Go," the woman says. "You can't miss your flight."

"What about…the person who attacked me?"

She meets my gaze, her expression calm, but bright. "Everything will be arranged."

A shiver runs over me, and I sense that I am in a small, rickety rowboat—the water looks calm, but underneath me, beasts battle.

THE AIRPLANE DOORS close right after we settle into our individual pods. I sink into the seat and take a deep breath. Julian leans across the aisle. "You okay?" he asks again.

I nod. "Yes, I'm fine," I give him a tired smile, like I'm a Good Samaritan who just had to help an ailing traveler, not a secret agent who just killed someone in the ladies room. "I feel bad for the woman."

Julian nods, brow serious—he's concerned for her too. "I hate stomach bugs."

An image of Red pushed into the closet, her broken face and unseeing eyes tilted toward her chin, sends a wave of disgust over me. *One more harmless nightmare? Like Vlad convulsing on the dance floor and Jack's teeth on my breasts…*

The flight attendant approaches, interrupting my train of thought. "Can I get you two anything before we take off?" she asks.

Julian orders himself a glass of wine, and I get a seltzer…"Wait," I say. The woman turns, her elegantly arched brow raised. "I'll take a brandy, too."

"I have a nice cognac." She leans toward me a little. "Basically the same thing," she almost whispers. *What a fantastic cap to this day.* Clearly I *so* belong here. The flight attendant moves off and Julian gives me a smile. The rumble of the engine vibrates up through my seat.

I may not know the difference between cognac and brandy but I survived.

Drink in hand, I begin to relax as the plane speeds down the runway and lifts into the sky. *This wasn't a nightmare. This happened.* An assassin attacked me, and I killed her. Jack attacked me, and I killed him. *I'm the one who lives.*

THE APARTMENT IS empty when I get home, everything is where I left it, as far as I can tell. Archie is at Mary's, and I'll pick him up later, but right now I need a shower. Dropping my bags on the bed, I move through to my bathroom and strip.

Holy crap.

A fresh layer of makeup and the dim light in the plane had kept the darkening of my chin hidden on the flight home. Now, in full daylight, I can see it clearly under the foundation. It's going to be a bitch to cover up as it changes color and will take weeks to fade.

The press rollout for the film is done, but I'm sure Mary will want me at meetings. Maybe I can tell her I need a vacation. That sounds so nice...just going away. Archie and me in a convertible, a scarf fluttering behind me as we race up the California Coast.

My hip is a mottled storm cloud of bruising. And as I peel off the bandaging on my shoulder, I discover red swollen skin around the stitching.

I still have the pen.

What am I supposed to do with that? And what is stopping Red's friends—whoever they are--from coming after me? Should I go stay in a hotel? I need to reach Temperance.

Steam from the shower curls around me, fogging the mirror and hiding my reflection behind misty gauze. My grandmother, holding a broom, reaching onto her tiptoes to knock down a spider web—the delicate artistry clumping around the worn wood handle—flashes across my mind

A sound in my bedroom shoots adrenaline into my system. *There is someone in here.*

Stepping silently to the bathroom door, I turn the lock, tensing at the sound. "Angela." It's Temperance calling out to me. My shoulders relax, but the adrenaline is still spiraling. His footsteps reach the closed door. "Angela," he calls louder. "I've been knocking."

"You should wait outside until someone answers," I try to put bite into my words but they come out shaky. *Crap, I can do better than this.* "I was about to get in the shower." That's closer—higher octaves, steadier tone. "Give me two minutes."

"I'll wait in the living room," he says.

Turning off the water, I grab a robe and wrap it around my naked body, slipping on a pair of clean panties as I move through the bedroom.

Temperance is waiting on my couch, all relaxed male, legs wide, phone in his hand. He's wearing a sport coat over a T-shirt and dark jeans. "Are you okay?" he asks, those tiger eyes of his locking on to the bruise on my face.

"I survived," I say, indignation starting to bubble. "But I did get attacked. What the hell, Temperance? How did that woman know who I was or what I was carrying? I don't even know what I was carrying!"

Temperance is unfazed by the sudden hysteria creeping into my voice. "Give me the pen," he says, slipping his phone into his jacket pocket.

"That's all you have to say to me?" Now there are tears in my voice. *Great.* "I killed her." The words come out on a whisper—almost an accusation. *He made me kill her.*

His gaze remains even, tempered... his mother named him well. "I'm sorry you had to go through that." He doesn't sound sorry. He sounds bored. Like murder is nothing to him.

But it's not nothing to me. "And Vladimir?" *Is it really three?*

Temperance stands, moving slowly, like I'm an injured animal he hit with his car that he doesn't want to frighten further—I might hurt myself trying to escape from him. "Where is the pen?"

I gesture back to the bedroom where I dropped my purse on the duvet. He gives a small wave of his hand, indicating I should go get it. Temperance follows me and watches as I unzip my purse and reach into the interior pocket, pulling the slim, black pen from inside. Anger rises in me again.

"Here's your stupid pen," I say, all *I'm an angry toddler.*

He takes it from me and slips it into an interior pocket. "You were injured?"

"Yes." I pull my robe aside, exposing the puckered, stitched wound.

His eyes narrow, and he leans closer, his breath not quite hitting the wound, but the nearness of him raising goosebumps none the less. "Not that bad," he says.

I pull the robe closed and step back. "Good that you don't wear a lot of strapless gowns. This is going to leave a scar." Anger is really gurgling now. This guy is messing with my life. I could have died! *I killed a woman.*

"You did well," Temperance says, his voice low.

I open my mouth and close it again, clenching my jaw. "I don't want to do this anymore," I grind out.

He raises one eyebrow at me. "That's not an option."

"Yes, it is. I just won't answer your calls," I'm making this up as I go along. "And I won't do what you ask. Seems pretty simple to me."

"That's not how it works."

"Really? Because I'm not interested in dying, or getting any more scars." I lower my voice. "Or killing anyone else."

"I'll have a doctor—a plastic surgeon—come over and look at that." Temperance's eyes focus on my shoulder.

I stamp my foot in a pathetic attempt to make him listen to me... to gain some power. *My anger and exhaustion have handed him all the cards.* Or maybe fate dealt Temperance all the aces—I never had a choice in this, and I still don't.

Depression, a stifling fog, surrounds me, and I slump under its arrival.

"Don't worry, you'll be safe here," Temperance says, his eyes scanning my bedroom.

"How can you say that?" I ask, all the anger leached away by the sadness. "Someone knows who I am, and that I'm working for you. If they can get to me in a secure airport lounge, they can get to me anywhere. I don't even know what I'm doing, but others—killers —do."

The skin around his eyes tightens. "Yes, but they wanted the pen. And you don't have it anymore. So you're safe." *For now.*

"The pen has something to do with Vladimir?"

"You're better off not knowing."

"Really? That's funny. Because if I had known I was in danger, maybe I would have been a little more prepared."

His gaze returns to mine. "Assume you're in danger then."

Oh, that's comforting. Hallmark should give this guy a show.

Temperance's hand lands on my good shoulder. "I'll get the plastic surgeon over here this afternoon. Don't worry, the scar won't hurt your career. You'll have some calls this week. Your next big role is coming soon."

"I'd like to be alone," I say, my voice wooden. I'm too tired for this.

Temperance steps back. "You did great," he says again, before turning to the door. I don't respond, just listen as he leaves, the front door automatically locking behind him. Taking a deep breath, I put the chain on before heading back to the bathroom for that shower.

All I want is to climb into bed and cry, but that's not me. I'm going to shower, then I'm going to pick up Archie…and I'm going to buy a freaking gun.

CHAPTER ELEVEN

Sweat beads on Temperance's forehead, dripping down his temple. His eyes are bright, hypnotic. I can't reach him. Searing pain lances through my shoulder, and I wake with a start, twisted in my sheets, damp from my own sweat. The light in my bedroom is the gray mist of dawn.

Archie stirs in his cage, flopping over so that his collar jangles against the metal. I should have taken it off last night.

My breath is evening out. The dream is fading quickly. I reach to my side table, feeling for the pistol I bought. I've got a lesson this afternoon. My eyes catch on the alarm clock. It's 5:45 a.m. I roll away from the window and close my eyes, but my heart is still hammering, and there is no way I'm going to sleep again.

So I grab my phone and check it. There is a text from Julian; it came in at midnight. He wants to see me today. I bite my lower lip. I've been avoiding him for the past week as my shoulder healed, but it's doing a lot better now, and I can just lie about it. The plastic surgeon Temperance sent to me suggested I say that I had a mole removed.

The thought churns my stomach. I don't want to lie to Julian. In the dusty light of dawn, with the memories of my dreams swirling, I can admit that I really like Julian. He's gorgeous, fun, attentive and great in bed. What's not to like?

He's a movie star with more notches on his bedpost than Don Juan.

I navigate to my Instagram and go through the comments on my latest post—a picture of Archie next to the pool. *Happy to be home after an awesome month promoting* The Tempest *around the world!* I quickly delete all the crazy comments. People are sick.

Checking my email, I find a message from Mary that came in at 2:00 a.m. *Call me as soon as you wake up. I have exciting news!*

"About time," I grumble to myself. Getting back to work is important. With the success of this movie, I should be beating back the offers. I email Mary a quick response—*I'm awake. Call me when you are* —then climb out of bed to make some coffee. Archie is still passed out so I let him sleep, making my way into the kitchen, stretching my arms over my head as I go.

I want to hit the gym today. The doctor said that I could start working out again. My shoulder doesn't even really hurt anymore.

I get the coffee maker going and grab half and half out of the fridge, my one indulgence. I'll be having egg whites and spinach for breakfast, but I can't live without my half and half. A girl has to get her fat somewhere.

My phone pings, and I settle at my kitchen table, listening to the coffee machine gurgle as I open the message from Mary. "Come into the office today."

"Okay, let's do it earlier though. I've got plans this afternoon." *Practicing with my new gun.* For *The Tempest* I had a lot of training—hand to hand and weapons. But the class I'm taking today is all about live combat. We went over that in my previous training, but action movies are not actually high stress—I knew what each person was going to do, didn't have to improvise at all.

Not like with Red.

The coffee machine beeps that it's done, and I pour myself a cup, adding my half and half…just a splash. Then a sprinkle of cinnamon. Since shooting and training ended, I've worked to stay in shape while on the road, but it's hard without my trainer, Synthia, on my case every freaking day.

I sink into my couch, coffee cup in hand, and shoot her a quick message to let her know I'm back and to set up a time to get together this week.

Flicking on the TV, I navigate to the local news. *I love the chipper morning news team.* There are fires outside of town raging out of control. Ugh. Again.

That's one of the problems with LA.

A knock at my door sends my blood pressure soaring. Who is showing up at my house at 6:00 a.m.?

I put my coffee mug on the table and flee into my bedroom, grabbing my gun off the side table. Just holding it makes me feel better. I step back into the living room to see the door opening. Retreating into the shadow of the hall, my heart in my throat, breath paused, gun clenched, I watch a large shoulder emerge.

Temperance's head pops in. "Angela," he calls softly as he moves into the room. His eyes catch on the coffee cup, and he closes the door behind himself. "Sorry to barge in." He waits by the door.

I let out my breath and lower the gun before stepping out of the hall. His eyes find mine, and he smiles as his gaze tracks down my body. I'm wearing a thin white T-shirt and a pair of panties. His Adam's apple bobs as he pulls his eyes back to mine.

I raise one brow and give him a smile. He likes what he sees. Most men do.

"Sorry," he says again, his voice a little scratchy. *Oh, it feels good to affect Mr. Statue Man.* "May I come in?"

"You're already in," I point out. "Give me a minute to put something on, and I'll get you a cup of coffee."

He nods, stepping toward the couch. Back in my bedroom, I put the gun on my side table and slip on a pair of jeans and a bra before letting Archie, who is now awake, out of his cage. I carry him to the balcony door and open it up, stepping into the warm morning.

Smoke from the wildfires tinges the air, and my nose wrinkles at the acrid odor. Putting Archie down on the wee-wee pad, I wait for him to do his business before grabbing one of the treats I keep out here for him. "Good boy," I coo, crouching down to offer the treat and scoop him up again.

Shutting the door behind me, I head back to the living room.

Temperance is sitting on the couch. He's muted the TV and is at the edge of the seat--looking ready for anything. "Can I get you that coffee?" I ask. He shakes his head. I shrug and drop into the arm chair, reaching for my own cup. "So this isn't a social call," I tease.

He gives me a wry smile. "No. I have another assignment for you."

I swallow the sip of coffee in my mouth and purse my lips. "I'm still recovering from the last one," I say. "And I haven't been able to find out what happened to Vladimir." He doesn't react, just stays very still. "I've asked Mary several times, and you know that woman can find out almost anything, but the status of Petrov is being kept pretty damn secret."

"You don't need to know."

Anger swells in my gut. "You don't think I have a right to know what happened to him?" I lower my voice. "To know if I killed him?"

"You did well. What you were supposed to. That's all you need to know."

I huff out a breath and sit back into the seat, pulling my knees up in front of me. "I don't agree." A small twitch in Temperance's jaw is the only sign that he heard me. "And," I continue, my anger flaring, "I don't like you showing up here and letting yourself into my apartment. You're lucky I didn't shoot you."

One brow goes up and he clasps his hands. "That's something else I wanted to talk to you about."

"What?"

"The gun you bought."

"I'm learning how to use it. Already have some experience," I say, getting defensive.

"I understand but—"

"I need to be able to protect myself," I cut him off.

His eyes narrow. "If you want a gun, I'll get it for you. A gun registered to you is a bad idea."

"Your offer is a bit late. I have my first lesson today."

"I know, that's one of the reasons I stopped by so early. You need to talk to me before you do things like that."

I sit forward. "How would I know that? You keep me totally in the dark. It didn't occur to you I might want protection after what happened in Shanghai?" I raise my brows at him. Archie, displaced by my movements, hops off the chair and heads into the kitchen, his little tail held high.

"I'm sorry that we've had communication issues." He purses his lips. *What, are we heading to couples therapy next?*

"Look, I told the training people it was all for a role so don't worry about it."

That tick in his jaw again—the man has some tells, I'm pleased to see. "I need you to go to—" Temperance is cut off by a bark from Archie.

"He wants his breakfast," I say, standing.

Temperance follows me into the kitchen. The sun is over the building across the street now, and the intimate space is filled with warm, yellow light. I pull out Archie's kibble and fill his bowl. He prances around my feet as I place it back on his mat, grabbing his water bowl. Temperance stands in the doorway, watching me. His gaze is almost like a touch, a gentle brush in a crowd...the almost-missed invasion of a pickpocket.

"Have you been following the election?" he asks me.

I glance at him before putting Archie's water bowl down next to his food bowl. "A little." I lean against the counter and cross my arms.

"Reginald Grand is interested in meeting you."

I raise my brows. "The Republican candidate for president?" Temperance nods. "Hold on," I say. "What do you mean 'he wants to meet me'—like, the way that Vladimir wanted to meet me?"

"No." He shakes his head. Then gives a small shrug. "Well, yes, his interest is that of a fan."

I bark a laugh. "Vlad wanted to fuck me, Temperance."

"As do many of your fans." He says it low, trying not to insult me or insinuate that he too wants to do me.

I shake my head and turn to my coffee pot, refilling my cup. "So, how is this not like Vlad? I'm not going to need to slip something into his drink?"

"Nothing like that." I turn back to Temperance and wait a beat, but he does not go on.

"So…what am I supposed to do with him?"

"Just meet him."

"Just meet him?" Temperance nods. "This smells like bad fish, Temperance."

"He asked to meet you. I'm facilitating." That ticking jaw again.

"You're not happy about this," I say, stepping forward. "Why?"

His sharp gaze meets mine, and he licks his lips. He takes a step into my kitchen. "It's totally inappropriate."

Both my brows go up. "What do you mean?"

"He's getting security briefings because of his position. So he knows what happened with Vlad."

"Maybe he can tell me then," I say, sullen and childish but not regretting it.

Temperance goes on, ignoring my grumbling. "The fact that he is asking for a meeting with an operative—it's just not done."

"He's married, right?"

Temperance huffs. "Yeah."

"But, like, a known philanderer."

"Yes, he's been married three times, leaving each for the next."

I nod slowly. "I don't want to meet him," I say with a shrug. "I don't want to get involved in politics. Never have. And this guy seems pretty toxic. You know Hollywood is a liberal town."

"It would not be public. We'd keep it a secret."

"I still don't want to meet him."

Temperance nods. "I'll let him know your feelings. But I can't guarantee he won't show up here. He is one election away from the presidency."

"You think he'll win?" I ask.

Temperance shrugs, his gaze falling onto Archie, who walks up to his feet and sits on one. "I don't know. I also try to avoid politics."

I laugh. "That's rich."

He bends down and picks up my dog. The small, white fluff ball in the big man's arms is cuteness personified, and something inside me melts a little. I'm suddenly not even pissed he showed up unannounced at 6:00 a.m. "You sure you don't want a cup of coffee?" I ask.

Temperance shakes his head, his attention on Archie as he scratches the little dog behind the ear. "I'll get out of your hair. But expect to hear from me soon." He glances up at me. "And congratulations." He grins.

"For what?"

"Ah, Mary hasn't gotten hold of you yet." Temperance smiles with some secret knowledge. "You'll know why soon."

"Give me my dog," I snap, pulling Archie from him. *Holding my dog with that smug smile. No thanks, bozo.*

"I'll let you know what Mr. Grand says."

Temperance shows himself out. I make my egg whites and spinach, eating at the kitchen table, then get into workout gear and head to the gym in my building. I've got it to myself and hop on the rowing machine. CNN is playing on the big TV.

Reginald Grand fills the screen—he's got reptilian eyes set deep into a puffy face. The man is balding with grey, oily skin, and jowls that shake as he speaks. The tv is on mute so I can't hear him but his lips are moving and there is something gross about them. The shot goes wide, and his wife is standing next to him. She is almost as tall as her husband, with brown hair pulled tight to her scalp and her mouth set in a deep frown. *Resting bitch face.* My heart goes out to her. She's probably a nice lady but with a face like that it's hard to tell. There is a bit of the librarian shushing unruly teenagers about her.

I plug my headphones in, and Grand's voice comes through. "We've got to keep these criminals out of our country. Rapist and murderers are flooding over our borders." He pauses, looking out at the crowd, his lips pursed and chin high. "I am the only one who can stop them."

I stop rowing to pull the headphones out of my ears and find the controller so I can turn off the TV. *I don't need to listen to that crap.*

My grandmother escaped the Nazis and found safety on these shores. Roma are often called gypsies and are thought of as thieves and beggars, but they are a persecuted people who did what they had to in order to survive. *Close to 500,000 didn't survive the Nazis.* My grandmother and I don't get along and I can't forgive her for the mistakes she made—not that she's ever asked for my absolution—but she's hard working. If she ever stole anything, or killed anyone, the crime came from desperation.

I pick up the rowing bar and push back, releasing a breath. *I've killed out of desperation and duty.* Pulling the rowing bar to my chest and leaning back so that my abs engage, I take a fresh breath. *I'll never kill out of hate.*

There are some lines I won't cross.

MARY IS all smiles when I show up at her office. She comes around her desk and hugs me. "I've got some great news," she says, motioning for us to sit down by the window, where she's got a couch and two chairs.

"I'm dying with anticipation," I tell her.

She grins. "Well, what is the one role that could make you an even bigger star than you are now?"

"I've had one successful movie," I point out. "So I imagine there are a lot of roles that would help."

She nods, too eager to listen. "*Star Wars!*" she blurts out.

My jaw loosens. *Star Wars...*

"They are making a new episode. And you're going to be the star —a young Jedi woman. The most powerful Jedi ever."

"Really?" A smile is breaking out on my face.

"Yes." She grabs my hands. "The money is amazing. And you're getting a piece of the box office." She smiles smugly. "I'm a hell of a negotiator."

"Mary, this is amazing."

"I know."

"Who's directing?"

"Troy Woods!"

He's huge—his last three films made as much as the freaking *Matrix* franchise. *Crap on toast.* Mary is squeezing my hands, and I can't even speak. She laughs. "You have a few months until you start shooting."

"I'm...this is..."

"Oh, I know. You've arrived."

I nod, my voice lost in the wonder of the moment.

Temperance's congratulations came back to me—he knew about this before I did. Did he help make it happen? He certainly acted like he did. Is Troy Woods an asset as well?

"Woods wants to meet you as soon as possible."

I shake myself out of my stupor. "Yes, of course. When?"

"I'll let you know." Mary stands. "Come on, I'll take you to lunch and give you all the details. We need to celebrate."

She goes to her phone and buzzes her assistant. "Bradley, please let the paps know I'm taking Angela to Petunia's for lunch to celebrate a major new role."

I look up at her…God, she plays this game well. She should work with Temperance. Maybe she does already…

Mary grabs her purse and a jacket out of the closet. Turning back to me, she laughs. "Come on, let's go."

I pick up the bag Archie is sleeping in and follow her out the door. When we arrive at the restaurant, a few photographers are already waiting. They snap shots of us getting seated at an outdoor table. The clicks continue as a bottle of expensive champagne arrives, and Mary and I click our glasses. They wander off by the time our appetizers arrive.

"This is obviously a game changer," Mary concludes after detailing the lucrative financial package, then going on about foreign rights and future roles. I sip my champagne and pick at my tomato and burrata salad, a weight growing in my chest. A game changer, yes —but whose game?

CHAPTER TWELVE

My LUNGS BURN and music pounds in my ears as I run around the empty indoor track. Sweat slicks my body, and there are no thoughts in my head, just the beating of my heart matching the throbbing of the song.

I'm in the zone.

My eyes flick down to my watch. I'm meeting Synthia in ten minutes. It took two weeks to get back on her schedule. I pump my legs harder, pushing against all resistance and breaking through another layer of myself. *This is power.*

When I can't keep up the pace for even one more breath I let myself slow down, my entire body tingling with effort, my chest heaving with exertion. I slow to a walk and continue around the track, slowly regaining my composure.

Synthia's fit form appears in the doorway, and she waves. I give her a big, breathless smile, crossing the large space toward her.

We meet in the middle. "You're looking good," she says, running her eyes over my body.

"Thanks, I've been trying to stay in shape." I give a sheepish smile. "It's not easy on the road."

"Lots of tempting food."

"And not enough time to exercise."

She nods, her brown eyes sympathetic. She is fit in the way that few humans will ever be. With long, lean, sculpted legs, a stomach carved by hours of hard work and a strict diet, and shoulders that could probably carry me around, Synthia is a pure professional.

"Come on." She waves me to follow. "Let's hop in the boxing ring."

I nod, pulling my hair tie out and gathering up all the locks that escaped during my run, then refastening it as we head into the next room, where several boxing rings are lined up.

It's empty now but will fill soon. The gym opens in twenty minutes. They let me in early because I'm a big star meeting a world-famous trainer. There isn't one cell in my body that feels bad about that.

Synthia ducks under the ropes, and I follow. She passes me gloves, a mouth guard, and helmet. I fit them all on, the plastic of the mouth guard satisfying against my teeth.

Synthia's eyes fall onto my shoulder, which has largely healed in the weeks since my return. "Something going on there?" she asks before putting in her own guard.

I give a small shrug and pull out my mouth guard to answer. "Had to have a mole removed."

She gives a sympathetic nod. *That's normal.* I slip my mouth guard back in and bite down. The lying comes easy.

We touch gloves and then begin our dance, circling each other, gloves up, eyes narrowed. Once again my heart starts to beat hard, my head clears out, and I feel weightless. Ready for anything.

Synthia lunges, surprising me with a kick that knocks me back, almost landing me on my ass. I catch myself, but she's still coming, a jab connects with my chin, knocking my head back. She's not playing today.

I get my hands up again but backpedal into the ropes, and she's on me, pummeling my stomach so that I have to drop my arms to shield my midriff. Synthia responds with an uppercut to the jaw, jangling my brain.

She punches my gut, and I curl over. Another uppercut and I'm on a freaking rollercoaster, her fists the track, my body the unwitting car.

I push off the ropes hard, forcing her backward, then roll to the side and flee to the opposite end of the ring. She stalks toward me. I lash out with a front kick, and Synthia pauses, just out of my reach. I retreat further, outpacing her. But she keeps on coming, like a lightning bolt determined to find me.

Once you've been struck by lightning, you're more likely to be struck again.

I wait for her to get closer then try another front kick. She blocks it and strikes out with one of her own. I jump back, just avoiding it.

My jaw and stomach are aching from her punches. I grip the mouthguard between my teeth and meet her hard gaze. Then I slow, letting her meet me in the middle of the ring. She jabs at me, testing the distance and my reaction.

I jab, then step forward into a cross punch, which she backs up to avoid. Taking advantage of my slight momentum, I crouch down and slide forward, coming up under her and landing an uppercut.

Yeah!

She stumbles but recovers fast, an elbow coming down on my injured shoulder. I spin away, throwing a body shot as I sidestep. She oofs out air at the impact. I step in close, striking with my other fist and creating the rhythm for a series of body blows.

Synthia kicks out, catching me in the knee so that it gives way, and suddenly I'm kneeling.

Her knee comes up, aiming right for my face, and I throw myself onto my back. She launches onto me. *Crap, the woman is a judo freaking master.*

Fresh sweat, clean soap and the musk of effort fills my sense as she covers me. Her arm wraps under my leg, trying to get me into a hold. I scoot away, inelegant and verging on desperate. Synthia has my leg, though. With a practiced strength, she flips me onto my front, leg pinned to my back. She leverages her weight so that my femur is at her mercy.

I strain for a moment, but she tightens her grip. She can break my leg. *I lost.*

Tapping the mat, I admit defeat.

Synthia immediately releases me and stands, offering her gloved hand while smiling around her mouth guard. "You're too good at this," I complain. It comes out garbled because of my guard, but Synthia laughs as I accept her help. The gym is filling up, voices and the dull thud of gloves meeting flesh echo in the cavernous room.

"Angela?" I turn toward the voice. Julian stands on the other side of the ropes. He's wearing workout gear—a pair of loose shorts and a T-shirt made of synthetic, moisture-wicking material that hangs off each well-defined muscle. His blue eyes are focused on me, hurt behind the lashes.

I'm such a dumbass. I've been avoiding him since we got back from Shanghai. I get my mouth guard out in a pile of spit. *Ew, classy. Jesus, could this go any worse?* "Hey," I say. *Super lame.*

He shifts slightly, looking almost nervous—to the extent a man that good-looking and assured can look nervous. "How have you been?"

"Good. And you?"

He gives a nod. "I heard about the new *Star Wars* film, congratulations."

"Thank you, I..." God, he is so cute. "Can—" I glance at Synthia, and she raises her brows in a *what the hell is wrong with you* expression.

I sigh and approach the ropes, crouching down so that I'm at the same height as Julian. "I'm sorry," I say quietly.

He gives me a half smile, just enough to bring out one dimple. "For what?"

I purse my lips. "I've been an asshole."

"Have you?" His smile grows to reveal the second dimple.

"I should have called you back."

He gives a shrug. "It's considered polite." Julian steps closer. "Treating a man like that can confuse him."

"Isn't that usually the girl's line?" I look down at my gloves. I'm still holding my saliva-covered mouth guard. *Awesome.*

"I don't know. But, I like you Angela. And..." he brings his gaze up to meet mine. "I thought you liked me too. I mean…in Shanghai…"

We had like the best sex ever.

"I did. I do. I think…would you believe that I got scared?"

Synthia clears her throat. "I'm gonna grab a juice. You want anything?"

I look over my shoulder at her. "No, thanks."

She looks at Julian. "No, thank you," he says. Synthia nods and starts taking off her gloves, headed for the in-house juice bar.

"Can I make it up to you?" I ask Julian.

"You want to take me to dinner?"

"Yes, please."

He gives a small laugh. "When?"

"Tonight?"

"I've got plans," I frown and he grins. "But I'm free tomorrow."

"Okay." That shy, *I like him* smile is tugging at my lips.

"Julian!" A guy calls from one of the other rings. I glance up at the big, muscled man, wearing gloves, and leaning on the ropes. "Come on!" he shouts.

Julian winks at me. "Trainers," he sighs dramatically. "See you tomorrow." He turns and jogs over to the other ring. I stand and grab my water, watching as Julian climbs under the ropes and pulls on gloves and headgear before slipping in a mouth guard.

Julian glances over at me as his trainer taps his gloves, and I raise my water bottle to him. He grins around his mouth guard, then focuses on his sparring partner.

They circle each other, gloves up, Julian's leg muscles in sharp relief as he dances on his toes. "Damn," Synthia says from behind me.

"I know, right."

"He's as gorgeous in person as in the movies."

"I know," I say again.

"You've been avoiding his calls?"

I look over at her. "Yeah," I admit. "My life's kind of crazy right now." *To put it real mild.*

She shrugs. "I'm never too busy for a piece that fine."

I laugh. "He's more than a 'piece,'" I say, attempting to make air quotes with my gloves on.

She shrugs. "Come on, let's get back to work."

We go two more rounds, and she wins them both. My legs and

125

butt are burning with exertion, and my shoulders are going to throb tomorrow, but it's a good feeling.

"You should come to my dojo," Synthia says. "I want to start working on some more advanced weapon training."

My heart gives a small thump. "Great," I say, my mouth dry.

"You're going to need to know how to look good with a light saber."

I laugh. "Too true."

A thrill of excitement races through me. I'm going to be the star of a freaking *Star Wars* movie. As we push into the changing room, I let gratitude grow inside of me. My life is good, even if it's so damn complicated.

THE NEXT MORNING, when I text Julian to confirm our date, he gets right back to me. "How about my place?" I suggest. "I'll cook."

"Sounds amazing," he responds.

"Wait until you taste my cooking."

"I like what I've tasted so far." *Damn.*

I bite my lip, not sure how to respond. Memories of his head between my legs rush over me, raising goose bumps. Why did I wait so long to get back together with him? Oh right, because I'm a freaking secret agent, and I'm pretty sure someone is trying to kill me. My eyes scan my living room. Not that anyone has tried anything since we got back from Shanghai; it's been all quiet on the secret-agent front. I have not even heard from Temperance about that whole Reginald Grand thing.

"Can't wait to see you tonight," I type, then delete. I want to write something sexy. Last time he saw me I was all sweaty, wearing headgear and holding a spit-covered mouth guard.

Should I take a sexy picture? No. That's the kind of thing that gets hacked and posted online.

"My skills in the kitchen are nothing compared to my bedroom skills." I delete that immediately. Archie jumps up on the couch next to me and circles once before snuggling into my side. *I need to say something!*

I turn my attention back to the phone. It starts ringing before I can respond. *Saved by the bell.*

I don't recognize the number so I let it go to voicemail like any sane person does. I'm left staring at Julian's message again, feeling all hot and bothered when a voicemail pops up.

I hit play.

"Hi, this is Reginald Grand. I'm sure you've heard of me." *Seriously?* "I'd like to meet you. There are some issues of national security I'd like to discuss. Call me back." He leaves a number.

I close my eyes. *Ugh.* My to-do list is getting long: call back a presidential hopeful, figure out something sexy to say to Julian, and make dinner tonight. *I haven't even decided on what to cook.*

First, Julian. I switch to that screen as another text comes in from him. "What can I bring?"

"You can carry the watermelon." It's a *Dirty Dancing* reference I'm hoping he'll get. Not sexy, but it is funny… I think. *I'm such a goober.*

Now on to figuring out dinner. I'll save political intrigue until later. Standing up, I grab my reusable shopping bags from the front closet, slip on my sandals, and heft my purse onto my shoulder. Archie follows me around. "Okay, boy," I say, pulling his bag out. He barks with excitement when I put it on the floor for him to climb in.

My phone pings. I glance at it quickly before heading out the door. Julian sent me an emoji of a couple dancing. *The man might be my soul mate.* Warmth spreads over my chest as I put the phone back in my purse and head to the market.

I'VE GOT eggplant roasting in the oven and marinara sauce bubbling on the stove, a bottle of red wine open—though I've limited myself to just one little jam jar full as I cook. Don't want to be wasted when Julian gets here. I'm making Mario Batali's eggplant Parmesan. A rare indulgence. Cheese…yum.

Inviting a man over for dinner and then offering him my usual platter of steamed vegetables and poached salmon is just wrong. Besides after that hard workout with Synthia I'm sure I can handle a little mozzarella. There is nothing fried here!

It's annoying that I'm even having this conversation with myself as I slice the soft cheese.

Wiping my hands off, I take another sip of wine and stare at my phone. *I should call Reginald Grand back.* Waiting more than a day when a presidential candidate calls you about "national security" seems just wrong. Not that I've ever dealt with something like this before, but common sense says return that call quickly.

A sigh breaks free as I pick up my phone. Grand picks up on the second ring. "Angela." His tone is warm, like we are old friends. The guy might be running for his first political office but he sure sounds like a politician. *Or a producer.*

"Mr. Grand," I say, putting a note of awe into my voice. It's seems a safe bet that a man trying out for leader of the free world has an ego that enjoys stroking.

"I'm so glad you called."

I stir my marinara. "Of course, how can I help?"

"I'm going to be in California for a few days—fundraising and the like. I want to meet you."

"That's flattering, sir. But I make it a point to stay out of politics." Check my Instagram, bro—it's all pics of my dog, sunsets, and me working out.

"I totally understand; it's a dirty business." He's injecting humor into his voice, trying to be self-deprecating but just coming off as slimy. "But the things I want to talk about can't be discussed on the phone."

Crap on toast.

"I see." The timer for my eggplants buzzes, and I grab a hot mitt.

"I'll send a car for you. We can meet at my hotel. I promise we won't let anyone find out."

Pulling open the oven, the soothing aroma of baking eggplant rushes out on a wave of hot air. "Um..." *Can I say no? How do I say no?* "When? I've got a really busy couple of days."

"I thought your new movie didn't start shooting for a few more weeks." *Two months actually.*

"Yes, but," I inject a smile into my voice. "I have a life, training, you know how it is." *We are both big time, right fella?*

"I can work around your schedule." His voice is getting colder. I'm starting to piss him off.

"Okay, when are you going to be here?" I put the eggplants on the stove and walk over to my iPad, opening the calendar app.

He speaks to someone in the room with him.

"We get in tomorrow evening. I've got a rally the following night and a fundraiser lunch. The best time for me is 3 p.m."

"I have training," I say, which is true.

"What about after the rally, midnight?"

"Plans with my boyfriend."

"You're dating someone?" He sounds surprised, as if he had intel that I wasn't dating. *I'm not answering that. Clearly this isn't as much about national security as he claims.*

"What about the following morning? Early?"

"Fine." His voice is flat.

"Six a.m."

"Fine," he says again, clearly annoyed.

"Great, do you need my address?"

"We have it. The car will pick you up at 5:45."

I hang up. Maybe I should move.

"I LIKE THIS PLACE," Julian says as he steps into my living room. "It's cozy."

Is that a nice way of saying small? "Thanks." I take the bottle of wine he's holding. It's a chilled rosé. "I was actually just thinking about moving."

He nods, slipping off his leather jacket, releasing his scent into the air. I have to work hard to keep my eyes from rolling into my head with pleasure. *It's wrong to just try to screw him on my couch, right?* I need to wine and dine him first, after all the no-getting-back-to-him stuff. "How many bedrooms?" Julian asks.

"Just the one. And it's all rental stuff. Mary got it for me last year when we started shooting *The Tempest.*"

He hands me the jacket, and I put the wine down on my entry table to hang his coat in the closet. "I can see how you'd be ready for an upgrade."

I give a short laugh. "This is really nice compared to where I was living before."

"Where was that?" he asks with a grin that pops his dimples.

"Housing for aspiring models," I say. "I had to share a bedroom." I give him a fake frown. "Growing up I had my own room—we lived in a farm house."

Grabbing the wine, I start to walk toward the kitchen. "Smells great in here," Julian says.

"I'm making eggplant parm."

"Oh, yum."

"Want some wine?" I ask, putting the bottle on the counter. "I've got red open." I turn to him. "Or we could open this?"

"Either works for me."

He leans against the counter, watching me as I open the wine. A blush creeps up my neck at his close inspection. "Is it wrong that I just want to kiss you?" he asks, and I almost drop the bottle. His hand comes out to steady it. "Sorry."

"No." I shake my head, screwing up the courage to look at him. "I just—" A grin steals over my face. "I was thinking I had to wine and dine you before attacking you."

He moves closer, smiling. "I'm easy," he smirks, taking the half-opened bottle out of my hand and putting it on the counter. His other arm goes around my waist, and my breath stops. He's so handsome I can barely even take it.

I want to say something witty and sexy that will make him chuckle, but I've got nothing. My eyes close at the feel of him against me. A small moan climbs out of me, and he gives me that chuckle I wanted. The warmth of his face grows close, and then his lips find mine. My hands remember they exist and slide up his arms, finding those shoulders. Another moan comes out as I dig my fingers into the strong muscle there.

His tongue swipes at me, and I open for him. His one hand drops down to my ass and pulls me tight, while the other roams under my shirt, skirting up my spine and breaking goose bumps over my skin.

I want to have sex—right here, right now—in my kitchen.

"You do?" he says.

Holy shit! "Did I say that out loud?"

"About having sex in your kitchen right now?" He's smiling against my lips. I open my eyes. He's right there, those big blue sapphires of his shining down at me. "Yeah, you did."

My mouth goes into a perfect little "O" of surprise. *Some secret agent I make.* "I..."

"I'm happy to oblige." He turns us so that my back is to the counter. He pushes the wine away and lifts me up so fast that I let out a little yelp of surprise, followed by a quick, sharp laugh as my grip tightens on his shoulders.

"Is that why you wore this skirt?" he asks, running his hands up and down my thighs, pushing the white material up slowly.

"I thought we'd have a drink first."

He grins at me then leans over and grabs my jelly glass of red wine, taking the last sip. "I'm good," he says. "You?"

I can only nod as I watch his tongue lick his lips. Running my hands up his shoulders into his hair, I bend my head to kiss him as his fingers push my skirt out of the way. He's wearing a dark, silky T-shirt. I reach down to find the hem and pull it over his head. He lets me and then pulls at my shirt, getting rid of it.

I giggle, and he growls. It's like we've been lovers forever, not just a night in Shanghai. He kisses me with his hands on my cheeks, holding me, worshiping me.

That sense of power I felt last time we were together fills my brain again. It's a heady mixture of raw hunger and the realization of my own physical capabilities.

Blood pounds in my ears, and I'm suddenly desperate for him, my fingers pulling at his jeans. He meets my passion, pushing them down and pulling me to the edge of the counter so that we fit together. So that we can be together.

So we can both get exactly what we want.

"This is really good," Julian says, moaning around another bite of eggplant parm. It's his second portion.

I sip my wine and watch his pleasure. "I'm so glad you like it. And I'm really sorry I avoided you." The words just spill out. I'm so relaxed right now, wearing his T-shirt and nothing else, an empty plate in front of me. I could not be more satiated.

His eyes find mine, and he smiles. "I'm glad to hear that." His gaze drops back to his plate. "So, you were afraid?"

I don't answer, instead just sip my wine again, feeling the warmth infusing my body.

"I get that," he says, bringing his eyes up again. "I think." A blush springs to his cheeks, and he looks away.

"What?" I ask, intrigued by the sudden change in color.

He shrugs, and I get to see all his muscles work to make that happen. *Stealing his shirt was such a good idea.*

"I'd like to spend more time with you. For us to be..." He turns his eyes to mine, and they are serious—the playful air that floats around him reined in. "Exclusive." Before I can respond, he rushes on. "I don't want to freak you out, or force you into anything. It's just—I've been at this longer than you, and I'm not into meaningless flings."

I narrow my eyes at him. "Since when?" I ask. He blinks, and I sit forward. "Sorry, but, you were, weren't you? Into flings. I mean…you have a reputation."

He shrugs again, and I drop my gaze to admire his chest until he speaks. "I was in my twenties, a huge star. So yes, Angela. I fucked around a lot. But, I'm in my thirties now. I want more."

"More than sex in my kitchen?"

He shakes his head. "Oh, no. Sex in your kitchen is all I want."

"Shhh," I hold my finger over my lips. He cocks his head. "Don't let my bed or couch hear you."

He laughs. "Fine, sex with you anywhere. Anytime. But only you."

I give a small nod. "I can do that."

"It doesn't freak you out."

"I'm not the kind of person who has sex with more than one person at a time anyway, Julian."

His eyes dart back to his food. *He's had sex with other women since Shanghai.* That's fine. "I thought, because I asked to hold your hand in public that day, that you..."

"Yeah, I know." *I can't explain why I had to pull away.* He didn't even notice the scar on my shoulder, it's so slight now. "I didn't believe it. That you'd really want me." I say it quiet, the lie feeling awkward on my lips.

He meets my gaze. "You still don't get it, do you?"

"Get what?"

"Angela, you're one of the most desirable women on the planet. And you're only going to get bigger, more desirable. Your star is going to eclipse mine when your *Star Wars* film comes out. Mary will probably have you do a drama after. I won't be surprised if you win an Oscar."

Oscar. The image of that bloodied statue cracks across my consciousness, and I have to drop my gaze to hide the pained expression. "Thank you," I whisper, knowing I need to respond. I take a deep breath, pushing that image away, back into the world of dreams. And I raise my gaze to Julian.

He thinks I'm just being shy about the stardom I've gained, about the brightness of my future. He doesn't understand. *Is there any way I can make this work without him knowing?*

CHAPTER THIRTEEN

I'm waiting on my balcony in the dull, gray light of dawn, watching for the car to pull up. The air is dusty with smoke from the fires. I scroll through my phone's news app, Archie warm in my lap.

The largest fire tornado in California history killed a firefighter last night. I hit play on the video. A whirling inferno blasts across my small screen, sending a shiver over my body.

The fear that man must have felt as that monster came at him. One hundred and sixty-five miles per hour…temperatures in the center of the vortex reaching 2700 degrees.

My heart gives a hard thump as I read the next headline. "Russian Interference in the Election confirmed by Intelligence Agencies." Vladimir's confidence that Grand would win the election comes back to me with startling clarity. It's like I'm back in that room, standing next to the bar, the chilled glass of champagne in my hand. *"Things will change," Vladimir said. "Reginald Grand is a good man. He sees the possibilities that bringing our two nations closer together can provide."*

Is that why Temperance sent me to deal with Vlad?

What was in the pen?

I Google Vlad's name again but find nothing after his collapse at the consulate event. He can't be dead then… that would be reported, right? I close my eyes and rub them, hiding in the darkness for a moment. The soft purr of an engine pulls my attention to the drive below. A black town car stops in front of the building. "Come on, Archie," I say, standing with him in one arm. "It's show time."

The driver is uniformed and gives me a professional smile as he opens the door. "Mr. Grand sends his apologies for not being able to meet you himself."

"No worries," I say, happy not to be stuck in the backseat of a car with the man.

The drive to his hotel is quick, the early-morning traffic light for LA. By the time I'm heading home it will be a clogged mess. A twinge of annoyance tightens my grip on my phone. *Why do I have to waste my time on this? I could be lying in bed finishing the latest Charlaine Harris book.*

I let out a sigh. I should be happy that this is the most annoying thing happening to me today. I could be starving. I could be hunted by freaking Nazis.

Closing my eyes, I practice some gratitude. *I'm successful, healthy, have a new amazing man in my life, and a great new role.* Temperance's face flashes across my mind's eye. *Do I give thanks for him?*

Opening my eyes, I decide not to think about it. I can be grateful for so much without even bringing him up-—or the shadowy world he coerced me into joining.

We pull into the hotel drive, and a liveried doorman opens my door. I give him an appreciative nod and see a flicker of recognition in his eyes. I've got on sunglasses, a casual white T-shirt, and a pair of designer jeans that hug every curve. "Lift and separate. That's what jeans should do." Mary's advice echoes in my head as I feel the doorman's eyes on my ass.

Archie peeks his head out of the top of his bag when we enter the lobby. A woman in low heels and a knee-length skirt suit bustles over to me. "Ms. Daniels," she says, her voice all wispy with excitement. Her lipstick is the wrong color for her skin tone and the suit far too conservative and heavy for LA. She must work for Grand. "I'm Tabitha Sanders, Mr. Grand's advisor."

I give her a warm smile and slip my sunglasses off to let her see the glint of friendship I'm putting into my gaze. *We are both women in this world. You can trust me.* "Hi Tabitha." I widen my smile.

"Mr. Grand is very excited to meet you."

I don't respond. Nothing nice to say, don't say anything at all…right?

"Please, follow me. We've arranged a private room at the restaurant."

I follow her across the lobby and up a large staircase to the second floor. The restaurant doesn't open until seven, but she leads me past the hostess desk, through the dining room, to a private door. She knocks before entering, and we step into a room with a table for twelve but only set for two.

Ah, an intimate gathering. A freaking breakfast date.

"Excuse me," a man to my left says, startling me. *Jeez, was he hiding behind the freaking door?* "I need to search you."

"This is Agent Patrick Maloney. He's Secret Service," Tabitha explains, her voice holding reverence.

Agent Maloney is tall and broad, wearing a dark suit. His brown hair is dusted with gray and shorn close to his head. Brown eyes with deep pouches under them assess me.

He motions for me to hand over my bags. Archie yawns as the big man places his bag on an empty seat while putting the purse on the table. "Please stretch out your arms and separate your feet?"

I clear my throat and consider protesting, but there is no glint in his eye, only pure professionalism. He bends down, starting at my ankles and patting his way up, hands skimming the tight jeans. *As if I could hide anything in these bad boys.* At my waistline, he uses the back of his hands to circle me, bringing them down over my butt cheeks before moving onto my arms.

His hands cup my shoulders and then slide down my sides, across my belly and up, not touching my breasts but also making sure I'm not squirreling anything between them. *But with the right bra I could hide something from this search.*

Maloney steps back and says something into his sleeve that I can't quite make out before reaching for my handbag. He searches through it with the air of a man who's searched a lot of purses and finds each one as boring as the last—it's not the same dreariness I'm used to from TSA agents, but he's not on edge, not expecting my lipstick to contain a weapon, even though he opens it to check.

Maloney hands me my purse and then eyes Archie for a moment, who wags his tail and lolls his tongue. *Clearly a threat to national security.* "Does he bite?" the agent asks.

"No," I say with a warm smile. "He's just a puppy."

"Please remove him from the bag."

I pull Archie out, his little body curling as I bring him to my chest. The agent opens the bag, looking inside at the gnawed-on bone and flannel blanket before turning his attention back to Archie. *Wait, is he going to pat him down?* The thought raises a giggle but I suppress it, giving the agent an amused smile which he pretends not to see. The color edging his collar lets me know the man is not totally immune to my charms.

Maloney runs a finger along Archie's collar, who bends his head and tries to turn it into a petting session. The agent ignores the adorableness, and after confirming that my dog is not a threat to Grand, gives me a sharp nod of approval and dismissal before exiting.

As if on cue, a door in the back of the room swings open and a waiter enters, offering me a big smile. Blond-streaked hair, perfect teeth, fabulous body—an actor or model for sure. "Good morning," he says. "Welcome to the Gentry."

"Good morning..." I leave the sentence hanging, asking for his name.

"I'm Steven," he says with a small bow.

"Morning, Steven. I'm Angela."

He blushes slightly. "Yes, I know who you are. May I offer you coffee?"

"Please, with half and half, if you have it."

"Of course." He leaves quickly, and Tabitha points to the table. It's got one setting at the head and one to its left. I take the seat at the head, and her face pales. *Thought so.*

A guy who thinks he's going to be president also thinks he gets the head of the table. But he made me show up; I'm not going to make this easy for him.

The door opens, and Reginald Grand himself enters in a swirl of cologne. Only about 5' 8" with the jowls of a mastiff, and his bald palette glowing under the overhead lights, the nominee is smaller than I thought. Spotting me, he breaks into a grin, revealing capped, overly white teeth. I stand and he comes at me for a hug. *Seriously.* He embraces me, and Archie squirms under the pressure. A wet smack of lips against my cheek leaves a trail of saliva. "Such a pleasure," he says, stepping back and running his eyes down to my tits.

Is he kidding? Could the guy be more of a freaking cliché.

"Tabitha, coffee and—" He turns to her, keeping a hand on my arm. "Get me some of that coffee cake they had yesterday." He turns back to me. "It's fabulous, you'll love it."

He squeezes my arm, and I move away, settling back into my chosen seat. *Do I look like I eat coffee cake?*

His lips press together at my retreat, but he doesn't say anything, dropping into the seat next to me. "You look great. You're a really gorgeous girl…great style too."

I give a small nod, the compliment somehow sounding like an insult. I'm also a talented actor and secret agent, but yeah, I am hot as hell. *Thanks.*

Steven comes in and pours us both coffee. "Thanks," I say, catching his eye. His brows are lowered. Not a fan of Mr. Grand. Could it be his running mate's stance on gays? That they are an affront to God and should all go through conversion therapy?

"Mr. Grand," I say. "You requested this meeting. I don't want to be rude, but I do have another appointment at eight. I hope we can get down to brass tacks."

He laughs and picks up his coffee cup as Steven leaves the room. Tabitha still stands in the corner. Grand looks over his shoulder and nods, dismissing her.

Once we are alone, he sits even further back in his chair, spreading his legs out…taking up as much room as possible. Part of me wants to scrunch down and make more space for him. But I force myself to maintain eye contact and to keep my body language neutral.

"What you did with Vladimir Petrov…very impressive."

I drop eye contact and bring a hand to my chest. "That was

horrible——the seizure was so sudden and powerful," I say. "I have no idea what happened afterwards and have not been able to find out." I bring my eyes back to his. "Is he okay?"

Grand licks his lips, leaving a shiny trail that turns my stomach. "Don't worry, I know. I've got clearance," he says, ignoring my question.

"I'm sorry, but I don't know what you're talking about."

He leans forward, his face suddenly way too close, and I can't help but lean away. "I want you to do someone for me."

"Do someone for you?" My voice is low, and I inject a note of confusion into it. *What could I possibly do for you?*

"I've got a lot of enemies. People who don't want me in the Oval Office." *I can't imagine why.* "And I need your help with that."

My brows go up. *Is he serious?* Holding his gaze, I realize that yes, he is serious. "I have no idea what you're talking about," I say again.

The door opens before he can answer, and Steven places a piece of cake at Grand's elbow. The man who hopes to be the leader of the free world doesn't glance at him.

"Thank you," I say as Steven sets a matching plate next to me.

Grand picks up the piece of the cake and shoves a bite into his mouth, moaning with pleasure as Steven makes his exit. "Have some," he says, pushing the plate in front of me.

"No, thank you." I pause to wrest control of myself. *This conversation has gone from nuts to coffee cake crazy.* "I came here as a courtesy, and now I'm leaving." I stand up. He moves quickly blocking my exit.

I pause. "Please get out of my way." I say it low and quiet, meeting his gaze.

His eyes are a pale yellow, green...reptilian. His skin shiny with sweat making his grey pallor moist. "Look, sweetheart—"

"I'm not your sweetheart." I grit through my clenched jaw.

He grins. *Every woman is his sweetheart.* "I want you to do this for me."

"And I want you to get out of my way so I can leave."

His smile widens. "That Temperance is a genius. You know there are a lot of you. Hollywood types working for us."

"Us? Last time I checked, the election wasn't decided."

His face goes a little blotchy at that, adding spots of color to his livid skin. "You are going to help me." A spark comes into his eyes, one that I recognize—an anger fueled by righteous rage. He thinks everyone should do exactly what he wants, and when they don't, it pisses him off. *Men.* "I'll send you a note with a name," he says.

This is dangerous. I go to sidestep him, and he blocks me, grabbing my arm. I twist out of his grip, holding back a punch to his stomach.

Stepping to the side, I go to move around him, but Grand reaches out and grabs me again, tighter this time.

"Let go," I hiss. *You're not the only snake in this room.*

"You'll get the note," he says, spittle stinking of coffee and bad teeth spraying my cheek.

"I don't work for you."

"I'll expose you," he threatens, a smile pulling at his wet lips. We are almost the same height, he's only got about an inch on me, but the grip on my arm is iron tight. He leans closer as if to kiss me, and I rear back, twisting free from his hold and moving quickly to the other side of the table, my heart hammering.

He is very dangerous.

Grand does not follow me. He's between me and the door I came in. Will he let me through? *Should I just lie, tell him I'll do as he asks?*

I relax my shoulders, allowing them to slump into a position of defeat. He smiles, predatory and victorious. A stupid, arrogant man. Why do so many of them have so much power?

"Fine," I say, straightening up. "I'll look at your note." A flicker crosses his gaze. *Mistrust.* I'm agreeing too easy. "You've left me no choice," I point out. The mistrust eases, and the thrill of victory sparks again.

"Come here," he says, waving for me to move closer to him.

He's not done with me yet. "I'm leaving," I say, sidling toward the door that the waiter passed through. I might end up in the kitchen, but that's better than going through Grand.

Color infuses his cheeks again as he recognizes my intention. "Come here." He says it more forcefully, his voice deep and rough.

I'm at the door now, Archie's bag gripped hard against me. He squirms his head out and looks at Grand with sleepy eyes.

"If you walk out that door, I'll expose you," he says. "Get over here."

My lips purse. He's a loose cannon. Or a liar. Probably both. "Expose me," I taunt, stepping back into the swinging door. It opens, and he starts toward me.

I turn, pushing into the hallway, the door swinging shut behind me. I break into a run, my sneakers quiet on the linoleum. He bursts through the door behind me, his dress shoes clacking.

Risking a glance over my shoulder, I see him slow to a stop, his breath huffing. I keep running. He doesn't yell any final threats. But I feel his eyes on me, boring into my back, hot as a laser, as I reach the end of a T and take a left.

I slam into Steven, who falls back with a yelp of surprise. "Sorry," I say, reaching out a hand to steady him.

He rubs at his chest where I barreled into him. "You okay?" he asks, concern wiping away the shock and pain.

"Yes. How do I get back to the lobby from here?" His eyes raise to stare down the hall behind me. "Not through the restaurant," I clarify. "I need another way out."

He nods, his jaw tightening. *He can guess what happened in there.*

"This way," he says, leading me down the hall. We pass a Secret Service agent on our way, who nods to us, his expression blank. *See no evil, hear no evil...*

ONCE I'M safe in a Lyft on my way home, I text the emergency number I have for Temperance. "Need to see you now."

He texts back. "I'll meet you at your apartment in twenty."

I'm shaking as I pour myself a cup of tea, the steam rising up and heating my face. Glancing at my bar cart, I consider adding a splash of brandy or whiskey but the clock on my phone reminds me that it's not even 9 a.m. Way too early to start drinking, no matter what the day's been like so far.

A knock at the front door jerks my attention. I grab my gun off the counter by the cup of tea and move into my living room, Archie on my heel, his small nose tapping my ankle.

The door begins to open, and I keep the gun down, standing at the entrance to the living room, my eyes riveted on the moving door.

Temperance steps in and smiles when he spots me. It quickly fades to a frown of concern when he sees the gun in my hand. "I told you to get rid of that," he says as he comes inside, closing the door behind him.

"Seriously?" I say, my voice coming out on the verge of hysteria. "This gun—" I shake it a little and he frowns deeper. "Is the least of my worries right now. In fact, it's the opposite. It's the freaking only thing keeping me from going crazy."

"What happened?" Temperance crosses to me, and I back up, retreating to my kitchen and cup of tea.

"Grand happened," I say.

"Grand." Temperance's voice is laced with disgust. "I was clear he needed to leave you alone."

"Yeah, well." I put the gun down next to my steaming mug and turn to Temperance, my back to the counter. A flash of Julian and me in here crosses my mind, and I swallow the lump of nostalgia for yesterday before continuing. "He made it clear I had no choice. So I went to see him this morning at his hotel."

Temperance cringes slightly, as if he knows where this is going. "He bragged that he knew all about what happened with Vladimir, dropping your name in the process. He told me I was a beautiful girl. And then he said that he has an enemy he wants me to"—I hold up my hands to form air quotes—"take care of."

Temperance starts slightly but almost instantly pulls the shield of secrecy back around himself, his expression returning to neutral. *The damn wizard.*

"Not only that," I go on. "When I said I would do it, just to get out of there, he wouldn't let me leave. He grabbed me, and I'm pretty sure he was going to *kiss* me, but I ran." Temperance doesn't speak, doesn't move. He is a statue in my kitchen. "Say something," I demand, anger bubbling over the shock and fear.

"That's unacceptable." He says it quietly, like it's true and he can do something about it.

His words calm me a little, and I manage a deep breath but it comes out in a stutter. "What are we going to do?" I ask.

Temperance's gaze is unfocused. "I need to talk to some people, and I'll get back to you."

"Okay." Dread tightens my gut again. If he has to go to higher-ups, I could lose this fight. Grand could be president soon, and then where will I be? Fucked. Possibly literally. "This isn't what I signed up for," I say, pulling my tea forward, cupping it in both hands, and breathing in the fragrance of ginger and spice floating up from the chai.

"I know," Temperance says it quietly. "This is not normal."

"Well, that's comforting." I say it with a small laugh. "It is in my business, though. I don't mean being given names of enemies to knock off, obviously," I say. "But using power to get sex? Yeah, that happens."

Temperance nods. He knows. Everybody knows. It's the way the whole damn world works. A shiver of anger floats over me again, and the sweet steam from the tea is suddenly too much for me. I need something else. My eyes wander to the bar cart again. No, I've got training in an hour, and I'm going to keep going with my life.

"Grand does not understand how anything works," Temperance says, pulling out one of my chairs and sitting down. He makes it look small and delicate, with his size and bulk.

"Or he understands it all too clearly," I mumble.

Temperance ignores me. "The president, let alone a candidate, does not get to use assets for their own personal vendettas."

"I would freaking hope not," I say, moving into the seat across from him. Archie jumps at Temperance, and the spy master picks up the small dog, settling him onto his lap, petting him absently as he stares out the window.

"Did he say when he'd deliver the name?"

"No, but soon, I imagine. I'm not sure. I ran out of there. Like, literally ran away out a service entrance. He didn't just want me to take care of his enemy—he wanted me to blow him or something along those lines."

Temperance shakes his head in disgust, looking down at Archie. "He didn't know who he was dealing with."

His words bring me comfort. That's right. He didn't. Grand made a mistake. He isn't going to get away with this.

"Will we expose him?" I ask.

"I don't see how we can do that without also exposing you, me, and the entire operation. And he knows that."

Right, of course.

"So…you'll just have a stern talking-to with him?" I ask.

A smile pulls at Temperance's lips…it's sly, scary. "Something like that." A lump forms in my throat. I'm not sure who is scarier, Grand or Temperance. But I guess I'll find out.

CHAPTER FOURTEEN

A FEW DAYS later I'm at Synthia's dojo showering after my training, letting the water pound onto my tingling muscles, hair slick on my back, eyes on the drain—letting everything wash away.

"Angela!" Synthia's voice reaches me from outside the door, and my face comes up.

"Yeah?" I answer, stepping forward out of the spray, peering through the fogged glass door at the empty bathroom beyond.

"There is someone here to see you." Her voice is laced with amusement, so it's not Temperance or Grand.

"Be out in a minute."

We met up at her dojo today. The main gym is always crowded on weekends, and she understands my hesitation about that...or at least she thinks she does. It's not all the staring; it's the exposure. I can't concentrate on Synthia when I'm thinking about threats all around me.

Turning off the shower, I grab a towel and dry myself quickly. Grabbing my body brush, I give it a couple of squirts of body oil and then begin to rub from my feet up. My already-tingling muscles light up again at the gentle massage. Moving toward my heart, I take my time, bringing color and energy to my skin.

Though they're now a favorite of Gwyneth Paltrow and the Goop crowd, I learned about body brushes from my grandmother long ago. But she did it dry before the shower—with a much stiffer brush so that there was an element of punishment in the self-care routine. *There is a note of punishment in everything that old woman does.*

Throwing on my wrap dress and slipping into leather sandals, I run my fingers through my hair, leaving it to dry naturally. It gets so abused through my work that I like to condition and leave it alone when I don't need to make it look any specific sort of way.

A quick application of face moisturizer, mascara and lip gloss, and I push out of the changing room. Synthia's private dojo is well equipped. Made up of two main rooms, it's a large and bright space scented of eucalyptus. I pass through the equipment room, which includes the standard weights and treadmill along with ropes hanging from the walls for yoga inversions and a full set of pilates apparatuses. The dojo itself has large casement windows, closed on this sunny, yet smoky day, with a mirrored wall and thick mats running from wall to wall. The wooden swords we practiced with today are hanging up alongside other mock weapons.

In the small reception area, with its water cooler and a few comfortable chairs, a man in a dark suit and tie with super-short hair waits with his hands behind his back. He's military, maybe, or used to be anyway. Or wants to be...

"Ms. Daniels," he says with a deferential nod. "This is from Mr. Grand." He holds out an envelope.

Crap on toast.

I don't want to take it. My hands are frozen by my side. *I can't take it.*

"Ms. Daniels?"

I swallow, dread trying to claw its way out of my stomach. Dread's cousin, terror, is sitting on my brow. But bravery thumps from my heart, and I lift my chin, extending my hand to take the slim envelope.

Mr. Military gives me a nod then turns on his heel and leaves. I hold the edge of the envelope, trying not to be afraid of the inanimate object.

"What was that all about?" Synthia asks. "Mr. Grand? That asshole running for president?"

I give a rueful smile and shake my head. "He's got a crush on me and has been trying to get in my pants."

She sneers with disgust. "Ew, he's married isn't he?"

"Yeah. And we all know how much that matters."

"What a scumbag." *If she only knew.* Synthia is still in her workout gear: skin-tight tank top and shorts, her hair pulled back into a bun. She crosses her arms as if to protect herself from men like Grand, as if there is any way to keep them at bay.

They come for us no matter what.

The thought is dark, a tendril of evil snaking through my brain, but it gives that bravery in my heart power. And I slip the envelope into my bag. "If that's a love note, you should go to the press."

I shake my head. "I'm not getting involved in politics."

Synthia's lips tighten. "You've got a lot of power these days, Angela. You may want to use some of it for good."

It sounds almost like an accusation.

"I don't have that much power. I've been in one successful movie and cast in another. Getting publicly embroiled in a political scandal could put that at risk. Everyone loves *Star Wars* no matter which side of the aisle they're on."

Synthia nods, her lips quirking to one side. She gives a shrug, dropping her shoulders and letting go of any shade she was trying to throw my way. "I get that. Tomorrow, you want to come back here?"

"Yeah, that would be great. Same time."

It's not until I get to my car that it occurs to me that Grand must be having me followed. How else would he know to find me at Synthia's? And not only that, he wants me to know that he is following me. Doesn't want me to feel safe anywhere. *Mission accomplished.*

I reach into my purse and pull out the envelope, my car engine humming quietly in the darkened garage. Inside is a single piece of paper—it must be Grand's assassination instructions. I unfold it slowly. Printed in Times New Roman is just one name: Temperance Johnson.

Temperance takes the paper from me, and I pick up my glass of wine. His brows raise. "Who dropped it off?" he asks.

"Didn't get his name. But I would recognize him."

"Do you think he knew what he was delivering?"

"No idea."

Temperance looks up at me and nods. "Well," he says, sitting back into the kitchen chair. "He's even bolder than I thought."

"So, what are we going to do?"

"What do you think we should do?"

"What did your superiors say?"

He doesn't respond, just glances down at the paper. I sip my wine, forcing myself to wait. Staying quiet is the best way to get other people to talk. But my simple mind tricks don't work on Temperance. *Big shocker.*

"Are you afraid of him?" Temperance asks me, his tiger eyes coming up to meet mine.

"Afraid? Sure," I give a shrug. "I'd be a fool not to be. A man with that much power and that much crazy? He's dangerous."

"He also has knowledge. The man has received intelligence reports for the past three months."

I sit back into my chair, my shoulders coming forward into a protective hunch.

"I'll take care of it." Temperance folds the paper and slips it into his jacket pocket. He's wearing a blazer over a black T-shirt, with indigo jeans and a pair of leather sneakers. The guy could be a successful producer or an agent—the Hollywood kind, not the spy kind.

He goes to stand, and I move with him. "That's it?" I ask.

His brows go up. "Is there something else?"

"I mean, what am I supposed to do?"

"Do you want to do something?"

"I thought—" I cut myself off. Dammit, Temperance is messing with me.

"Thought what?"

That you could solve this! "Never mind." I step back, picking up my water glass and moving to the sink. "I'll see you out." I put the glass down on the counter.

Temperance leads the way into the living room, but a knock at the door freezes us both. He steps forward, checking the peep hole, his body stiffening then waves for me to look. *It's Julian.*

Temperance heads toward my bedroom, and when I go to follow, he stops and leans close, his breath right at my ear. "Give me thirty seconds, then let him in. I'll go out this way."

This way? "The balcony?" I ask.

He smiles and nods. A thrill shoots through me. *That's hot. Sorry, but it is.* He cocks his head, seeing the spark that his words brought to my eyes, and then gives me a half smile, almost sympathetic. *Whatever, hot stuff.*

I turn to the door. "Who is it?" I call.

"Julian," he yells back. I glance toward my bedroom, but Temperance is gone, the sliding door to the balcony open and the wind playing with the curtain. We are five stories up. Is he going to shimmy down the freaking wall?

"Just a sec," I answer Julian, then take a deep breath, arranging my face into a happy and excited expression before opening the door for him. "Hey!" I say with a breathless smile. *I'm so happy you just showed up here.*

"I know you weren't expecting me. But I was in the neighborhood." I glance down and see that he is in running clothing.

"Come in," I say, widening the door. "You want some water?"

"Sure."

He steps into my apartment, his sexy smell coming with him. I'm still amped up from Temperance's visit. From the threat Grand made against me. But I'm happy to see Julian. The guy is like a balm for me. He heads for the kitchen, and my gaze falls to his ass in the loose shorts he's wearing. *Damn. Hot damn.*

In the kitchen, I pour him a glass from the Brita and hand it over. He drinks it down, sweat trickling from his hairline. "Want to grab some dinner?" he asks as he puts the glass on the counter.

I laugh. "You want to go out like that?" I raise a brow.

He grins. "I figured I'd change first and come back for you."

"Mm-hmm." I take a step toward him. "You can shower here, if you want."

He smiles. "I thought you might like to see my place tonight. You've never visited me."

"In Malibu?" I ask.

"Oh, no, that was just a rental while I renovated. I moved into my new place when we got back from Shanghai. It's in the Hollywood Hills."

"Fancy," I say before thinking about it.

Julian laughs and warmth spreads through my chest. "It's a gorgeous place—mid-century modern from 1961—that I spent way too much on, bringing it back to its former glory." His cheeks are bright and eyes dancing. *He loves his home.*

I might be in the midst of an international incident that is going to get some people— hopefully not me—killed, but at least my boyfriend is freaking adorable and wants to keep moving forward.

Am I putting him in danger?

I push the thought aside. Temperance would have said something…right?

"What?" Julian asks, and I realize I'm chewing on my lip.

"Oh, nothing," I say, forcing a smile onto my face. "I definitely want to see your place."

His hand comes out and holds my hip as he leans in for a quick kiss. Memories of what we did last time in this kitchen flash through, heating me from my hair to my toes, and I wrap my arms around him. He makes a small appreciative sound as his other hand comes around to grab my ass.

God, he smells good. How can someone so sweaty smell so good?

My cell phone rings, and I groan. *What now?* He laughs as I pull free to grab it out of my purse. "Sorry," I say.

"No worries. I'm going to head home and get ready. I'll be back in about two hours to pick you up."

"Sure." He leans in and gives me a quick kiss before leaving. I finally find my phone in my bag and pull it out.

Mary.

I've missed her but return the call. "Hey, doll," she says.

"Mary, what's up?"

"Troy Woods wants to meet you tomorrow." The director of the *Star Wars* film. "Can you come by the office? Ten a.m.?"

"Of course. I'm excited to finally meet him."

"He is thrilled you're on this project. He just got back from shooting in New Zealand, or he would have set this up earlier."

"Sure, I understand."

We hang up, and I clench the phone in my fist, feeling pretty darn good. I've got a great, hot boyfriend, a starring role in a huge film, and Temperance is taking care of my only problem without me. *Life is good.*

A small warning bell rings inside my head; often the clearest skies hold the most danger.

JULIAN TAKES me to a trendy place where paparazzi swarm, and we hold hands. It's fun, and the food is great. We cuddle in the booth and dance until my feet ache. "Come on," he whispers into my ear. "Let's go home."

The idea that we may one day share a home warms my drunk little heart. Could I really have everything? Why not?

His home is up in the hills, with a security gate. "When did you get this place?" I ask as the wooden gate trundles open for us.

"About four years ago, after *Dusk* came out." Dusk was his first big heartthrob film. It grossed over a billion worldwide and cemented him as a star. "I've been renovating."

"Wow, four years to renovate?"

"It's a hell of a process, and I don't recommend it." He laughs at himself, and I reach out and run my hand over his shoulder, just wanting to touch him as he pulls onto his property.

"I'd love to get a place like this someday," I say.

He laughs again. "You haven't even seen it yet."

"That's my point! A driveway this long, this much land…" *Hard to just stroll right in with that kind of security.*

I look away as I think of Jack Axelrod's house. He had a driveway this long…

Julian's home comes into view: a white, mid-century modern masterpiece. All clean lines with an absence of Hollywood excess. It takes my breath away. "Wow."

"You like it?"

"I love it." I look over at Julian, and he's smiling. There is pride in his expression but not ego. He is proud of the house itself—not that he can afford it.

Julian pulls around the circular drive, stopping at the front door. Climbing out, he comes around for my door, and I let him open it for me. Not because I'm some damsel who requires old-fashioned courtesies or who doesn't have the strength to pry open a car door, but because I like the way he looks leaning in for my hand.

Julian enters a code into the lock at the front door. I glance away to give him privacy. Maybe one day I'll have that code. Or my own code. A shiver of want runs over me. *I want him and this relationship. I want us to work.*

He glances up at me as he swings the door in, giving me a shy smile.

The sound of a car engine in the drive pulls both of our attentions back out into the night. A marked police car rolls into view, closely followed by an unmarked sedan.

Julian straightens, his brows arching. The hair on the back of my neck rises. *Oh no.*

The passenger door of the unmarked vehicle opens and Julian moves to stand slightly in front of me…to protect me. But I can tell. I can *just tell* this is my fault.

I recognize the fedora first—it's Mr. Cliché from the night I killed Jack Axelrod. Detective Jacobs. My throat goes dry, but I force my face to remain neutral as if I've never seen him before.

His eyes land on me, and he smiles, slow and pleased. "Hello officer," Julian says as the detective approaches. He's not worried. As a prominent, law-abiding citizen, why would he be?

"Mr. Styles, I'm Detective Jacobs." Julian extends his hand, but Jacobs doesn't take it. "I'd like you to come down to the station with me; we have some questions for you."

"Excuse me?" Julian stiffens, his hand dropping to his side.

Uniformed officers climb out of the marked car, the tools of their trade jangling on their belts. Jacobs flicks his gaze to me. "You sure you want me saying anything in front of the lady?" he asks Julian. Jacobs gives me a sly, almost-not-there smile—as if calling me a lady is at once an insult and a lie. *I'm no lady—I'm a killer.*

My lips tighten, and Julian stands taller. "I think you're confused. I've done nothing wrong and have nothing to hide."

"Then come with us and answer some questions, please."

"What is this about?"

Jacob returns his attention to Julian. "An incident with a young woman." He drops his voice, the tone becoming almost sympathetic. "She's accusing you of some pretty serious crimes."

Julian shakes his head, his curls bouncing. "I have no idea what you're talking about."

"You should call your lawyer," I say quietly.

Julian glances back at me. His blue eyes are wide, but his expression is confused, unknowing. *He doesn't realize the danger he is in…yet.* "Right." He returns his attention to Jacobs. "I'll be happy to come down to the station at a more convenient time with my attorney."

"Look—" Jacobs steps closer. "I don't want to have to arrest you." He says it like he's doing Julian a favor. "Then it's going to show up in the blotter, and the press will get hold of it."

"Arrest me?!" Julian's voice jumps—hitting the first note of fear.

"Just come with us now so we can get this over with." Julian doesn't move. I put my hand on his back, an attempt at comforting him. "Come on," Jacobs says, tilting his head toward the officers standing behind him.

"Who's your lawyer?" I ask. "I can call for you."

Julian looks over his shoulder at me again. His eyes are wide…so blue. "Diane March, but she does entertainment."

"Your agent is Lawrence Fishberg, right?"

He nods. "I'll call everyone." I lower my voice, though I'm sure Jacobs can hear me.

Julian's jaw stiffens. "No." His voice has gone cold, and he turns back to the detective. "Let me see the arrest warrant."

Jacobs's mouth tightens. "Look, you've been accused of rape. I can arrest you for that without a warrant."

"Can you?" Julian straightens, reaching into his pocket and pulling out his phone. He scrolls through, Jacobs watching with a scowl on his face. "Diane," Julian says into the phone. "I've got a detective here who wants me to come in for questioning about a rape accusation. He says he can arrest me."

Julian waits and listens, then holds the phone out to Jacobs. The detective does not take the slim handset, just steps back and waves to the uniformed officers. They move forward, the one in the front, a tall white guy with pockmarked cheeks, pulling out his handcuffs.

"You're under arrest," he begins. There is squawking from the phone. Julian holds it to his ear.

"They are arresting me." Then he hands the phone to me before offering his wrists.

My heart is hammering. *This is my fault.* How can I stop it? I put the phone to my ear.

"Which station are they taking him to?" a female voice on the other end asks.

"Where are you taking him?" I ask the officer.

"The Hollywood station on Wilcox Avenue," he answers.

I tell the lawyer on the line. "I'll meet him there." She hangs up, and I am left clenching Julian's phone as they walk him to the back of the cruiser.

Jacobs steps up close to me. "Brave fellow you've got there," he says, humor lacing his voice.

A chill runs down my spine, but I keep my face neutral as I meet Jacobs's dark gaze. "Screw you." I bring false bravado into my voice.

"You better do what Grand asks…and soon." Jacobs smiles a toothy grin. "This is just the beginning. We're going after your grandma next."

I step closer to him, and his eyebrows twitch, but Jacobs does not retreat. There are only inches between us. I can feel the heat of his body and smell the stink of sour coffee. "You'd regret that," I say. "She survived the Nazis when she was nine. Nine." I raise my brows. "I think she can handle you." My eyes drop down between us, examining his body, and when my gaze returns to his, I make it obvious that I find him lacking.

"We'll see who has regrets," Jacobs says, but his voice has lost its edge. I affected him. *I'll do much more than that.* He moves off toward his vehicle as anger churns in my gut.

Julian makes eye contact from the back seat—sparkling sapphires shining in the dome light. I take a step forward. "Your lawyer will meet you there," I say. He nods and forces a smile.

"This is all a misunderstanding," he says, his voice rough with emotion.

"I know."

The cars pull out, their tires quiet on the freshly paved drive. The rise and fall of nocturnal insects fills in the soundscape. The distant smoke tinges the air as I pull out my phone to call Temperance.

I chew on my lip while I wait for him to answer. "We need to meet," I say when Temperance picks up.

"Okay." His voice is quiet, and I can hear the sounds of a restaurant behind him.

"I'm at Julian's house. He just got arrested."

"Did he?" There is a hint of curiosity in his voice but no fear or shock.

"Yes, get here now." I hang up and clench my phone tight to keep my hand from shaking.

Turning to the house, I stare at the partially open door. Should I go inside? I need a glass of water and to sit down. Julian certainly wouldn't mind.

I enter a large living room with a glass wall exposing the glittering city, an infinity pool in the foreground. Modern yet comfortable looking couches and chairs are grouped in seating areas. Along the wall to my left is a kitchen with a large central island.

Closing the door behind me, I find the light switch, illuminating the space in soft white and rose. *It's beautiful.* Julian is not only hot, smart, and talented, but he also has incredible taste.

And I'm ruining his life.

CHAPTER FIFTEEN

TEMPERANCE ARRIVES TWENTY MINUTES LATER, driving a sleek black Mercedes. He unfolds from the driver's seat and comes around the front, the engine ticking as he passes.

I stand in the doorway, hands clasped tight. He doesn't wait for an invitation into the house, just strolls in, like he's been here before. The fragrance of leather and wine wafts off of him.

Temperance pulls a device out of his pocket, about the size of a cellphone, and turns it on. Quickly scanning the room, he nods to himself and then waves for us to leave.

In his car, the air conditioning makes me shiver as he pulls away from the house, passes through the open gates and begins to wind down from the hills. "Tell me what happened." I explain about Detective Jacobs. "He's got people everywhere," Temperance says, nodding as if he expected something like this to happen.

"Grand? That just doesn't make sense. He was a celebrity and business man a year ago. How does he have so much political power?"

Temperance's jaw tightens before he answers. "White supremacists."

The words hit me like a punch to the stomach. *Nazis, they always come for us.*

"My grandmother survived the Nazis." It comes out quiet but firm.

"She survived by fleeing," Temperance points out.

"I guess sometimes you have to flee. Besides, she was a child. What was she supposed to do?" I sound angry, almost scared. I bite my lip to banish the weakness.

The road twists and curves down the mountain. Mansions hide behind high walls and lush landscaping.

"Fleeing won't work this time," Temperance says.

"I'm not trying to flee. I want this life. I want everything I've worked for." *Everything I've killed for.* "What are we going to do?" I turn to Temperance. *We're in this together.*

"I have a safe house we can stay in tonight. I'm not sure you'd be safe at home." He checks his blind spot and merges onto the highway.

"I have a big meeting tomorrow. The director of my new movie, Troy Woods. I need to go see him. And what about Julian?"

"We will do everything we can for him." A ball of nausea swirls in my stomach. Julian doesn't deserve this; he should be with some nice girl. "Don't feel too bad about it," Temperance says, as if reading my thoughts. "It's not your fault."

"Isn't it?" My voice comes out sounding soft, edged with regret.

"Is it your fault Jack Axelrod attacked you? That I approached you?"

"It's my fault I said yes. I could've taken the punishment due, and Julian wouldn't be in jail right now."

"Right." Temperance says it like it's not right. "And your grandmother could have stayed in Romania and been gassed with the rest of her family. But she chose to flee. She left them all behind, and she made it out alive."

"And she's a bitter old bitch. She survived. She's still breathing. But she's been miserable her whole damn life."

Temperance glances over at me, pulling his eyes from the road for just a moment. I don't meet his gaze. "You're saying she would've been better off dead?"

"I don't know. I don't know what I'm saying. All I know is that my choices landed Julian in jail tonight."

Temperance lets out a laugh. "No, they didn't—at least not on their own. Grand's choices did, or even Julian's. Or just fate." Traffic slows and the brake lights in front of us throw a red hue across Temperance's face. "Nothing is any one person's fault. It's all a kind of elaborate chain reaction."

"Or it is all just chaos, atoms crashing into each other?"

"Either way, not your fault."

I can't help the laugh that releases.

TEMPERANCE'S safe house turns out to be an entire floor in one of the newly renovated old factory buildings downtown with junkies nodding off outside the plush lobby. *Very LA* Sunshine, celebrity and incredible wealth in the high rises and hills, with drug addicts and desperation huddled at its base.

The elevator opens right into the apartment's living room. Distressed, painted wood floors, high, iron-beamed ceilings, and the redolence of sandalwood greet us. There is a kitchen along the back wall, and a lanky, nerdy guy is standing behind the marble-topped island, his brown eyes huge behind thick glasses. "Justin, meet Angela," Temperance says, moving through the uncluttered space.

Justin stumbles as he comes around, grabbing at the counter to stay upright. *He's recognized me and can't quite handle it.* The man's face goes beet red. *So, not an agent.* "Angela, this is Justin," Temperance says as he pulls out one of the leather stools for me.

The nerdy guy works his jaw a couple of times before finally squeaking out a hello. He's still holding onto the counter where he caught himself. "Evening," I say.

Justin's eyes jump to Temperance, who smiles at him. "We need to discuss a problem," Temperance says. Justin swallows and straightens, releasing the counter and nodding. Temperance turns to me. "Can I get you a glass of water or a cup of tea before we begin?"

"Sure, water," I say.

Moments later, we are at the large dining room table. Justin projects from his laptop onto a screen lowered from the ceiling. A photograph of Detective Jacobs wearing a uniform and looking about twenty years younger glows in the dim room. "Detective Abraham Jacobs," Justin says, his voice deeper and more confident now that's he behind his computer screen. "He's been a suspected 'ghost skin' since 1991."

"A ghost skin?" I ask, turning to Justin.

His screen reflects in his glasses, hiding his gaze. "It's a term for white supremacists who hide their beliefs in order to further their cause."

"Oh." My voice comes out sounding small.

"In 1991, Jacobs was working in a local branch of the LA county sheriff's department where a neo-Nazi gang of officers were convicted for habitually terrorizing black and Latino residents. Jacobs was suspected of being a member of the group but never faced prosecution. He's continued to move up the ranks of the LA police department. In 2006, when the FBI released a report warning of white supremacists infiltrating police forces across the nation, we started tracking him closely. He's a leader and recruiter for a 'social club' that calls themselves the 'blue brotherhood.'"

"Why is he still on the force? Can't he be arrested and tried?" I ask.

Temperance shifts in his chair before answering. "Not enough political will." He sits forward, resting his elbows on the table, his gaze holding mine. "To put it bluntly, the history of law enforcement in the United States is linked to the history of white supremacy. The origin of U.S. policing lies in the slave patrols of the eighteenth and nineteenth centuries." He looks down at his hands where they are interlaced on the wooden table.

When his gaze returns to mine it's softer, gentle—like he is about to impart some sad news. "In 2009, three years after the initial report warning of the infiltration of police forces, a joint report between Homeland Security and the FBI was issued, warning that white supremacist groups were recruiting 'disgruntled' veterans and law enforcement officers due to their skills and training. The report concluded that 'lone wolves and small terrorist cells embracing violent right-wing extremist ideology are the most dangerous domestic terrorism threat in the United States.'" A shiver runs down my spine, and I have to look away, staring at my glass of water.

"Conservative groups freaked out and the report was rescinded," Temperance goes on, his voice calm, free of accusation, though his words are sickening. "In fact, Homeland Security stopped tracking the groups altogether, and now it's just the FBI." Temperance pauses. "And us."

He sits back into his chair. "The military took action—they began to screen members for white supremacy tattoos and have done a relatively effective job of rooting out the extremists in their ranks, but police departments are not centralized. There is also a lack of will to rid many departments of racists. Fifty years ago, in many parts of the South, entire departments were made up of Klan members. And beyond that, being a member of a white supremacy group isn't in itself illegal. Freedom of speech."

"So you"—I look between the two of them—"keep track of the racist police officers?"

"We have a team," Justin says. "Temperance has a lot of autonomy." Pride deepens his voice even further. His back is straighter—the nerdy guy is looking more like a secret agent all of a sudden. *But he's still overly affected by a beautiful woman.*

"It's sickening," I say, feeling the truth of it my gut. "Is what's happening with Grand and Jacobs connected to Vladimir in some way?" I ask. "I've read about the suspected Russian interference in the election."

Justin looks over at Temperance, who gives nothing away, his face that strong, stone statue again. "I can't go into details about Vladimir," Temperance answers. "But we can draw a straight line from Jacobs to Grand now, thanks to you." Temperance gives me a predatory smile. It's chilling... almost like he's happy about what happened to Julian. Or even manipulated it into happening somehow.

"We suspected that Grand had ties to white supremacist groups," Temperance goes on. "They support him on Twitter and other social media. And while he is not about to admit a close connection, he has avoided opportunities to condemn them."

"I don't think he's going to admit it now," I point out.

"No, we don't need him to." Temperance nods to Justin, who types into his computer for a moment.

My watch beeps, a reminder to take Archie out for his final pee. "I've got to go home," I say. "Archie is alone."

Temperance pulls out his phone. "I'll have him picked up."

Right, because you can access my apartment whenever you want. Awesome.

After sending off a quick message, Temperance returns his attention to me. "Grand has made several mistakes. This proof of his connection to Jacobs is the nail in the coffin."

"What were the others?" I ask.

"Besides trying to get you to assassinate me?" Temperance raises an eyebrow. "I can't go into details at this time."

"Will there be a time?"

"Perhaps." *Come on.* I give off a dramatic sigh, and Temperance smiles, almost like he is enjoying my frustration. "You know other things about him from the news—the accusations of sexual assault." The screen flashes, and images of the women who have come out claiming that Grand forced unwanted touching on them glow to life.

"But that can be easily challenged," I point out, the bitterness in my voice coating my tongue. "We all know that women are often not believed when they claim sexual assault." Temperance nods. "It's what got me into this situation in the first place," I mutter.

"And what we assume is a false accusation against Julian is what has brought us here tonight."

"Right," I say, sitting forward. "And what are we going to do about that?"

Temperance smile grows into a grin. "We have to kill Grand." His words strike me like a fist to the solar plexus, stealing my breath and numbing my limbs.

I pull in a breath, my mind racing and stumbling and coming up empty. *Kill a presidential candidate?*

"He asked you to assassinate me," Temperance goes on. "He knows I'm a thorn in his side. That I am your contact and protector." *That I'm black.* He doesn't say it, but I hear it. "He also knows I'm pursuing his ties to white supremacists and other dangerous connections we can't go into at this time."

I put up a hand, asking him to slow down. Closing my eyes, I pull in a deep breath. "That is so extreme." I finally find some words, though they hardly do justice to the swirl of confusion in my mind. *This all sounds crazy!* "Your superiors can't...I mean, who has the ability to authorize this?"

Temperance ignores my questions about his superiors. "I have a lot of leeway. And we're going to use it." Glancing over at Justin, I see that the young man's jaw has gone slack with surprise again. *This guy does not have a poker face.*

"Reginald Grand is a danger to the country." Temperance's voice thrums through the large room. "And our mission is to keep this nation safe. We have to stop him."

IN THE MORNING, Archie and I take an Uber over to Mary's office, and I show up looking like I'm not hiding from a presidential candidate who wants me to kill for him...and who I'm plotting to murder in return.

Mary meets me at the elevator and, looping an arm through mine, she bustles us to her office. "Did you hear about Julian?" she asks, her voice low.

"I was there when they arrested him. It's bullshit."

"This is a disaster. A goddamn disaster."

"I know, even an accusation can be devastating." Archie squirms in his bag and pops out his head. I rub under his chin, and he sighs appreciatively.

"You're so sure he didn't do it?" Mary asks me, brows raised, mascara-shrouded eyes wide.

"Yes."

Mary's lips press tight, and she nods once before crossing the room and pouring herself a coffee from a silver carafe. She holds it up, offering me a cup. I shake my head. "Just water please." She pulls a chilled bottle from the mini-fridge. Bringing it over, she puts it in my hands and smiles. Her *be brave* smile. "We'll get through this," she promises me.

She has no idea. I give her back a smile that says *I'm glad you're with me.*

"So you two have been dating?" she asks, her voice pitching up.

"Yes." There's no need to be shy about it; we've been photographed together numerous times.

"So this can affect you," she says. "We have Jennifer on staff. But for crises like this I like to bring in some extra muscle. Do you know Damon Schwartz?"

"By reputation." He's the master at hiding or spinning the biggest scandals in Hollywood.

"Good." Mary nods once. "I talked to him this morning, and he's willing to take you on. His fees are astronomical, but he's amazing. These accusations could screw everything up——turn you into tabloid fodder as the wronged woman. We need to get out in front of it."

I don't have time for that. I've got to meet Temperance. "Mary, listen."

She interrupts me. "No, you need to listen to me. Damon's coming in after your meeting with Troy, and we're formulating a plan. It's what's happening."

Mary crosses to her office door and opens it, waiting for me. We're headed into the meeting with my new director. Right now I'm not fleeing or fighting. I'm getting ready to create.

TROY WOODS IS thin on the verge of emaciated. The bones of his wrists are clearly visible when he reaches out to shake my hand, and his fingers feel like sticks in my grip. The Oscar-winning director smiles at me, the skin around his eyes crinkling. He's in his late forties and has spent the last decade making hit movies and apparently not eating.

"Pleasure to meet you." He's nodding and smiling as he releases my hand, his straw blond hair bouncing around his face, reminding me of a friendly scarecrow.

"I am so honored," I gush. "It's a dream to work with you."

He waves his hand as if trying to bat away the compliment. "I'm excited to work with you too but, please, let's not turn this into too much of a love fest." He laughs. Mary and I laugh with him.

Troy moves toward the conference table, taking control of the room and the meeting. Mary moves to follow us, and he catches her eye, cocking his head slightly. *He wants us to be alone.* Mary nods and excuses herself, the door whispering closed behind her.

"I am so excited to get started," Troy says, motioning toward the table. There are two scripts waiting, and I feel a thrill run through me.

Usually they send the script over early—in most cases I'd read it before accepting a role. But this is the *Star Wars* franchise and Troy Woods, so this is my first chance to see it. I ease into a chair, pulling the manuscript toward me.

"I've been working on it, and I think it's really good," Troy says, taking the seat catty-cornered to mine. He's got a nervous energy to him, as if there's a vortex of creativity swirling around inside his chest trying to burst out.

"I'm sure it's excellent." I go to open it, and he puts his hand on the cover, stilling me.

"I'm sorry. But can you just wait a minute?" I look up at him. Troy takes a deep breath and closes his eyes. "There is a method to my madness. I swear." He gives a self-deprecating laugh.

"Sure." I take my hands off the manuscript and fold them in my lap to keep from grabbing at it.

"I want us to get to know each other a little bit first." His eyes meet mine. "And then I want to talk about who your character is and how I see her for this film."

That would all be easier if I could read the script. But I just nod and smile.

Troy sits back in his chair and folds his hands over his thin chest. He's wearing a simple gold wedding band, scratched and patinaed. He and his wife have been together for twenty-five years—they are one of those famed Hollywood couples that have managed to make it. Does he cheat on her? Does he force actresses to give him head?

I try and push the idea out of my mind. *Not every man is a predator.*

"First, I want to get something really simple out of the way." He takes a deep breath. "Temperance."

I can feel the color draining from my face. My hands grip each other in my lap. "Temperance?" I stutter out.

"The name of your character," he says.

I feel like I'm choking. "I'm sorry." I look down at my hands and then force my eyes up to meet his gaze. "I wasn't…Right, of course. I didn't realize that was her name." Color is rushing back to my cheeks —a blush, the type of which I have not suffered since middle school, is surging over me.

"That's fine, you haven't seen the script. Of course you don't know her name." He sits forward quickly. "You've got a pretty terrible poker face."

I manage to keep my expression neutral, just raising one brow. I have no idea what's happening. Or where we are in this conversation. All I know is that I need to *not* react.

"Your character's name isn't Temperance." He gives a quick bark of a laugh. "I'm just fucking with you. I'm talking about Temperance. Temperance Johnson."

My heart is hammering in my chest, but the smile I give him says: *I have no idea what you're talking about, and I'm indulging you because you're my director.*

He sits back in his chair. "That's much better."

"So." I reach up to touch the script again. "Should we get started?"

He does that strange bark of a laugh again, his narrow chest shuddering. "Okay, you're actually very good. I wasn't so sure when Temperance suggested that we work together. But I have grown to trust the man. He's got an eye for talent. We've worked together for about a decade now." Troy holds my gaze—his eyes are green with flecks of gold, like a wheat field in early summer.

I don't say anything. I don't want to give anything away. Is he really working for Temperance? Or is he on Grand's side and just playing me? And why would a big-time Hollywood director be involved with any of these people? *What did he get caught doing?*

"He told me about the issue with Grand." Troy sits forward and picks up a plastic water bottle from the center of the table. "Tricky business, that." He cracks the lid and takes a slug, his Adam's apple bobbing. "But I think I can help."

"I'm sorry. I'm not entirely sure what you're talking about." I keep my voice neutral, once again a woman letting a powerful madman spin his tale.

"Oh please, you've recovered well, but you gave it all away with that first flush of color." He runs his hands over his face and gives me a mock look of utter shock.

Uncomfortable, I wiggle in my seat, embarrassed by my behavior. Scared by it. *I exposed myself to him.* But isn't that a director's job? To get you to expose yourself? No wonder Temperance likes working with people in my industry.

"I'm telling you I can help you. There's a party tonight. Grand's back in town, you know?"

I did know. The final presidential debate is scheduled for tomorrow and Grand and his Democratic opponent had flown in a couple days early to adjust to the time change while prepping for the debate. Given the stakes, I assumed he'd be squirreled away the whole time with advisers at some quiet location.

Troy goes on, "I can take you as my date." He takes another sip of the water. "Your face is getting red again."

I clear my throat. Look down at my hands and try to rein in some of the insanity raging in my brain. "Are you," I lean forward, keeping my voice low. "Are you suggesting that you—and Temperance—want me to kill him? *Tonight?*"

He gives a nod, that scarecrow hair flopping forward. Then Troy taps the script. "The dilemma you're facing now is very similar to what your character goes through. This is going to be great prep for the part." I don't say anything. Can't. "This is the kind of work that'll make you a star."

THE GOWN, borrowed from a top designer, looks like a Jackson Pollock painting—sprays and dots of colors—with spaghetti straps, a corset, and a skirt that comes to my knees.

I run my hands over my hips, turning to the side. *I look good.* Gorgeous, famous, everything I ever want to be. I'm staring at my ass. At the firm roundness of it. I have spent countless hours working on this ass, perfecting its shape. Denying myself delicious food in service to it. *It does give me power in return.*

My eyes rove to the script Troy gave me, which sits on my dresser. I have everything I came to this city to get…with just this one small caveat.

My grandmother's face flashes in my mind; wrinkled and gnarled with age, features twisted with bitterness. But we have the same dark hair and thick lashes…the same strength of will. Did she have to kill to escape the Nazis? *She was a child.*

A sudden, pressing need to hear her voice makes my skin itch. I've got my phone in my hand, and I'm dialing home before I even fully realize it. *Home.*

My maternal grandmother moved into my parents' house after I lost them. A small farm that they worked in addition to their other jobs. Dad was born and raised in the Midwest, his accent thick and bland, his hair blond and wavy. A good and simple man. The kind you read about: hard working and married to the same woman his whole life. In many ways, he lived the American dream…until he died.

There are a million ways to live the American dream.

My mom grew up without a father. She didn't remember him and questioning my grandmother never led to answers. They didn't get along, Mom and Grandma, but a fierce loyalty kept them in touch.

And when I had no one else, Grandma raised me.

The phone picks up and the TV murmurs in the background but no one speaks. A lump blocks my voice. I haven't talked to her in almost a year. Not since my last visit.

I clear my throat and force my tongue to work. "Hello."

"Stacy?" My grandmother's voice, thin as paper and strong as iron, crosses the line.

"Yes, it's me." Silence stretches between us. "I just wanted to call and say hi."

"I don't believe you, child. What are you doing out there?"

"My most recent film was a big success." I stand up, suddenly feeling this ridiculous urge to defend myself, as if her opinion matters.

"Well, what do you want? A gold star?"

I look at myself in the mirror, at the stunning figure that I strike. I square my shoulders and lift my chin.

I am a queen.

But am I a coward? *Ask her.*

"I wanted to ask you a question."

"Well, spit it out."

"Have you ever killed anyone?"

Silence. "That's a rude question."

"I'm not trying to be rude. I just want to know when you were a kid and..."

"And the Nazis wiped out my entire family. Did I kill any of them?" There's anger in her voice, old rage seething. The kind of anger you can never fully release.

Could it be so strong that it's passed down in our DNA? My mother was the opposite of angry—shy and compliant. All she strived for was to make everyone around her comfortable and happy. She wanted a normal life, and she got it as best she could. Married my father, who was as cornfed as America makes them, and worked hard. *She lived the American dream too.*

I read about a study that found fear was passed down in mice DNA. The scientist filled a cage with acetaminophen—which smells of almonds—while administering electric shocks to mice. Soon the small creatures shook at the scent of acetaminophen. Their pups did the same even though they never suffered the shocks.

Did my grandmother's bloodlust get passed down to me?

"Yes," I say to her. "I am asking if you killed any of them."

"I never got the chance. But I wish I could have. I really do." Her coldness, the anger in her voice, stokes that fire inside of me.

"Thanks, Grandma."

"For what? Are you going to use this for some role?" Disdain drips off her words.

I meet my own gaze in the mirror—the unique violet color stunning—framed by my long, dark lashes. "Yes. For a very important role."

TROY WOODS and I move down the red carpet together, telling reporters about my role in his upcoming film. We smile, we laugh at each other's jokes, we answer questions about how excited we are to work together. *Very.*

Inside the event space, away from the cameras, the light is low. Buffet tables heaped with gourmet food line the walls. Chandeliers hang from the ceiling, throwing purple light around the room, making all the meticulously displayed food look odd and unappetizing.

Waiters dressed in black move through the space with trays of drinks. Troy grabs two champagne glasses and hands me one.

"Grand isn't here yet," he says.

There is surveillance on every exit and entrance.

Troy is the lead, and I am but a weapon. *The actress to his director.*

But is that fair? That takes all the responsibility of this and lays it on his shoulders. *I agreed to be the weapon…to the role.*

I fiddle with the ring on my finger. It's very similar to the one I used on Vladimir, but the stone is ice blue. Temperance assured me that this time would be different. *It is a delayed-reaction drug that will take days to go into effect—his death will look like a heart attack, unconnected to sharing a drink with you at a crowded event. Grand is overweight, older, and loves junk food. We're really just helping nature along.*

"I'm going to get a bite to eat," Troy says. My brows raise. The guy is so thin you'd think he didn't consume food at all, let alone in a high stress situation.

My stomach is bursting with thoughts and feelings; I couldn't add one morsel.

"Wait," I put my hand on his arm. "Don't leave me alone." The words spill out. I didn't even know I was going to say them. Didn't realize I needed him by my side in this crowd.

He throws me a smile, the thinness of his face making him look skeletal under the strange purple light.

"Come on." I follow him through the crowd, my full champagne glass spilling over the sides and wetting my hand.

Eyes track me. People are whispering.

Julian's situation is public. I didn't get asked about it by the press out front because of the work Mary and her team have put into shielding me.

Will eliminating Grand solve Julian's problems? Temperance assures me he can take care of it. But I'm not doing this solely for him. I'm doing this for the country. A man like Grand, ruthless, racist and unscrupulous—willing to risk national security for his own personal vendettas—shouldn't be the ruler of the most powerful country on earth.

Who am I to decide? Just one woman playing a role.

We reach a buffet table, and Troy grabs a plate, beginning to pile sushi onto it. My stomach twists. He glances over at me, cocking his head as he listens to the small device in his ear.

"Grand is here," he says, popping a shrimp into his mouth. Troy chews thoughtfully as he continues listening.

Will I ever be so used to this that I can snack on shrimp while plotting an assassination?

The lights flicker, and the music screeches off. My heart thumps in my chest. *What is going on?*

There are small cries of alarm, and the crowd seems to surge, everyone moving closer to each other and then away—bodies are bouncing against us. Fingers grip my arm, and I recognize the bony touch of Troy.

People are pulling out their phones and flashlight apps glow. The room is suddenly sparkling with them. A couple hundred spotlights— everyone has one in their pocket.

"What's going on?" I ask, reaching into my purse for my phone.

"It's a power outage. Probably from the fires," Troy answers.

"What are they going to do?" I ask.

"There are generators. The lights should be back on soon."

He pops another shrimp into his mouth. I can see his jaw working in the dim light of the flashlights.

My own phone out, I flick on the app and shine it down at my feet.

"We've lost Grand in the darkness," Troy says, his mouth half full of shrimp. "Secret service might evacuate him. We may have lost our opportunity."

Relief and dread war in my chest. "Can you stop eating?" I say, my voice coming out harsh. Annoyed. "Sorry," I say immediately. "I'm feeling a little tense." I let out a small laugh, the word *tense* does not do justice to what I'm feeling. I'm on the verge of puking. I'm on the verge of taking a life. And there's a freaking blackout.

"No worries." Troy swallows before putting his half-full plate down on the edge of a nearby table. He takes my arm, moving me through the crowd. People are starting to enjoy the darkness. Laughter grows louder without music. People are still drinking. *This is exciting.* This is an adventure for all of them now.

"Do we have eyes on him yet?" Troy asks. His lips pull down into a frown, and his eyes find mine in the dancing light. He gives me a small shake of his head. "Secret Service evacuated him." I don't know if I'm relieved or dissapointed.

CHAPTER SIXTEEN

THE LINE of limousines stretches down the road and around the bend. "Ms. Daniels!" a red-vested concierge waves me toward a stretch limo at the curb. I glance at Troy who's flicking through his phone.

"Go ahead," he says, not looking up at me.

Red Vest opens the back door, and I hesitate. *This is not the car we took here.*

The interior of the car smells like leather and perfume—floral, feminine high notes with whiffs of masculine musk. It fits the woman sitting on the far bench with her crossed ankles, androgynous navy pants suit, and hair brushed back into a helmet.

Vice President and Democratic Party presidential nominee Natalie Stone.

I slide into the seat across from her. Stone's green eyes are lit with intelligence and deep knowledge—her gaze holds a confidence I'm used to seeing only in men with too much power. The presidential hopeful's lips are curled up into a closed smile that crinkles lines around her eyes. *Has she had work done?*

Guilt and loathing instantly churn in my stomach at the question...practically an accusation in my mind.

Clearing my throat, I smile at her, banishing all thoughts of plastic surgery and physical appearance. My lizard brain will never give it up, but there are bigger issues here than how much poison either of us has pumped into our faces in an attempt to stay young and relevant.

"Angela." Her voice is low, with a roughness to its baser notes, as if she is recovering from a cold. "Thank you for taking the time to see me."

I nod, not sure how to respond. *She didn't request my company.*

The overhead lights dim as the car engine thrums. *We are moving.* Glancing behind me as we pull away from the curb, I see Troy Woods talking on his phone, gaze cast down to the sidewalk.

"I hope you don't mind if I give you a ride home."

"Uh, no, I just…"

"Troy won't mind." She says it as if she knows him. Natalie Stone's hands are folded in her lap, her gold wedding ring glowing softly in the overhead lights. Her nails are painted a soft, feminine pink. *How many advisors did it take to pick that color?* My own nails are lacquered in blood red, a color chosen by the stylist to match my dress. "Do you know why I've asked to speak with you?" Her head cocks ever so slightly—a dog picking up the taste of fear on a summer breeze.

I offer up a timid smile. "I'm not sure."

"My opponent," Natalie maintains eye contact, her voice even, "is a dangerous psychopath." I can't help a nervous smile taking over my face. "I must win this election. For the security of not just our nation but the world."

"I'm not really into politics."

Her eyes narrow, and a spark of anger brightens the green into a shimmering gold. "What a lazy thing to say."

She's stolen my breath, and I can't respond. Clearing my throat, I try to come up with something, but her eyes have me pinned in place, weighing on my lungs, sparking fear in my chest. *She's not a bully like her opponent, but she is dangerous.*

"Sorry," I finally sputter out.

Her lips curl again, and she settles back into the seat, glancing down at her lap and dusting at something. "Can I offer you a drink?" Her eyes raise back to mine. They are calmer, the deep green of moss in the shade of a large tree.

"Water?" It comes out a question.

She nods with her chin toward the bar by my side. There are plastic water bottles lined up, and I grab one out of the well. Cracking off the top, I take a long sip. She waits for me to put the lid back on before continuing.

"While I'll agree this is a messy business—politics—I hope you'll agree that someone has to do it."

"Yes," I say.

"And from what I know of your interactions with my opponent, you're not a…fan, shall we say?"

"We could say that."

She nods and shows a bit of teeth with her next smile. "Good." It sounds as if something has been decided, though I'm not sure what… if anything.

We are merging on a highway, and the street lamps are casting tiger stripes of light into the close space. "There are only a few weeks left until the election, and I'm almost sure he will pull something unexpected." She smiles at me again, those crinkles around her eyes deepening. "I have skeletons." Natalie waves a hand dismissively. "As do we all. But a woman's old bones…are not as accepted as a man's."

She pauses, as though waiting for a response. The water bottle sweats in my grip. "Yes," I say again, feeling, once again, like a parrot repeating words its master wants it to say.

"I know what Temperance planned." I keep my face neutral—not one twitch or flash of acknowledgment. Natalie's eyes stray behind me, and I follow her gaze. We are getting off at my exit. "But that is unacceptable. He will be disciplined for his actions." Her eyes return to mine, and Natalie Stone, the first woman to make a real run at the highest office of the land, pins me again with her gaze. "I hope that we can work together in some other way in the future."

The car pulls up in front of my building, and the driver gets out. "It was a pleasure to meet you, Ms. Daniels." Natalie does not extend her hand, and when the door opens, I slide over to get out. A hot, smoke-tinged wind greets me as the driver begins to close the door. "One more thing," Natalie says.

I bend down to see her. She looks suddenly small in the large car

—her hair too big, the cross of her ankles too practiced. Natalie is a woman from another era trying to use the traditional weapons of female apparent subservience to win a war against male brutality. It's worked for her up until now, advancing cautiously through the system by working hard and appearing to follow all the rules. But she's got skeletons because you can't get to where she is without leaving bodies behind. And a woman like her, petite, elegant, whip smart in a world that isn't, *she can't win.*

We need new weapons. New tools. *How can women stop the violence and oppression against them?* Not by crossing their ankles, spraying their hair into submission, and toning their asses to perfection.

But right now it's all we've got.

"I've arranged for Mr. Styles's release." My eyes go round. "I will protect you from Mr. Grand until the election." She gives me a predator grin. "And then once it's over, his power will be greatly diminished."

"You'll win, won't you?" My voice is tinged with a desperation whose authenticity is so unique and pained. Immediately, I take note of the places where it came from—a tightness in my chest, the angle of my neck, a tremble in my jaw—and lock it away for a future role.

Natalie's brows raise. "I'll do my best," she says. The driver closes the door and bows to me slightly before heading back to the front seat. I stand there in that hot, harsh, smoky wind and watch the sleek black car pull away.

If her best isn't good enough we are all screwed.

A BLACK SHOPPING bag hangs on my doorknob. I pause when I see it, my heart rate picking up speed. I glance back toward the elevator doors; they are closing quietly on the empty chamber.

I'm alone in the hall.

But is someone inside my apartment? I pull my phone out of my bag as I approach my door and cue up Temperance's number.

The bag is small and slick, shining in the hall's bright lights. I peek into it without touching and see pink tissue paper and a business-card-sized note. It is embossed with the initials VS. Flipping it over, I see a note in tight black script. *This is the book I told you about. I think you will like it. -Vlad.*

The card trembles in my fingers. *Vladimir is alive and giving me gifts.* Pulling the bag off the doorknob, I swipe my fob and push into the apartment. I flick on the lights and find the place as I left it...or at least I think it's the same.

Archie gives a bark from his crate in the bedroom.

My gun is stashed in the first drawer of the entry table, and I check the chamber and the safety before moving further into the apartment, leaving the black bag by the door. Sweat trickles down my back as I move toward the kitchen, my gun gripped in both hands.

The kitchen is empty, the door to the balcony locked.

Blood rushes in my ears, and I force myself to breathe evenly as I head to the bedroom. I left the door open, and the bathroom light on. It spills into the dark space, splashing across the made bed, throwing dark shadows into the corners. I flick on the lights, illuminating the room. Archie barks again, a high, happy sound from the far side of the bed where his cage sits.

It's just the two of us.

I check my closet and the shower stall before letting Archie out onto the balcony to do his business. My dog back inside and the balcony door locked, I return to my living room and the waiting black bag.

It looks like it should hold jewelry or lingerie, not a book. Placing my gun on the table I pull out the tissue paper and unwrap a worn paperback. The cover features the Soviet sickle and a pistol resting on a spread of hundred-dollar bills. *The Twentieth of January.*

I thumb through the paperback, the yellowed pages releasing a fragrance I adore—old books. *Nothing like it in the world.* I take my pistol and the paperback with me. Archie follows climbing into his cage and circling twice before settling. *It's late, after all.*

I put the book and gun by the sink as I take off my makeup and wash my face. Keeping them with me, I return to the bedroom and slip out of the dress, pulling on a nightshirt and climbing into bed.

Leaving the lights on in the living room and kitchen, as if electric bulbs can keep the bad guys at bay, I settle into the pillows, my gun next to me on the bedside table, and begin to read the thin volume.

THE LAST PAGE crinkles between my trembling fingers as I turn it. *I finished the book in three hours.*

The swirling rumors about Russian interference in the election, and the acknowledgment from the intelligence agencies of that reality, storm my brain.

The Twentieth of January, published in 1980, is a classic spy novel with a Manchurian candidate—except this one is the presidential candidate himself, not the brainwashed assassin. The book weaves a tale about an American businessman from a wealthy East Coast family who, with very little political experience, and spouting populist rhetoric, manages to win the presidency against far more experienced opponents.

A CIA operative discovers the plot and realizes that the Kremlin is in control of the president-elect. This creates a crisis for the intelligence agency: let a man with hidden ties to the Soviet Union become president, or create a possible Constitutional crisis by exposing the plot?

A no-win situation.

The book, however, has a satisfying ending. The President-elect's wife is shown the compromising materials being used to blackmail her husband and confronts him. Overwhelmed with shame, he commits suicide before inauguration.

Why did Vladimir send me this?

I reach for my phone on the bedside table and call Temperance. It's two in the morning, but I don't care. Temperance picks up, his voice smooth—he wasn't asleep or is excellent at faking wakefulness.

"Have you read *The Twentieth of January*?" I ask.

There's a brief silence, behind which I hear the shifting of bed sheets followed by the sound of a door closing. *He was in bed with someone.*

"Yes," he answers. "How did you hear about it?"

I pull off my own blankets and begin to pace. "Vladimir Petrov first mentioned it to me in Shanghai—"

Temperance cuts me off. "What did he say?" His voice is like a laser, so hot and intent I stop walking, standing still in the middle of my bedroom.

"He just asked me if I'd ever read it. It was small talk. I'd been telling reporters how much I love to read. Spy novels specifically, because *The Tempest* was an adaptation."

"All he did was ask if you'd read it?"

"Yes, but when I got home tonight, there was a bag on my door with a note from him and the book inside."

"Why didn't you call me immediately?" His voice has dropped to a dangerous rumble.

"I don't know, I thought—"

Temperance cuts me off again. "Get out of there now."

My eyes scan my bedroom, which moments ago felt safe but at Temperance's words has become a shadowed and dangerous place. "Why?" I ask.

"Just do as I say. Now."

A sound at my front door sends my heart racing. "Temperance," I whisper. "I think someone is breaking into my apartment."

The whine of the lock disengaging closes my throat even as I'm moving to my bedside table, the phone still pressed to my ear.

"I'm on my way," Temperance says, quick movements evident in the sounds behind him. I leave the connection open but place the phone on my side table as I pick up my gun.

When terrified and in desperate need of my hearing, why does my heart beat so damn loud that it drowns out everything else?

Pulling in a deep breath, I kneel behind my bed, using it to block my body from anyone entering my bedroom. Arms extended on the mattress, I aim my gun at the door.

Archie, in his crate behind me, wakes and snuffles at the bars.

There is no sound from the living room.

I should just wait here.

I'm safe here in my nightshirt and underpants, with my gun and my bed for protection. If I stand up and try to go investigating, I'm just begging to get killed.

Blood rushing in my ears is like the ocean roaring during a hurricane. I can't hear a damn thing except the pounding heartbeat that caused the internal storm and now Archie's soft whine of concern. *Why are you up in the middle of the night? I kind of have to pee now.*

My bedroom door, already slightly ajar, eases open. My shoulders burn and my hands ache with tension as my eyes narrow into a pinpoint on the entryway.

Vladimir Petrov steps into my bedroom, his eyes quickly finding me hunkered on the floor, using the bed as a shield, the gun gripped in my fist. *Just shoot him.*

But I can't. He's so damn alive. And just standing there.

Those sharp blue eyes of his trace from the barrel of the gun down my arms and meet mine. "Angela," he says, his voice slightly slurred, that thick accent turning my name into something exotic—almost precious.

Oh, his face is…slack on the left side.

His left shoulder is dropping as well. *Did I do that to him?*

He's wearing all black—a turtleneck and dark pants making his pale hair and skin that much lighter, those beady blue eyes that much brighter.

"What are you doing here?" I ask, my voice steady. *I'm the one with the gun.*

A faint smile toys with the right side of his mouth. "I wanted to see you. Did you like my gift?" He steps further into the room—his shoulders are almost as broad as the doorway, his head practically brushing the lintel.

"Stop walking," I say.

That twisted version of a smile broadens, and he puts his hands up as if to placate me. "I'm not here to hurt you."

"Then why are you here?"

"I just wanted to see you. Our last parting was so…" He raises his brows. "Dramatic." A hint of anger has entered his voice.

"Get out," I say again. "Breaking and entering doesn't work for me."

He shrugs. "I didn't break in." He holds up a key fob. *I am so moving if I survive this…*

"Just because you can get into my apartment without smashing anything doesn't mean you have an invitation."

His eyes darken, something about my words bringing fresh anger into his gaze. Vladimir takes another step forward, and my finger tenses on the trigger. "One more step and I'll blow you away." *What the hell, am I in a Western now?*

"You are much more than I ever dreamed of—a real tigress." *Ew.* "Did you like the book I gave you?"

"It seemed like a far stretch. Not that well-written, either."

His brow lowers, as if he's taking my literary criticism seriously. "You have so much faith in your country that you don't think your elections can be influenced in this way?"

I did. "No," I answer. "It just all seems a little cliché, doesn't it?" *The new theme of my freaking life.* "I mean, a Manchurian candidate?"

"The Communists in that Cold War drama could never accomplish what we have done."

He's going to kill me. That's why he is here. No way would he tell me any of this if he didn't plan to take me out. I have to shoot him. It's him or me!

"The election isn't over yet," I say, taking in the breadth of his chest.

An awareness comes into his gaze. *He saw my look, honing in on my target.* Vladimir's muscles tense, and he launches himself at me. My finger squeezes the trigger, but it's all a blur.

His shoulder slams into me, rolling us both onto the floor, my head crashing into Archie's crate. He barks with surprise and upset.

Vladimir is on top of me—the softness of his cashmere turtleneck contrasting with the roughness of his grip. He gets the gun away from me as easily as the sun melts ice cream on a summer day and flings it across the room. The small, useless thing hits the wall and thunks onto the carpeting.

Thick, strong arms circle me—he's hugging me. Dry lips brush my neck and he takes in a deep inhale, reminding my own lungs to start working again. I breathe in mint and aftershave along with something musky and raw.

"Angela." He says my name with a strange, horrible reverence. "You are magnificent."

I wriggle under him, and he sits up, getting some of his bulk off me so I can breathe more easily. His face above mine, Vlad looks down with that crooked smile. "Come," he says. "We should go."

"Go?" I squeak, incapable of keeping the fear out of my voice. Archie is still barking, and Vladimir looks up at him and growls, a deep rumble in his chest that vibrates through me and makes Archie whine and then go silent. *Scary dude.*

Vladimir returns his attention to me, brushing a strand of hair from where it's tangled against my lips. "Grace Kelly gave up her career for Prince Rainier III."

My brain trips over itself. He doesn't want to kill me, despite what I did to him. He wants to *marry* me. The hiccup of a laugh that is trying to break free gets stuck in my throat as his gaze lowers to my body—his inspection is like a frigid wind, and I tense under it. Vladimir's eyes light, and he moves a hand off my shoulder down to my breast, cupping it so that I whimper and shiver. "You like that?" he asks.

No! But I keep my mouth shut even as my entire body grows rigid against his touch. "You're so beautiful," he says. "And"—his eyes return to my face—"brave." That twisted smile distorts his mouth again. "Grand made a mistake with you—he went too far. But don't worry. Vladimir is here to protect you now."

"Oh," I whisper, letting my voice go breathy and bringing up a hand to cup his face. *I need to play this just right.*

"You won't need to work anymore," he explains. "I will take care of everything. And I can protect you from Reginald Grand. From Temperance Johnson. No one will make you do things you don't want to do anymore."

Except you, huh, buddy? "How?" I ask, infusing my voice with awe.

"Reginald Grand is under our control," Vladimir says.

"Like in the book?" I ask. "You're blackmailing him?"

"Yes, *moy pitomets,* my little spy-in-training. You see, I am much more powerful than even your president. Only I can keep you safe."

Vladimir's hand is slipping down the side of my body, following the curve of my waist. "Well, he's not president yet," I say, keeping my voice meek.

Vladimir stills. "He will be," he lowers his mouth toward my breast, so slowly that I make out every glint of stubble on his jawline, the tiny scar of a healed piercing in his earlobe, every detail of this moment searing itself into my mind.

I didn't kill Jack to lie here and take this!

Raising my head, I take his earlobe in my lips. Vladimir shudders with pleasure as I flick it with my tongue. His fingers find my panties, and he shifts, rolling his hips to the side so that he'll be able to remove them.

Blocking out the sensation of his fingers against my thigh as my panties slide down my legs, I shift to roll him over. "I like to be on top," I say into his ear.

Vladimir's laugh rumbles through his chest and shakes my will, but I have to keep up this charade for just a little longer. I find his lips and kiss him like a director is filming every second—this is the man I love, and he's going off to war. *He's about to die, and this is the last time I'll ever get to touch him.*

Vladimir's hands squeeze my waist as my thighs press around him. I raise up over him and reach for the hem of my shirt. He watches, his eyes wide as saucers and dark with hunger, as I pull it over my head. I'm naked astride him, his eyes roving over my bare flesh. I smile down at him. *We will be the greatest lovers of all time. Better than any novel. We are meant to be.*

Vladimir believes the lie.

I spin the T-shirt above my head, joking now. *Playful.*

The old rotary phone is right there, right above his head, but I don't look at it. *Don't telegraph my intentions this time.* I keep my gaze on him, keep spinning that T-shirt. Until I release it, letting it fly away, and his eyes follow it for just a moment—one tiny moment.

I grab my white phone—the antique behemoth I bought so that I could take this city by storm, one promising call from my agent after another—and bring it down onto his face with every ounce of strength I've willed into my body.

Every push up, every punch, every weight lifted and calorie

counted comes down onto him. He jerks and cries out, and I strike him again. I keep going until Vladimir is still, his warm blood splattered over my burning, naked flesh. Then I stop.

I breathe.

I won.

"Angela." I whirl around at the sound of Temperance's voice, a snarl ripping from my chest.

He is standing behind me, looking down at the scene. His eyes trace the blood on my breasts, the phone still gripped in both hands, the pulpy mess that is Vladimir's face.

Temperance gives a curt nod and holsters the pistol in his hands, his movements practiced and calm. He reaches out, offering me his hand. Both of mine still hold the phone. "You can put it down now," he says, all calm confidence. It soothes me, and my fingers loosen enough to place the phone on the once-white carpet.

Temperance helps me up, and I stand on unsteady legs. "Go take a shower," he says.

I do as he says, making the water so hot that it practically scalds me. I use my dry brush with such vigor that I'm sure my grandmother would be proud. *She was always punishing herself.* My hand stills as an unbridled clarity overcomes me. *She hates herself for surviving.* It's not a new thought—not original—but I *understand* it this time. Because there is a hate brewing inside of me…for me.

My hair in two braids, wearing sweatpants and an oversized T-shirt, I open the bathroom door. The air feels cold compared to the steamy lair I'm leaving.

Temperance waits for me, Archie in his arms. The little dog is wet and shaking. *He must have had blood on him.*

He wriggles, trying to get to me. I reach out, tears welling in my vision as I wrap his soft body against my chest. He licks my jaw and snuggles his head under my chin with a soft sigh. "I'll keep you safe," I promise in a low whisper, talking half to him and half to the weak, sad part of me that is surrendering to self-hatred.

"You did good," Temperance says, his voice deep with a hint of pride.

I bring my eyes to meet his tiger gaze. "How do you deal with…" I tilt my head toward the destroyed body, keeping my eyes locked on Temperance.

"I have a team on the way," he says.

"No." I shake my head, my thick, wet braids waving back and forth. "I mean, mentally. How do you not…*hate* yourself?"

"Put it in a box," Temperance says, his voice even. "Lock the box. And don't open it unless you need it."

"Why would I ever need it?" I ask, letting the figure on the floor draw my attention. *It's horrible. Disgusting.*

"Don't worry about that until you do. But remember that one day you will need it. So don't try to get rid of the box. Just keep it in a dark, safe place. Can you do that?"

I swallow and take a breath. "I think I can."

"You can," Temperance agrees. "You've got it, Angela. Whatever *it* is, you've got it in spades."

He doesn't touch me, but his voice is like a warm arm over my shoulder, comforting me…and welcoming me into a club. One I'm not sure I want a membership for. Temperance begins to move into my living room, and I follow. "What was the deal with the pen?" I ask.

Temperance pauses on the threshold and turns back to me. "Digital kompromat," he says.

"Kompromat? Do you mean blackmail material? The dirt the Kremlin has on Grand?"

"Basically everything relevant on Vladimir's computers. It includes blackmail fodder against Grand, as well as evidence of ties between US white supremacy groups and the Kremlin. Everything we'd ever need to bring Grand down."

"But you won't."

Temperance gives a sharp shake of his head. "It's too dangerous."

"Just like the book."

Temperance nods. "Life imitating art."

A laugh bubbles up, and I let it escape, ballooning into my death-filled apartment. "You're telling me that the Kremlin got this idea from a freaking spy novel."

Temperance shrugs one shoulder. "There is credible evidence that when Grand traveled to Moscow back in the early 80s for business, he came home with a copy of that book." His eyes flick to my bedside table where the paperback still rests—only a few droplets of blood marring the cover. "We suspect it was the KGB that gave it to him... it is shame that kills the character in the book. Grand seems immune to that emotion."

"He 'wishes to be in politics for business reasons'," I say, quoting the book. Temperance's attention is drawn to his phone. "So he's not a pawn, you don't think. He is working with the Russians to win the election."

"Yes," Temperance answers without looking up from his screen.

"Grand is not going to kill himself, he is going to follow through," I say. "The man is a total egomaniac." Temperance is typing into his phone now. "But we can't kill him?" I ask.

"He won't win the election," Temperance says. "The Russians have not penetrated our electronic voting systems. They are using propaganda to try to win votes for their candidate." His eyes reach mine. "That's powerful. But we must have faith that the American people won't be so easily manipulated into choosing such a divisive leader. We just have to trust the democratic process."

My brows rise. "Since when do you have that much faith?"

A sad smile tugs at his lips. "I have to. My hands are tied."

Temperance returns his attention to his phone, and I glance back at the room one last time. I didn't want to become a member of this club, but now that I have my entry card, maybe there is something I can do with it.

CHAPTER SEVENTEEN

"THEY LET JULIAN GO THIS MORNING," Mary tells me over the phone. My heart thumps loudly. I'm out walking Archie up in the hills of Griffith Park. Dry brush rattles in the hot wind and golden slopes stretch out before me, the silver and black of the city below, the ocean twinkling in the distance.

"That's great to hear."

"There is a press conference arranged for this afternoon, and the accuser will be there, saying she made a mistake and apologizing."

"That's good," I say as three other female hikers pass me. We nod at each other. *One has a can of mace at her waist.*

"He asked that you come too, as his girlfriend, to show support."

"He did?" I say. "Because he hasn't called me."

"Well," Mary sounds curt. "It was actually Billy's idea." She references Julian's publicist. "We are all against it over here. You don't need to be there. Have dinner with him tonight or something. Let the paps see you together, but I think showing up to this press conference is too much. You've only been dating for what? A few weeks."

"I'll give him a call and see what he says."

"Just so you know, we strongly recommend against it."

"Objection noted."

"What?"

The connection is breaking up the higher into the hills I get. "I'll call you later," I say, but Mary is gone. Slipping my phone back into my bag, I slide my hand over my own mace can before re-zipping the pack. Pulling my hat lower against the bright sun, I keep climbing, legs burning, mind settling into the rhythm of the hike.

When I get back to my car, I'm sweaty and tired. Archie sits in the passenger seat, and I tune the radio to the news.

On the day of the candidates' final debate rumors circulate around both campaigns. According to the FBI, a new investigation is being opened into Vice President Stone's handling of campaign finances, and a warning from the State Department this morning of Russians meddling in the election has both camps scrambling to control the narrative.

I pull out of the parking lot and navigate the twisting roads toward home. The news announcer's voice is paused when my phone rings. Julian's name comes up on the screen, and I answer. "Julian," I say. "Mary told me you'd been released. That's great news."

"Yes." His voice is rough, like either he's been using it too much or not enough. "Apparently, it was all a big misunderstanding." There is bitterness in his tone. "We are having a press conference later."

"Yeah, Mary said you wanted me to be there?"

He sighs. "No, that was Billy's idea. I don't want to involve you more than necessary. I wish we didn't have to do it at all. But can I see you later?"

"Sure." My grip tightens on the wheel. *This is all my fault. I have to end it with him to protect him.*

"How about my place? Seven?"

"See you then."

My other line beeps as Julian and I say our goodbyes. It's a New York number I don't recognize. I take the on ramp for the highway as I answer it. "Angela Daniels," I say in my most professional voice.

"Angela, so glad I caught you. This is Tabitha Sanders from Reginald Grand's campaign."

My finger hovers over the disconnect button on my steering wheel, but I restrain myself. "I remember you," I say, keeping my voice neutral.

"Reginald wants to see you again. He has matters of great importance to discuss."

Like why Temperance Johnson isn't dead. And Vladimir Petrov is…and how I got Julian released from prison perhaps?

This could be a golden opportunity…Natalie Stone asked us to leave him alone. Temperance and Troy seem to have given up on the idea of taking him out. But maybe…

"I'm very busy at the moment preparing for a new role, but I could make some time tomorrow." I keep a neutral tone in my voice.

"We can send a car again," Tabitha suggests. "We will be out at Mr. Grand's resort in Santa Barbara. Do you know it? Grand Golf and Conference Center."

"I've never been, but I'm sure I can find my way. I don't need a car."

"Tomorrow at, shall we say 6 p.m., then?"

"Yes, perfect."

We hang up, and a grin spills over my face. *I'm coming for you, Mr. Grand.*

I ARRIVE at Julian's place up in the hills as the sun is setting over the ocean and throwing a pink and peach mirage across the landscape. A shiver runs down my spine. *It reminds me of when I arrived at Jack's house.*

So much has changed since then…

Julian answers the door in jeans and a black cotton T-shirt. He smiles at me, but there is a wariness to his eyes that wasn't there the last time we saw each other. He reaches for me without a word and pulls me into a warm embrace. Julian's face nuzzles my neck, and he kisses me there, setting another shiver—this one fueled by desire—racing down my spine.

I have to be strong. Have to end it with him.

"Angela." His voice rasps against my skin and even though my brain is telling me to pull back, my body is melting against his… maybe one more time…

No. That's not fair to him. Or me.

His lips move up my neck, nibbling my chin and finally reach my lips. I open my mouth—to protest, I swear—but he devours me instead, pulling me closer, moving us into his house, kicking the door shut behind us.

His hands find the zipper on my dress, and it slips off my shoulders, settling on my hips, his fingers unclasping my bra and shoving it away so that his mouth can move south.

I try to take a deep breath, but he steals it with his touch, making me crazy and dizzy. The back of his knees hit the couch, and he sits, his hands securely around my waist, holding me in place so that he can control my every move. *I love the way he touches me.*

He asks for everything and demands nothing.

Tears spring to my eyes, and I bite my lip as he worships me. *I want this, him, me... us.*

I lean down and cup his face, kissing him back, lowering to my knees in front of him so that we are at the same height. *I'm not ready to let this go yet. No matter how selfish that might be.*

I'm going after Grand. Yet I want to keep Julian--and everything else about my miraculous career. But I know I can't have it both ways. There will be no delayed-reaction pills involved when Grand and I meet, no way to mask the killer. And to my surprise, it's a sacrifice I'm prepared to make.

"THANK YOU FOR COMING, MS. DANIELS," Tabitha Sanders smiles at me. "I know Mr. Grand is eager to speak with you again." She turns and begins to move down the hallway.

My low heels make no noise on the carpeted floor. We are in Grand's hotel outside of Santa Barbara, a golf resort and conference center. He's taken over part of the top floor with his entourage. Secret Service line the hall, standing as silent, watchful sentries. Tabitha slows to a stop in front of an agent I recognize as the same one who patted me down when I first met Grand for breakfast.

"Maloney, right?" I say.

"That's right, Ms. Daniels."

I offer him my purse, and he takes it, opening the small leather bag and searching through it. Satisfied that I'm not concealing a weapon within its silky interior, he turns to my body.

Ah, my best weapon.

I suppress the smile that toys with my lips, moving my feet apart and spreading my arms for his inspection. His touch is the same as last time, professional and thorough… and he does not discover the tiny pistol tucked between my breasts.

Maloney opens the door for me, a waft of stale air seeping into the hallway. Taking back my purse, I step into the dark room, alone. The shades are drawn, and the only light in the office comes from a television tuned to a twenty-four-hour news station. Grand is sitting behind a large desk, a breathing shadow in the dark room.

The door closes behind me, and I sip air, waiting for Grand to turn his attention away from the announcer, who's sputtering with rage about something.

"Angela," Grand says, muting the TV and swiveling his chair to face me.

"Mr. Grand." I mimic his tone—syrupy sweet and dripping with ownership.

"Please, sit." He gestures to one of the two chairs facing the desk. I approach it, resting a hand on the upholstered back, keeping it between us.

"No thanks," I say.

He shifts forward, his large leather chair creaking as he puts his elbows onto the empty desk top. "Temperance is still alive. Get rid of him, or I'll expose you."

"I'll expose you right back," I snap.

"You'll be dead." He says it like it's final, as if there is nothing I can do to stop him. *He is a powerful man, and I am just a woman.* My chin juts up, and a spark of anger ignites in my chest. *I am so sick of this power dynamic. So done with it.* "I'll expose you to our enemies," he goes on. "Let them know you are an asset. That you are dangerous to them."

"What makes you so sure I'm not dangerous to you?" My voice is quiet and sure. *I am dangerous.*

My hand takes the pistol from between my breasts without even really thinking about it. *The anger made me do it.*

There is power in women's rage.

He grins when he sees it, bright teeth flashing in the darkness. "You can't shoot me."

"Can't I?"

"No," a man's voice says behind me, followed by the cocking of a gun. *It sounds bigger than mine. But it's not the size of the weapon that counts. It's how you use it.*

"I may not be able to shoot you and survive. But I can shoot you."

A side door opens, and a man, his white head bent over some paperwork, strides in. "Numbers in Michigan are looking great," he says, raising his eyes to Grand, sitting behind his desk. He then scans the room and quickly finds me, the gun in my hand, and then the man behind me, and the gun in his. What a picture. The man's face goes almost as white as his hair. "What's going on?" he asks. Then his head cocks slightly. "Aren't you Angela Daniels?"

I smile my movie star smile at him. "Yes," I answer. "Do you know that your boss is a Russian puppet?" His eyes widen but not enough. *The man is a bad actor.*

Grand laughs and stands, moving toward the employee, my aim tracking him. "Trying out her role for an upcoming movie, Philip. We are going over lines together." Philip takes a step back as Grand's thick hand lands on his shoulder. "Why don't you see Angela out," he says, turning to me.

My options are limited: shoot Grand and die. Or leave with Philip and hopefully survive. Our threats to expose each other are as menacing as Moscow and Washington's threats of nuclear annihilation. *We both want to live.*

Grand raises his brows, and I take a step backward, my gun lowering. "I hope to see you again after the election, Ms. Daniels," Grand says as I turn towards the door. "We will have much to discuss then."

Philip approaches to escort me out. He's tall and lanky, the opposite of Grand's short and stout. I can feel Philip struggling not to shy away from me. "I'm sure we will see each other again soon," I say to Grand, making it sound like a promise.

I turn my gaze to Maloney, his back to the door I need to pass through, his gun still in his hand but no longer aimed at me. I wink at him before turning to Philip and lacing my arm through his.

MY STOMACH IS IN KNOTS, my throat barely open enough to breathe as I watch the returns two weeks later. I'm alone in my apartment. Julian wanted to get together but I begged off—afraid I'd expose my deep connection to the outcome. Archie raises his head off my thigh and stares at me with those big brown eyes of his—but the dog's got nothing to say. "The popular vote doesn't count." My voice is a whisper. "Millions of votes in California were just wasted." Archie sits up, his tail thumping once. *Reginald Grand has won the electoral college.*

Temperance may have been technically right to have faith in our people—Stone is narrowly winning the popular vote nation-wide—but a whole lot of people went for Grand and he's going to be our next president.

I want to throw something. Punch someone. Puke. I want to give up but at the same time strike out.

This is why I don't want to care about politics.

But I don't have that luxury anymore.

My phone rings. It's Synthia. "This is horrendous," she says.

"I can't even."

"I'm moving to Canada." I try to laugh but it comes out scratchy —like bare tree limbs clacking together in a winter storm. "I can't believe she lost. This country is so misogynist."

"She had skeletons in her closet."

"So does he! The man was accused of sexual assault by dozens of women. He's been married three times and is an admitted—nay—a proud philanderer. He makes fun of disabled people and is an unabashed freaking racist!" Synthia lowers her voice. "And it sounds like the Russians were involved with getting him elected. Did you hear about that?"

"A woman's old bones are not as accepted as a man's," I say, repeating Natalie Stone's words, my gaze locked onto the TV screen.

"That's for damn sure."

A knock at my door pulls my attention away.

"I have to go," I say, my voice sounding wooden.

Synthia sighs. "Me too. I'm going to get drunk."

I hang up the phone, my vision clouded with tears, but I take a deep breath, steadying myself, and then stand.

Archie follows me to the door. I check the peephole and find Temperance filling it. I open the door, sighing. He steps into the living room, that predator's gaze of his taking in the space. It looks the same as it ever was. My bedroom, on the other hand, has new hardwood floors.

"How are you?" he asks as I close the door behind him.

"Terrible, you?"

He gives me a tight-lipped smile. "Got anything to drink?"

I point to the open bottle of wine on my coffee table. "I'll get you a glass."

When I return from the kitchen, Temperance is leaning back into my couch, Archie resting on his thigh. Filling his glass, I hand it to him. He clinks it against mine.

"How can we keep fighting, risking our lives for a country that would elect him—" I point at the TV as I flop onto the couch next to Temperance. "Russia might have interfered, but a lot of people cast their vote for that monster. A sexual predator. A racist, misogynist..." My voice fades.

Temperance's face is shadowed. "This country is bigger than any one man."

"Sure, but I wouldn't have fought for Hitler's Germany. Would you?"

His jaw tightens. "He's not Hitler." *Yet*, his voice seems to imply.

I wave my hand. "Look, I'm not political. Never have been. Okay? All I ever wanted was to act. Not exactly a unique dream." My voice is rising, the apathy that's been sucking at my bones all evening lifting as anger spreads her wings.

"People show up in this city every day with the same aspirations as me. But then *you* barged into my life and made me a part of this—" I struggle for the right words. "Machine," I spit out. "A cog in this wheel, but I'm not metal or wood, Temperance. I'm a woman. And I'm not going to follow orders from that man. Ever." I'm breathing heavily, my chest heaving. Temperance doesn't respond, doesn't even look at me, keeping his eyes fixed on the red wine in his cup. "Say something," I demand.

His lips tighten before opening. "This *machine* is about keeping our population safe. What matters are the lives of the American people."

I slam my glass down onto the coffee table so hard that wine spills over the rim and Archie jumps off Temperance's lap. I lean over, getting right in Temperance's face, force those tiger eyes to meet mine. "That's bullshit, Temperance. A war criminal's excuse. I'm not going to work for a corrupt, power-hungry, *insane* man. *I'm* going to keep the American people safe by resisting."

"Yes, but quietly."

"Women have been quiet far too long." My voice trembles but sounds strong anyway.

"We can't expose him, for all the same reasons I explained before."

"Why can't we kill him? Make it look like a heart attack—like we planned."

Temperance shakes his head. "Look, we have to play the long game here. There will be an investigation. There are proper channels to deal with this sort of thing."

"You wanted to kill him a few weeks ago."

"That was before he won." Temperance's voice is quiet; it sounds almost betrayed.

"You were promised he'd lose," I remind him. Temperance eyes meet mine, and I see the truth in them. *This wasn't supposed to happen.* Fear ripples through me.

"I need you to be in—one hundred percent in," Temperance says quietly. "We can fight this, but we have to do it quietly. This is a long game."

"As long as it ends with him dead or in prison, I'm in," I answer, the conviction in my voice vibrating straight from my chest.

Temperance nods. "Good."

"I'll take it," I say, turning away from the spectacular view—the city, the Hollywood sign, and the sparkling ocean all on display for me —to the real estate agent.

His eyes glow with success. "Do you want the furniture too?" he asks.

"No, thank you."

He nods. "I can recommend a fabulous interior designer."

Mary walks out onto the patio, the clip-clop of her heels mixing with the pleasant rushing sound of the water feature of the infinity pool.

"It's perfect," she decrees. "I love everything about it. You should take the furniture too."

I look back into the modern home behind her—three bedrooms, two baths, a long drive with a big security gate. "No," I reiterate. *I'm making this into my home.*

She shrugs. "You start shooting next week. You're not going to have time to decorate. At least take the bed and some kitchen stuff." She makes it all sound so reasonable, but that's not what this decision is—I need something that is *mine*. Where I feel safe. Where I can be myself, all the disjointed, dangerous parts of me.

I've found my citadel. I am a queen. I am a girl. And I'm going to run this world.

Turn the page for a sneak peek of *Unleashed*, book 1 of the Sydney Rye Mysteries.

SNEAK PEEK

UNLEASHED, SYDNEY RYE MYSTERIES BOOK 1

Chapter One

My dog once took a bullet that was intended for me. A bullet that ripped through his chest, narrowly missing his heart, and exited through his shoulder blade, effectively shattering it. This left him unconscious on the floor of my home. Amazingly, this bullet did not kill him.

Ten years ago I adopted Blue as a present to myself after I broke up with my boyfriend one hot, early summer night with the windows open and the neighborhood listening. The next morning I went straight to the pound in Bushwick, Brooklyn. Articles on buying your first dog tell you never to buy a dog on impulse. They want you to be prepared for this new member of your family, to understand the responsibilities and challenges of owning a dog. Going to the pound because you need something in your life that's worth holding onto is rarely, if ever, mentioned.

I asked the man at the pound to show me the biggest dogs they had. He showed me some seven-week-old Rottweiler-German shepherd puppies that he said would grow to be quite large. Then he showed me a six-month-old shepherd that would get pretty big. Then he showed me Blue, the largest dog they had. The man called him a Collie mix and he was stuffed into the biggest cage they had, but he didn't fit. He was as tall as a Great Dane but much skinnier, with the snout of a collie, the markings of a Siberian husky, the ears and tail of a shepherd and the body of a wolf, with one blue eye and one brown. Crouched in a sitting position, unable to lie down, unable to sit all the way up, he looked at me from between the bars, and I fell in love.

"He's still underweight," the man in the blue scrubs told me as we looked at Blue. "I'll tell you, lady, he's pretty but he's skittish. He sheds, and I mean sheds. I don't think you want this dog." But I knew I wanted him. I knew I had to have him. He was the most beautiful thing I had ever seen.

Blue cost me $108. I brought him home, and we lived together for ten years. He was, for most of our relationship, my only companion. But when I first met Blue, a lifetime ago now, I had family and friends. I worked at a shitty coffeehouse. I was young and lost; I was normal. Back then, at the beginning of this story, before I'd ever seen a corpse, before Blue saved my life, before I felt what it was like to kill someone in cold blood, I was still Joy Humbolt. I'd never even heard the name Sydney Rye.

Chapter Two

My foot tapped against the spotted linoleum as the subway squealed over the Manhattan Bridge, and clacked up the East Side. I scolded myself for my constant tardiness and vowed that from that day forth I would change my life. I would get organized. I would become better.

Three hours later, a pastel-clad woman with bad hair asked if she could have a macchiato, which didn't make any sense. A woman wearing pastels, obviously from a place where they still wore scrunchies, asking for a shot of espresso with a touch of frothed milk on top. She should have been asking for a Frappuccino just like all the others who walked into the shop assuming that it was a Starbucks, because who could possibly imagine that there was coffee that was not Starbucks?

"Do you know what a macchiato is?" I asked.

The woman smiled benignly. "Yes, I want a caramel one." She obviously had no idea what she was talking about. You don't put caramel in a macchiato.

"So what you're saying is that you would like a shot of caramel and a shot of espresso with a touch of frothed milk on top."

"Why not? Let's give it a go." She smiled at me and I thought, this is amazing. She is willing to try a new drink--not only a new drink but a drink that she practically created for herself. Had anyone else ever ordered this? I swear, in that moment, I was filled with a renewed sense of life. I had been wrong--not all dowdy women dressed in pastels were unadventurous lemmings.

"Oh, this isn't what I ordered," she said, looking down at my small cup of perfect caramel macchiato from above her two chins.

"Yes it is. It is a shot of caramel and a shot of espresso with a touch of frothed milk on top." I had been wrong. She was like all the rest of them.

"No, I've ordered this before at Starbucks and it's iced and in a very large plastic cup with a straw. It's not at all like this," she said as she waved her pudgy hand at my creation.

"Actually, this," I pointed at the little cup, "is exactly what you ordered. Exactly." I looked at the line of tourists that snaked out the door behind her onto 60th Street and continued, "I asked you if you wanted a shot of caramel and a shot of espresso with a touch of frothed milk. You said, 'Sure, let's give it a go.' " I used a high-pitched nasal voice to imitate her. "Now, I will make you a new drink," I said, "but it won't be any Starbucks knockoff and you won't get whatever it is you want unless you first admit that you are an idiot." The woman's face turned red and all her features made a mad dash to the center, leaving her with only cheek, forehead, and chin.

"That's right," I was really rolling now, "an idiot, a dumb-ass who has no idea what is in her coffee. I bet you don't know that Frappuccino is a Starbucks name, not the name of a real coffee drink. Frappuccino is a trademark, not a beverage." I was still explaining the finer points of coffee in an outdoor voice to the tourist when my manager, a guy named Brad who always seemed to be staring at my tits, came out from the back and fired me. Although the way I stormed out of there, you would think I had quit. I threw my apron on the floor and told Brad to fuck himself and stop masturbating in the coffee grounds. Yeah, the customers liked that one.

By the time I got home, I was crying.

It is not often that the weight of daily existence catches me in public. I usually have to be in bed, alone, in the dark. But this time I was standing outside my apartment crying so hard I could barely get my key in the door. The thing is, I wasn't crying because I got fired or because I'd broken up with my boyfriend, Marcus. My job was stupid, and Marcus was an ass. Breaking up with that dick-wad was something on the list of "shit I've done lately that I can be proud of," but it was pretty much the only thing.

I got the door open and Blue whined and circled me, desperately happy at my return. I sat down, my back against the door, crying. Blue nuzzled me and licked my face. I hugged him and he squirmed. "You've only known me less than a day and already you like me this much, huh?" I asked him, sniffling back my tears. He flopped onto his back, exposing his belly and warbled at me in answer.

Blue followed me down the hall and into the kitchen, where my answering machine sat blinking. "Five messages," I told Blue, wiping my face with the back of my hand. He leaned his weight against me and nuzzled my stomach.

I hit play and heard Marcus's voice. "Hey, listen." I heard Marcus's tongue slip out to wet his lips. My chest tightened. "I was thinking I'd come over later and we could…I don't know…talk or something. Call me back." Beep. "Hey, it's me again. Look, I'm in the neighborhood. I guess you're not home yet. I think I'm just going to head over…all right, um, bye." Beep. "What the fuck, Joy. I was just at your house and there was a huge fucking dog trying to kill me. I--" Beep. "Your fuckin' machine sucks, and where the fuck did you get that vicious dog? I mean, we just broke up last night and you already have a new dog. I don't know what that means, but I just don't know about you anymore." Beep. "Listen, just call me, OK?" Beep.

I exhaled. "Did you really attack him?" Blue wagged his tail and sat. "I suppose it would be your natural instinct," I hiccuped. "He was invading your home, right?" Blue looked at me blankly. "You don't look mean." He really didn't. He was tall and very skinny. I could see his ribs under his thick fur coat. With the snout of a collie, the markings of a Siberian husky, and the body of a wolf, with one blue eye and one brown, he was a very unique mutt. It occurred to me that I knew nothing about this dog. Our history was barely 12 hours long. I'd basically moved a large, hairy stranger into my house. The phone rang as I stared at my new dog, a little confused.

"Hey." It was my brother, James. "You want to get some drinks tonight?"

"Yeah sure, I have a lot to tell you."

"Anything good?"

"Not really. Well, I guess one thing." Blue had curled himself into a ball at my feet. "How about Nancy's at-- " I looked at the clock. It was 6:30. "How about a half hour?" I asked, planning a quick walk around the block for Blue.

"Perfect," James said.

The sun was slipping behind the brownstones across the street and turning the sky pink when I left for Nancy's. "Hey," said the guy on the corner who always said hey. I ignored him. "Hey, pretty lady, you got a beautiful ass," he tried again. I watched the concrete and power-walked away.

Ten minutes later I was at Nancy's, a low-key lesbian bar with a nice backyard. If you wanted to talk to a stranger you could, but there was no pressure. If you wanted to take someone home you could, but again there was no pressure.

I ordered a 'Tequila Gimlet, straight up'. The bartender, whose name I was pretty sure was Diane, nodded and moved off to make my drink. My face, reflected in the mirror behind the bar, peered from between a bottle of Blue Curacao and Midori. I needed a haircut. My fashionable bangs had grown out, and now I just pushed them behind my ears. Last night's fight with Marcus and my early-morning journey to the pound had left puffy, blue-tinted circles under my eyes. All those tears had left the white around my gray irises streaked with red and--I leaned forward a little to make sure--my upper eyelids a bizarre orange.

Diane placed a martini glass brimming with a sheer red liquid on the bar, and I handed her a ten. I moved toward the backyard, trying not to spill my drink all over my hand while spilling my drink all over my hand.

One overly cute couple sat in the soft candlelight cooing. I took a table close to the door and artificial lighting. As the tequila burned in my mouth, I wrangled with the memories of the past 24 hours. I usually shoved thoughts I didn't like to the back of my mind. But they never went away--they're always back there-- lurking right on the other side of my self-control.

James appeared in the doorway, smiling, holding a Tequila Gimlet, splash of cran (but his was on the rocks). He was a head taller than me at around six feet. We shared the same gray eyes and blond hair, though James's was short and styled while mine was reaching past my shoulder blades. Edging towards 30, James liked to talk about how his green-bean physique was morphing into eggplant. But the guy was still a pole.

"You look like shit," James said as he sat down. I smiled weakly and slurped my tequila. "Seriously, what the fuck happened to you?"

"Well, I broke up with Marcus"--this elicited a gasp--"and bought a dog."--an even bigger gasp--"Oh, and I got fired." I raised my glass in a mock toast to myself and polished it off.

"I talked to you yesterday! All this happened in one day?" I nodded, tried to finish my drink, then realized I already had. I went and brought back another.

"It's not really surprising," I said as I sat down. "We all knew it was coming."

James nodded. "Are you OK?" he asked.

"Well, I did lose my job because I went kinda crazy at work."

"Crazy?"

I told him about the plump tourist, her misorder, my insane reaction, and Brad's management decision. Then I told him about the masturbation comment.

James laughed. "I love it," he said. "I'm proud of you, Joy. That job sucked. Marcus was a tool. You've got a whole new fresh start."

"Easy for you to say. How exactly am I supposed to pay my rent?"

"You'll figure it out. Now, tell me about this dog. I can't believe you're such an asshole that you went out and got a dog because you broke up with your boyfriend. It's so pathetic."

"You're a real sweetheart."

"Somebody has to tell you."

"Jesus, I wanted a dog, so I went and got a dog."

"Oh, this was something planned?" James leaned his elbows on the table with mischief dancing in his eyes. "It's just a coincidence that you happened to break up with your boyfriend the night before." He smiled at me.

"Oh, just shut up. So what if I bought a dog to console myself?" He was right, of course. I had gone and bought a dog because I broke up with my boyfriend. And, yes, that was pathetic.

"So, what kind of dog?"

"He's really beautiful. He has one blue eye and one brown. Oh, oh, the best part is he attacked Marcus when he tried to come over." James laughed. "I know. Can you fucking believe it? He left me five messages today." I held up my hand with all five fingers extended.

"Your dog attacks people?"

"Not people, intruders," I said with more confidence than I felt. For all I knew Blue attacked all sorts of people. Maybe it wasn't that Marcus was breaking into the house. Maybe Blue would attack any douchebag we passed on the street. The thought made me laugh.

James smiled at me. "Not to talk badly about Marcus, Lord knows he was sexy as hell, but the guy is kind of an idiot. Not to mention that he tried to control you way too much. Low self-esteem fucks up a lot of men." James sat back, his hypothesis fully expressed.

I laughed. "I guess. Whatever, I'm over it." I sat up and scooped up my drink taking a long sip. "I'm so over it."

"Well, are you going to call him back? I don't think you should. Make a clean break."

I knew he was right, but I also knew that I had no control over myself whatsoever and would probably call him. "How's Hugh?" I asked, changing the subject. Hugh was James's boyfriend of four years.

"He's good," James smiled. "Actually, we're really good ... Our offer was accepted." Hugh and James had spent the last eight months trying to find an apartment. Two months ago, they'd found it. A fifth-floor walk-up with a roof deck, two bedrooms (OK, a bedroom-and-a-half) and a kitchen that was recently renovated.

"Holy shit. That's awesome. How much?"

"It's a little out of our price range, but you always pay more than you want, right?"

Later, I stumbled into my building blind-drunk. I climbed the steps humming to myself, swinging my keys. I was feeling pretty good. Sure, I had no job, no boyfriend, and a weirdo of a dog, but life was not so bad, not so bad at all. I would make it; I could fix it. Everything was going to be just fine.

Blue greeted me at the door. "Hi, boy." I crouched and rubbed his ears. He nuzzled my chest, knocking me against the wall. Blue wrapped himself in my arms. I breathed into his neck, smelling the pound. "We're going to be OK," I said into his neck. "I'm going to take care of us. Starting tomorrow, I'm going to fix this mess of a life of ours." Then I passed out.

Click here to download and keep reading Unleashed!
OR...

Sign up for my newsletter and receive a link to download Unleashed as a FREE welcome gift:
emilykimelman.com/sydneyryebonus

AUTHOR'S NOTE

Dear Reader,

I hope you enjoyed the first book in my Star Struck Thriller series!

Obviously, this book is a work of fiction but I stole a lot from current events. *The Twentieth of January* is a real spy novel by Ted Allbeury. There is a conspiracy theory that the KGB gave the book to Trump back in the 80s which set off a chain of events leading to his Presidency. The original book was always thought to be too far fetched until now…

Check out *Benjamin Walker's Theory of Everything Podcast* titled *The Twentieth of January* for a full telling of the conspiracy theory. It's a crazy and fascinating story no matter which side of the aisle you're on. And the idea that a spy novel could affect the real world so drastically is pretty irresistible to a novelist.

The information that Temperance shares with Angela about white supremacists—the FBI report and the history of law enforcement—is all true. Sadly, I didn't fabricate any of that. I wish I could write a novel that would change it.

Right now, white supremacy is making a comeback the likes of which I never expected to see. Despite my grandfather's warnings that it could happen again—most of his extended family died in the Holocaust—I always thought that white supremacy had been permanently driven from political power. This just goes to show my white-person blindness. Ask anyone of color, or whose Jewish ancestry is obvious in their appearance, and they are not shocked like blue-eyed, blonde-haired me.

But the pendulum has swung us back to a time where nationalism is swelling all over the world again. We need to hold on to our values and our rights.

I hope that my story let you escape from reality for awhile. I know fiction does that for me.

Until next time fair reader.

Be brave,

Emily

EMILY'S BOOKSHELF

SYDNEY RYE MYSTERIES

Unleashed

Death in the Dark

Insatiable

Strings of Glass

The Devil's Breath

Inviting Fire

Shadow Harvest

The Girl with the Gun

In Sheep's Clothing

Flock of Wolves

Betray the Lie

STAR STRUCK THRILLERS

A Spy is Born

SCORCH SERIES ROMANCES

Scorch Road

Cinder Road

Smoke Road
Burnt Road
Flame Road
Smolder Road

ABOUT THE AUTHOR

Emily Kimelman not only writes adventure, she lives it every day. Embodying the true meaning of wanderlust, she's written her Sydney Rye mysteries from all over the world. From the jungles of Costa Rica to the mountains of Spain, she finds inspiration for her stories in her own life.

While living under communist rule in the former Soviet Union, the KGB sprinkled her with "spy dust", a radioactive concoction that made her glow and left a trail they could follow. She was two. She was destined for amazing things after that, and she continues to find adventure to inspire characters like the badass Sydney Rye.

Sign up for my newsletter and never miss a new release or sale.
www.emilykimelman.com/#

I now have an exclusive Facebook group just for my readers! Join *Emily Kimelman's Insatiable Readers* to stay up to date on sales and releases, have EXCLUSIVE giveaways, and hang out with your fellow book addicts.

If you've read Emily's work and want to get in touch please do! She LOVES
hearing from readers.
www.emilykimelman.com
emily@emilykimelman.com

facebook.com/EmilyKimelman

twitter.com/ejkimelman

instagram.com/emilykimelman

Made in the USA
Columbia, SC
11 May 2019